WHEN THE PITCH GETS PERSONAL

Atlanta Skyline's star Swedish wingback Oz Terim—or as the fans call him, the Wizard—has an airtight plan for his life, his career, even his meticulously renovated house, but he barely gives a thought to the Islamic faith he inherited from his Turkish parents. So no one's more surprised than he is when he's the victim of anti-Muslim hate crime. Refusing to take the threat seriously, he resists the security detail Skyline insists on . . . until he meets Kate Mitchell. There's no room for her in his plan and she's the exact opposite of what he wants. Then why can't he keep his hands off her?

After ten years in the military—and getting fired from her first post-Army job in Saudi Arabia—Kate Mitchell has slunk home to her Georgia roots. Private security isn't the career she dreamed of, nor is she thrilled to work with an uptight professional athlete who plays a sport she has no interest in. She never expected to be attracted to him—or for him to fall for her, too. As their opposite lives tangle up—and the threat against Oz grows more serious—Kate has to decide who she wants to be in life and in love.

Visit us at www.kensingtonbooks.com

Books by Rebecca Crowley

Atlanta Skyline
Crossing Hearts
Defending Hearts

Published by Kensington Publishing Corporation

Defending Hearts

An Atlanta Skyline Novel

Rebecca Crowley

LYRICAL PRESS
Kensington Publishing Corp.
www.kensingtonbooks.com

Lyrical Press books are published by
Kensington Publishing Corp. 119 West 40th Street New York, NY 10018

First Electronic Edition: September 2017
eISBN-13: 978-1-5161-0264-8
eISBN-10: 1-5161-0264-9

First Print Edition: September 2017
ISBN-13: 978-1-5161-0265-5
ISBN-10: 1-5161-0265-7

Printed in the United States of America

Chapter 1

Kate hissed a curse as the pen rolled down the slanted cover of the three-ring binder and onto the floor. She ducked under the desk to catch it and grimaced at the array of too-personal objects stored in the footwell: a half-full bottle of aftershave, scuffed leather Oxfords, and a nail clipper with a rusted hinge.

She snatched up the pen, blew off the dust it gathered on its journey and righted herself in her chair, wrinkling her nose as she stifled a sneeze. If her boss was going to insist that VIP client meetings were held in his office, he could at least vacuum occasionally.

Not that he had any interest in this account, having pointedly informed her most soccer players are football rejects. She wasn't super excited about selling private-security services to an athlete who played a sport she'd never watched, either, but she didn't exactly have a long line of potential clients knocking on her door. She thought of her monthly sales target, the fees for her niece's after-school tutor, the hundred dollars her mom blew on online poker last month. Then she opened the binder to the first page—a printout of the logo for Atlanta Skyline, the local Championship Soccer League team.

She rolled her eyes. If Lorraine spent less time fighting with the antiquated printer in order to fill these binders with grainy copies of websites and focused on the actual content of the client's request, maybe these briefs would be done more than three minutes before the VIPs arrived.

She sighed and flipped to the next page.

A Wikipedia article about soccer.

"For God's sake, what the actual—"

A rap on the door had Kate swallowing the expletive and bolting to her feet, wobbling momentarily on her high heels.

The door opened just wide enough to admit Lorraine's teased hair.

"Clients here to see you," she announced before shoving the door open the rest of the way and ducking back into the hall. With a sinking feeling Kate realized Lorraine hadn't given her the clients' names, nor had she gotten that far in the binder, but it was too late. The two men crossed the threshold and stood uncertainly before her, glancing around the shabby office. One was in his late forties with graying, ash-blond hair and hipster glasses. The other was younger, taller, and appeared even less thrilled to be there.

"I'm Kate Mitchell." She stuck her hand out to the older of the two, assuming he'd be the one paying the bills. "Thanks for coming in."

"Roland Carlsson," he replied. "And this is Oz Terim."

"Nice to meet you, Oz." She brightened her smile as she extended her hand, committing the unusual name to memory. Its owner offered no reply, regarding her coolly through remarkably large, remarkably dark eyes.

She gestured for them to sit and did the same, noting the way they both inspected the fraying cushions before lowering themselves into the rickety chairs.

She picked up her pen and hastily scribbled their names on the back of the logo page, including a phonetic *Cher-eem* for Oz's last name. Then she folded her hands on the desk. "What can I help you with today?"

Roland and Oz exchanged cryptic glances. Then Roland leaned forward while Oz crossed his arms and leaned back, the sleeve of his form-fitting T-shirt riding up to reveal a tattoo wrapping his biceps.

"I manage Atlanta Skyline, and Oz is a left-back on the team," Roland began, offering a hint of an accent before cutting himself short. "Sorry, maybe you know all of this already. How much background do you want?"

"As much as you feel is relevant," she responded, quickly jotting their roles beside their names on her piece of paper. She added a question mark beside left-back as a reminder to look up what the hell that meant.

Roland looked again at Oz, who arched a challenging brow at his manager before taking a committed interest in the wall on his other side.

"This is Oz's third season at Skyline. He came with me when I joined from Boston Liberty," Roland continued, and Kate nodded, though she had no idea what he was talking about. "We've never had any problems before, here or in Boston. In fact, Oz has become a fan favorite. They call him the Wizard, because he executes so many tackles yet never seems to get booked."

She blinked. Tackles? Booked? Soccer was the kicking game, right?

Belatedly she cracked a smile she hoped was convincing. "Right. Funny."

"He's always gotten a few bigoted comments on social media, but lately the attention has become slightly more..." Roland trailed off, his gaze drifting to the ceiling as he chose his next word. "Sinister."

Kate frowned. "Can you be more specific?"

Oz remained resolutely silent, arms folded tightly across his chest, his expression blank as he left Roland to elaborate. "The comments on Oz's social-media accounts have become hateful, and increasingly threatening, since someone posted his address in one of the Citizens First forums."

She snapped to attention at the name of the hate group gaining highly publicized traction across the country. Citizens First claimed to be an anti-immigration coalition, but they always seemed to find time in their busy schedule of xenophobia to be anti-gay and anti-woman, too. They were also notorious for flouting privacy laws and publishing private data.

She gave Oz another, more thorough onceover, wondering what about him could piss off a group like Citizens First. His name was fairly exotic, though she couldn't place its origin. He was well dressed, leanly built, and she supposed his angular face would be considered handsome if you liked that gaunt, underwear-model look.

She was more a blond-stubble-and-pickup-truck type herself, or would be if she had any interest in dating. After eight years of being told where to live and what to do—and in Saudi, what to wear and how to behave—she was done taking orders. She wanted to reconnect with her family, get her career going, and plant her feet on the ground.

If the perfect man fell into her lap and fit in with all that, fine. But she sure as hell wasn't going looking for him.

"The post was removed almost as quickly as it went up, so we couldn't do much about it," Roland explained, tugging her back to the present. "But my concern is the damage is done, and I think it's time for us to look at putting security measures into place in Oz's home. That's why we're here."

Maybe he's gay. He must be gay. "May I ask in what context the address was posted?"

"The thread was "Raghead Terrorists Infiltrating America's Sports." As far as I remember." Oz spoke for the first time. His voice was deeper than she expected, and softly accented, but his sarcastic monotone fit his ornery posture to a T. His eyes found her intently as he added, "I'm Muslim."

"Really? I thought tattoos were *haram*."

It was an unprofessional, unnecessary reply, but it generated the reaction she wanted. Shock cracked Oz's detached façade for a split second.

"What do you know about *haram*?" he asked, his tone wavering between annoyed and impressed.

"Eight years in the army with deployments to Iraq and Afghanistan, and I spent the last year working in security services for an American oil company in Saudi Arabia. I'm fairly familiar with the core tenets of Islam."

The beat of silence that followed was delicious. She resisted the urge to punch the air.

"Well, I'm non-practicing. Mostly."

She nodded, briefly enjoying a secret sense of triumph at Oz's rattled composure before refocusing on the task at hand. "Did anything happen to trigger your inclusion in the list? Any particular reason you've become a target?"

He shrugged, flattening his palms on his knees. "I pray on the pitch before each match, but I've always done that."

"He was in an article about Muslim athletes a couple of weeks ago, in one of the national papers," Roland offered. "It was about a few different athletes, but the photo was of Oz at an event here in Atlanta."

"Yeah, an interfaith event at the Peace Institute," Oz scoffed, re-crossing his arms. "This whole thing is ridiculous. My parents are Turkish, I was born in Sweden, I've lived in the United States for ten years—the article even says I don't fast for Ramadan. I'm a pacifist, not a terrorist or even a fundamentalist. So one racist asshole told his racist friends where I live. They're all such cowards, I'm probably at greater risk of being hit by a bus than one of them crawling out from behind their computer and showing up at my house."

"Don't underestimate these people," Roland warned, taking the words out of Kate's mouth. "Hatred and rationality don't usually go together."

"And reacting to their hatred empowers it, and empowers them."

"I'm not having this discussion again," Roland informed him between clenched teeth. "Your safety is paramount, so let's see what Kate recommends."

Oz rolled his eyes and retorted angrily in what Kate assumed to be Swedish. Roland replied in kind, and she didn't need to be bilingual to understand the heated, clipped barbs the men exchanged. While Roland kept his composure, Oz's voice rose in volume, his speech quickened, and his expression intensified. He turned to face his manager, giving her a view of his perfect jaw, tightened and defined in irritation.

Okay, he was actually pretty hot. Shame about the personality.

She sighed inwardly, turning a page in her binder. She really did need to get laid if she was lusting after a pretty-boy soccer player.

"Moving on," Roland said sharply in English, recalling her attention. Roland's gaze landed on her resolutely, while Oz shook his head and stared out the window.

"At the moment he has no security at all, and that needs to change," the manager stated firmly. "What do you recommend?"

She looked from Roland's resolute expression to Oz's sulky one and back again. This was a wide-open opportunity to sell a long-term suite of services to a wealthy, successful, famous-in-some-circles client.

It would require a lot of contact with Oz, particularly at the beginning. But if she got this right, Peak Tactical could become the preferred provider for Atlanta Skyline. Not only could they offer personal services to the players, there was stadium and game-day security, partnerships with other firms when the team traveled, pre- and post-season event staffing, background checks, bodyguards for VIP fans...

She folded her hands on the desk and smiled. "Let's start with the basics. Oz, does your home have an alarm system?"

* * * *

"They're not putting an alarm system in my house," Oz insisted in Swedish, shoving his hand through his hair as he followed his manager across the parking lot.

An oversized, Peak Tactical-branded pickup had parked beside his two-door Mercedes AMG, and it hung over the line so badly he wasn't sure he could get the driver's-side door open. He exhaled in disgust.

Roland stopped beside his own, larger Mercedes, apparently oblivious to the pickup's violation of Oz's parking space. "What's wrong with an alarm system? Everyone has one nowadays. Mine was preinstalled when I bought the house."

"It's invasive, that's what's wrong with it. It's an intrusive, pervasive, *aggressive* assertion about faith in humanity, and it's not the kind of statement I want made in my home."

Roland unlocked his car, opened the door and rested his elbow on its top edge. "It's a white box with lights and buttons that makes a noise and alerts the security company if someone forces open a window or a door. How is that a statement?"

"It says my house is a fortress that needs to be protected. It says I can't trust people outside its walls. I don't want to live like that."

"After a week, you won't even know it's there."

"Of course I will," Oz protested. "I'll have to set it every time I leave the house and disarm it every time I come in. And where are they going to put the panel—right beside the front door? What if I want to come in through the garage? Or the back door? You know how hard I've worked to get that house exactly how I like it, and—"

"Özkan," Roland interrupted, and he instinctively shut up at the use of his full name. "Enough. You can't intellectualize at me until I go away, not this time. I wouldn't do this if I wasn't genuinely concerned. These people are dangerous, and they're getting braver by the day. Did you see that story about the mosque in Idaho?"

Sobered, Oz nodded. "The one they set on fire."

"And put three people in the hospital with severe burns. This is more serious than your interest in minimalist design, or pacifism, or whatever other abstract philosophical point you want to make. Understood?"

Oz studied the man he'd followed for the last ten years, from Gothenburg to Boston to Atlanta. Roland was the only manager who'd been able to penetrate his arrogance as a prodigious teen, teaching him the discipline, patience, and humility that had saved him from becoming yet another early-twenties burnout whose potential was never quite fulfilled. Oz trusted Roland implicitly, and he knew he wouldn't win this argument.

Maybe he *shouldn't* win this argument. As much as it annoyed him to admit it, the outpouring of hatred on his social-media accounts had shaken him. He never imagined anyone could be offended by his cherry-picked commitment to Islam, and certainly not to the vehement, violent extent that had been unleashed. Roland was right—this was too much to handle on his own.

"Fine," he huffed, shoving his hands into his pockets. "And, thank you. For putting the team's money behind this, and for coming with me today. I know you could've asked me to do this on my own, or sent one of the Assistant Managers, but it was good to have you here." He exhaled before his next admission. "Apparently I still need you occasionally."

Roland gripped his shoulder briefly. "We'll get this nonsense sorted out."

Oz nodded, then added with a smile, "I do want it on record that I think alarm systems are cynical symbols of mistrust that degrade civil society."

Roland grinned. "If you find someone who cares, I'm sure they'll be happy to make a note of your objection. See you tomorrow."

"Later." Oz climbed into his car—that pickup wasn't as close as he thought—and started the engine, then threw the car into reverse and beat Roland out of the parking lot.

That's my one victory for today. He turned up the volume on a Swedish techno track as he headed for his home in Ansley Park, distracted and unsettled as he navigated the busy Atlanta streets.

When his best friend, Glynn, had texted that his address was on a Citizens First website, he'd laughed. Then he'd put his phone in his locker and spent the next several hours training with Skyline. When he picked up his phone again it had flashed with missed calls and panicked messages from a slew of friends and relatives. Although it had been removed within an hour, news of the list had found its way onto a lunchtime segment on one of the major broadcasters and taken off from there.

Suddenly his publicist was fielding calls from reporters asking how it felt to be outed as Muslim, whether he'd received any death threats, and vying to be the first to get his exclusive interview.

"You can't out someone for something that was never a secret," he'd told her over the phone in the hallway outside the locker room, still wearing his training kit. "And I'm happy to be interviewed on the subject of American professional soccer, since none of them seem to care enough to cover it on a regular basis, but my personal life is off-limits."

Except the messages kept coming. Hundreds of Islamophobic comments littered his social-media pages, punctuated by racist images and hideous language, each one worse than the last.

Oz took advantage of a red stoplight to scrub his palm over his eyes as comment after remembered comment flashed behind his eyes.

Get ready to die, filthy haji. We're coming for all you sand rats. Run back to the desert while your head is still attached to your shoulders.

But the one that scared him the most—the one that still sent a chill down his spine whenever it popped up—was by a user whose comments were always the same. Several times each day, across all the social-media platforms Oz used, a brand-new commenter appeared with a random jumble of numbers as a username. No amount of blocking seemed able to stop the phrase that posted over and over again: Ausonius 70.

Ausonius was a reference to a serial killer who'd shot immigrants in Stockholm in the late 1990s. Seventy was Oz's house number.

Oz exhaled a wave of anxiety as he turned into his neighborhood, forcibly shoving his thoughts in a different direction. Hateful though the comments were, he still wasn't convinced hiring a security company was the answer. And their erstwhile account manager, Kate Mitchell, hadn't done much to convince him.

He didn't like her, that much was clear. That she took Roland's side didn't exactly set them up to be best friends, but his distaste didn't end there.

He didn't like her accent, for a start, that deep country drawl that he heard most often from fat white men calling him queer through the windows of pickup trucks. As a pacifist he disliked her military record on principle, and her subsequent move to an oil company was even worse.

Of course, his opinion was based entirely on ideology. It had nothing to do with the way she'd utterly failed to respond to his provocation, or buy into his lofty objections, or laugh at his jokes…

He couldn't stop his smile. Okay, maybe she wasn't all that bad.

She wasn't bad-looking, either, if he was honest. Chin-length brown hair, blue eyes, a tall, athletic build. Nothing like his type, though. Not the sophisticated, erudite, professional woman he could count on to see him through what would inevitably be his short-lived soccer career to his life beyond. In fact, she reminded him a lot of his uncle's ex-wife—the woman who'd divorced him after an injury brought his uncle's high-flying soccer days to a screeching halt, whose abandonment sent his uncle into the depressive spiral that ultimately killed him.

He shook his head. No way was he falling into the same trap. He had The Plan.

Still, maybe they could at least—

Oz slammed on his brakes, the seatbelt digging into his neck as the car jerked to a halt a few feet from his driveway. He checked his mirrors, glanced out both windows, twisted in his seat to confirm the road was empty. Then he picked up his phone, found Kate's business card in his pocket and dialed her number.

She answered on the second ring.

"Kate? It's Oz Terim. I was just in your office."

"Of course, what can I do for you, Oz?"

"I think I might have a problem," he replied, studying the crude symbol spray-painted on his mailbox. The handiwork wasn't great, but the intention was clear.

A swastika. Bright, white, and so fresh the paint was still dripping.

Chapter 2

"Can we put it here?" Kate indicated a space beside the back door.

Oz shook his head. "No."

"Why not?"

"I don't want to have to look at it every time I go into the backyard."

"Can we put it over there, next to the fridge?"

"Won't work."

"Why?"

"It'll ruin the backsplash."

She swallowed an exasperated sigh as she propped her hands on her hips, surveying his enormous, white-glass-tiled kitchen and the even larger, even whiter dining and sitting rooms beyond it.

"I like the open concept, Oz, but it doesn't give us many walls to work with. And this alarm-system panel has to go somewhere."

He crossed his arms, brows furrowed in thought as he gazed across the space. Kate resisted the urge to roll her eyes for what must've been the thousandth time that morning.

On one hand, she had to give him credit. She'd prepared herself for non-stop conflict when she arrived with her crew, resolved not to leave Oz's house until she was satisfied with his security upgrades. Maybe she'd overestimated the force of his will, or more likely, underestimated the extent to which yesterday's graffiti had shaken him, because he was surprisingly receptive to her reasoning and suggestions.

On the other hand, he was decidedly not receptive when it came to practical issues like the placement and installation of infrared beams, motion-activated lights and alarm-system control panels. As much as she was grateful for his acceptance of the big picture, the constant back-and-forth about the details grated on her nerves.

Not that she blamed him. Much. If she owned a multi-million-dollar pile like his, she'd also be picky about what went where.

Thankfully she was at very little risk of ever having that problem.

"I can't see it," he said finally, shaking his head. "Let's stick with just one control panel on this floor, next to the front door."

Kate drew a steadying breath. "But as we discussed, you normally come into the house through the garage, right?"

"Right."

"And you don't want a control panel in the garage because you're still deciding where to install shelving in there."

"Right."

"But you also don't want a panel next to the back door, because you rarely use it to access the house, preferring to go through the garage to get to the backyard."

"Right."

"And we can't put a panel anywhere else in the kitchen because it'll mess up the tiling."

"Exactly."

"So." She exhaled. "You're about to go out. You turn on the alarm on the panel by the front door, and it gives you fifteen seconds to get into the garage before you set off the interior motion sensors. How far do you think it is from the front door to the garage?"

He squinted, calculating. "Well, the whole house is seven thousand square feet, so I guess you halve that to get the bottom floor. It's a pretty straight shot except for the slight curve around the kitchen island, which—"

"It's far," she interrupted. "Too far for fifteen seconds."

"I don't know," he countered, thoughtful and maybe, just maybe, a little bit playful. "My highest burst speed on the pitch was clocked at twenty miles an hour."

Lord, give me strength.

"You need a second panel on the ground floor," she informed him sternly. "Garage or backdoor. Pick."

He huffed a sigh, but she could swear she saw a hint of bemusement on that handsome face. "Fine. Garage."

"Great. Let's choose the location for the one in the bedroom."

She followed Oz up the stairs, which—like the banister and landing—were sealed instead of painted so the dark wood stood out against the white walls.

"This house is stunning," she told him truthfully. "All this white—how do you keep it clean?"

"I pay an extremely talented and thorough housekeeper. Also"—he paused on the landing, peered at a place on the wall, pulled one of those reusable cleaning pads from his pocket and scrubbed the nearly imperceptible mark until it disappeared—"I'm obsessive."

As if on cue, the sound of a drill whined from the direction of the kitchen. Oz leaned over the banister to have a look, but Kate ushered him up the stairs before he saw what she could: a fine spray of white dust as one of her workmen drilled holes to install the new panel.

"Well, it's worth it, because this place is amazing." She nodded for him to precede her to the second floor. "When was it built, originally?"

"Nineteen twenty-five. It had been totally modernized when I bought it—too modernized, in fact—and I wanted to strip everything back to a simple, minimal, Scandinavian style." Distracted by what was clearly one of his favorite subjects, Oz's posture eased as he led her down a carpeted corridor to the master bedroom. "The previous owners gutted it so the interior is all brand new, but at least it still has the gabled windows, the mature trees, and the carriage house out back."

She joined him inside the master bedroom, refusing to hesitate at the intimacy of the space, and then biting back a surprisingly affectionate smile as she took in her surroundings. The light gray carpet, pristine white walls and teak furniture were in line with what she'd seen downstairs, but this room actually looked vaguely lived-in. The bed was made, but not immaculately. A towel hung on the back of a chair. One of the dresser drawers was slightly ajar.

She cast a sidelong glance at her frosty new client. Maybe he was human after all.

"I don't know where we can put a panel in here. I like to sleep in pitch-black darkness. Those curtains are custom-made from special light-exclusion fabric. I can't have that little green light from the alarm glowing all night long."

Okay, half-human.

After twenty minutes of what Kate thought was impeccable patience on her part, they agreed to install the panel just inside the door to the en-suite bathroom. It wasn't ideal, but it was better than nothing, and she dashed downstairs to inform the installer so he could start work before Oz changed his mind.

When she returned to the master bedroom she found Oz staring thoughtfully at the place they'd agreed on, and she quickly directed him into the hallway before he could object.

"Ideally I'd like to put one more panel on the second floor. Is there another room up here you use a lot?"

"The study," he answered promptly.

"Perfect. Let's have a look."

The study was at the opposite end of the house from the bedroom. Oz pushed open the door and she almost burst out laughing the instant she glanced inside.

"So this is how you keep the house clean," she remarked. "You hide the clutter in here."

"You could say that," he admitted. And then, to her astonishment, he smiled.

After their meeting the day before Kate spent a couple of hours trawling Oz's social-media sites, trying to understand what had provoked Citizens First's ire. His Twitter feed was inoffensive, active only once or twice a week as he wished a teammate happy birthday or made a comment about Skyline's wins or losses on the soccer field (or "pitch" as Lorraine's binder belatedly informed her it was called). He was more prolific on Instagram, where every couple of days he uploaded a photo.

She'd flicked through them methodically, building a concept of her new client. Oz with his friends. Oz in the gym with his teammates. Oz at an awards ceremony. Oz at the beach without a shirt—maybe she'd lingered a little longer on that one.

Click after click, photo after photo, a theme emerged: Oz never smiled.

He clenched his fist and shouted in triumph on the pitch. He narrowed those big eyes and stared broodingly in professional shoots. He arched a brow or glanced haughtily at the camera in casual shots with friends.

But the smile she'd caught as they walked into the study was rare.

Which was a shame, because it was delightful. His chiseled features warmed, the corners of his eyes creased, and for a split second he looked younger. More fun. Much less serious.

Then it disappeared. Back to the task at hand.

She put her hands on her hips, surveying the study. In the rest of the house, where everything was vacant, she had to fight Oz to make an addition. In this room, she wasn't sure where they'd carve out space amidst all the clutter.

What he called the study was so big, she suspected it was actually a bedroom he'd turned into a man cave. A huge television occupied one end with an extremely comfortable-looking sectional positioned in front of it, easily big enough for six people. Built-in shelves overflowed with DVDs, comic books, and video games, and flags and posters covered the walls, including several variations on the same red-and-orange logo.

"What does this mean?" she asked, wondering if it was an Islamic affiliation she wasn't familiar with that could've contributed to the Citizens First attack.

"Galatasaray." At her blank stare he elaborated, "Soccer team in Istanbul. My uncle used to play for them."

"Oh. Right." Her face heated as she turned to scan the walls beside the entrance. At times Oz's dry, flat tone made her feel so stupid. She had to get over that. Immediately.

"This should be easy." She nodded to the wall left of the doorframe. "How about we move the Swedish flag up three inches, the Gala-whatever—"

"Galatasaray," he repeated.

"We move that one down three inches, and put the panel in between."

"Fine."

"Good. That's the last one. I'll tell Darryl."

She was on her way down the hall when Oz grabbed her arm. She pivoted, lungs tight, breaths rasping, not because of what he might say but because his loose touch seared through her polyester suit jacket, heating her arm from fingertips to shoulder blade.

Her jaw slackened as she sought the dark depths of his eyes, looking for some sign that he felt that, too.

She found none.

Her ears heated as his hand dropped, his expression impassive. What was wrong with her? He wasn't her type at all. He was too skinny, too brainy, and if the contents of the study were any indication, too nerdy to ever pique her interest.

She snapped mental fingers to halt her wandering thoughts. The complication of romantic interest was the last thing she needed. Laster than last, even. So far down her list of priorities for her newish, old-ish, ex-Army life, it wasn't even in the same notebook. She couldn't start crossing things off until she took care of the first item at the very top: Figure out who you are.

And right below it: Decide who you want to be.

Neither one ended in: with a man at your side. That was the whole point. She wasn't Kate the Soldier anymore, she was sick of being Kate the One-Night Stand or Kate the Fuck Buddy and she'd never even met Kate the Girlfriend.

She was done hiding behind versions of herself that gave other people control—her commanding officers, her erstwhile lovers. She had to answer these questions on her own, make her own decisions, finally pick her own path and sprint all the way down it.

"So?" Oz prompted, ripping her out of her thoughts. "Anything?"

"Sorry, what?"

"Yesterday you said you'd look through my social-media stuff to see if anything jumped out as a credible threat. What did you think?"

"Sure, yeah, I had a look last night." She exhaled. "I'll be honest, my expertise is physical security—alarms, response teams, bodyguards. I won't pretend to know anything about the psychology of stalking or cyber bullying. In general you seem to have a lot of admirers, and most of what I read was really positive. Then there's the streak of stupid, over-the-top racism that seems to be just part of the Internet, which I wouldn't consider credibly threatening. On the other hand, there was one comment that kept appearing—"

"Ausonius seventy," he filled in.

"Exactly. What is that?"

"John Ausonius was a Swedish gunman. In the early nineties he targeted immigrants in Stockholm, shooting them using a laser sight. Luckily he was a terrible shot, so most of them survived."

"Charming. And seventy?"

"My house number."

Kate paused, digesting this information, careful not to let the shrill warning siren whining behind her eyes show in her expression. "Well, that's creepy."

"Yes, it is."

"Maybe we should price out bulletproof glass," she murmured, foolishly thinking out loud.

That set him off, shattering the accord she'd worked so hard to build over the last two hours.

"Stop." He held up his palms, speaking quickly and forcefully, his clipped accent becoming more pronounced as his agitation grew. "Let me make something absolutely clear. I agreed to basic security measures. *Basic.* An alarm system, beams in the yard, a couple of motion lights. Not ideal, but I'll live with it. Anything else is a step too far, an admission of fear that I'm not willing to make. First, there's no way you're replacing the glass in this house. Second, I don't want any visible changes to the outside. I'm not building a fence, or stringing barbed wire, or installing bars on the windows—"

"Of course not, bars won't stop a bullet."

That shut him up.

"I'm not trying to scare you," she told him, keeping her voice calm and reasonable. "Probably someone's just being provocative, throwing in Ausonius's name. Your job is to shrug it off and keep living your life. My job, though, is to be overcautious and paranoid and respond to the slightest perceived threat. We won't make any additional changes today, but I have to think about the best way to respond to the mention of a long-range gunman."

Oz's tight jaw and thinned lips illustrated his unhappiness with her answer. She braced for another argument when a crash resonated from the kitchen. Oz was past her and racing down the stairs before she could say his name.

She should chase after him, she thought, be ready to smooth over whatever catastrophe had occurred. She should shield the poor technician who was probably already on the receiving end of Oz's misdirected anger. She should fix this situation. She should own it.

Instead she drifted to the window and gazed over the front yard.

Oz's house was beautiful. His life was beautiful. He had more money than he needed, more space than he needed, more cars than any single man needed. He was a professional athlete, paid ridiculous sums to play a game, and not even a particularly popular game. According to his Instagram, he had friends, family, and plenty of time to take exotic vacations.

Why was he so pissed off?

Her vision focused on the mailbox at the end of the lush lawn. He'd clearly made an effort to remove the graffiti—a desperate effort, leaving rough scrape marks from what she guessed was steel wool. It hadn't worked. Though some of the interior of each stroke had disappeared, the outline of the swastika was unmistakable.

She imagined Oz bent over the mailbox in the evening twilight, scrubbing futilely at the awful symbol while his neighbors slowed their cars as they drove past. Despite everything, her heart tugged.

She jogged down the stairs, grateful for the website which had informed her Oz was five-foot-eleven—only three inches taller than her—and as such gave her permission to never, ever wear heels in his company. She found the left-back by the sink, examining a superhero-printed coffee mug.

Bryce, the youngest of the workmen, raised his hands to her in innocence. "It fell into the sink and made a racket but it's not broken, I swear."

She winked at the nineteen-year-old, then spoke in a commanding tone. "How about you quit throwing this man's possessions around and do something useful. There should be some solvent and scrub brushes in the truck, go outside and fix that mailbox."

"Yes, ma'am."

Kate watched Bryce scurry out of the room, and when she looked back, Oz's gaze was on her. His expression had changed very slightly—softened, warmed. She dared a fleeting a smile, but got nothing in return.

Maybe she was seeing things.

"I thought of something," he said, his tone unreadable. "There's one more room I spend a lot of time in, where it might be hard to hear the alarm or get to a panel quickly."

"Which one?"

"The gym. In the basement."

"That's no problem," she assured him. "We'll put a fifth panel down there."

He shook his head. "Impossible. The walls are all mirrored."

She smiled around gritted teeth. "Let's have a look and see what we can work out."

Had she ever wanted to punch someone as bad as she wanted to punch Oz Terim in that moment? Not enough to remember.

Chapter 3

"I had a really nice time tonight, Oz."

"Me too."

"Let's do this again soon."

He hesitated. He didn't want to mislead her, but the curb in front of her waiting taxi wasn't exactly the best place to deliver the let's-just-be-friends speech, either.

Thankfully she had more to say. "Or we could keep going, right now. Do you want to come back to my apartment, meet my dog? She'll love you, I promise."

He exhaled in relief. She opened the door. He only had to walk through it.

"I don't think so," he said as gently as he could. "I'm not sure this is going anywhere romantically, but I had a lot of fun. Maybe you should come to my box for a Skyline match. Bring some friends, meet my friends, and we can all hang out. What do you think?"

Disappointment shimmered in her eyes, but to her credit she kept her chin up and her smile seemed genuine. "Actually, that would be great. Thanks for being honest."

"Pick a match and it'll happen." He opened the taxi door. "And let me know you got home safely."

"I will." She hugged him, briefly but warmly, then slid into the backseat and pulled the door shut behind her.

He waved as the car pulled off into the sparse, Thursday-night traffic. As soon as it was out of sight he spun back toward the restaurant and wiped his hand over his eyes.

What was going on with him lately? This was the third date in as many weeks that was perfect on paper and even better in person, yet he had zero inclination to take any of them further. Jamie was intelligent, hilarious, a medical student at Emory who'd spent two years after college working for an AIDS-prevention charity in Uganda. She was gorgeous, said all the right things, even had a minor interest in soccer. She would absolutely fit into his long-established plan for his post-soccer future—essential criteria for even considering a second date. There was no good reason he shouldn't want to see her again.

But the thought of another getting-to-know-you dinner with her filled him with dread.

He unlocked his phone and swiped to a taxi-hailing app. His thumb hovered over the Request Car button, then he closed the app and looked up. He wasn't ready to go home yet.

A neon sign flickered in the window of a rundown, fake-Irish pub three storefronts from the restaurant. Normally he hated dives—the stale-beer smell, the scarred tables, the sing-along-friendly soundtrack of cheesy pop hits—but after his pitch-perfect date he craved a little grime. He shoved his hands into his pockets and walked over.

The interior was slightly less shabby than he expected, and his sneakers barely stuck to the floor as he made his way to the bar. Only a few other people filled the large space. A couple in a booth, two men in work attire at a high table, and another couple playing pool at the far end of the room.

"Evening." The short, curvy, redheaded bartender was exactly his type. More so when she smiled. "What can I get you?"

He paused, taking stock of his physical response. Any hint of attraction? Anywhere? Even a twinge?

Nothing.

"Whiskey. Neat," he replied glumly.

She arched a brow, pivoting so he could see the rows of bottles behind her. "Which label?"

He peered past her, pointed to one on the top shelf. "Actually, make it a double."

She poured the drink and slid it over. "Rough night?"

"You could say that."

"Should've swiped left."

He shrugged. "Not her fault."

"No?" She crossed her arms and leaned against the shelf at her back. "I'd swipe right."

He sighed inwardly. Another beautiful, available, interested woman he couldn't be less excited about. Was this some cosmic joke? Tomorrow he'd probably fall in love with someone who hated him.

"Hey, can I get another—Oz, hi."

He turned at the sound of his name, and then his night got even worse. "Kate. Hello."

"Sorry, I didn't see you. Have you been here long?" She flicked her gaze to the bartender, pointing to her empty pint glass.

"Just arrived."

"He had a bad date," the bartender quipped, passing Kate a fresh beer.

She looked at him expectantly. He closed his eyes for a second, hoping that when he opened them this might all have been a bad dream.

Kate came back into focus. No, still awake.

"It wasn't that bad."

"Bad enough for a double whiskey," the bartender added. Belatedly he realized the two women knew each other.

"Really," Kate mused. "But I thought—"

"Alcohol is *haram*, I know." He rolled his eyes. "I think we've established I'm not the poster boy for devout Islam."

"I thought professional athletes didn't drink during the season," she corrected.

Irritation tightened his jaw. As if she knew anything about his grueling training schedule, the aches and pains and recovery periods, trying to ignore social-media onslaughts from angry fans after a loss while trying to focus and harden for the next match.

"Call my manager if you want to make a complaint," he retorted icily. "He'll make sure you get your season ticket refunded."

"Whoa, don't take your bad date out on me. I was merely going to suggest a way to work it off." She raised her palms in innocence, her smile mischievous as she nodded to the pool table. "I seem to recall you had one of these in your study. Can I tempt you?"

Without a second's hesitation he stood and swept up his glass, briskly nodding for her to follow. "Let's go."

Minutes later, as Kate finished racking the balls, he realized how expertly she'd defused him. Even stronger than his tendency toward self-righteous indignation—not his best trait, he'd be the first to admit—was his competitiveness.

He watched her with a mix of admiration and suspicion. How did she know?

She selected her cue. "I'll let you break since you're having a bad night."

He shook his head. "Ladies first."

"If you insist." She leaned over and shot, expertly sending two solid balls into pockets. She sank another one before missing her third shot and finally giving him a turn.

"I gather you've played before," he remarked dryly, then lined up his cue and sank his first ball.

"Lots of downtime on deployments. Not much else to do in the desert."

He sank one, missed one. "You mentioned. Iraq and Afghanistan. Army, right?"

"Combat support services, in a transportation battalion. Not the most action-packed job on the ground but not bad for female enlisted." *Crack*, another solid into a pocket.

"And then Saudi Arabia."

She missed. "And then Saudi Arabia."

"What was that like?" He squinted, lining up his shot.

"Hell."

He missed, put off by her frank response, but too interested to care. "Really? Why?"

She considered the layout on the table before positioning her cue. "The money was amazing, but everything else was awful. I did personal security for the wife of an American oil executive. The company had a chemical plant in the middle of nowhere, and all the Americans and their families lived in a compound outside the local town. The houses were big, there was a pool, a community center, a school—sounds great, right? It wasn't."

She missed. He picked an angle. "Why not?"

"The whole place was creepy." He caught her shiver of distaste in the second before he pocketed a ball. "Everyone knew everyone's business. Half of the husbands were sleeping with the other half's wives. I spent all my time with this one woman, who was either too smart to say anything about her husband's blatant cheating or too dumb to notice. Women aren't allowed to drive there so we were restricted to the compound, and if we left we had to wear *hijab*."

She raised her cue to take her turn. "After serving in the Middle East I thought the *Sharia* stuff wouldn't bother me, but living like that all the time is a whole other kind of crazy. I don't know how the women in these Muslim countries—" She stopped, looking up guiltily as she missed her shot. "Sorry, I didn't mean it like—"

"It's fine," he said mildly, lining up his cue. "There are over a billion Muslims in the world. We're not all the same."

"I know, I didn't mean to suggest—"

"I have as much in common with a Saudi Arabian Muslim as you do with a Nigerian Christian." He sank a ball. "If you are Christian, that is."

"Only by default. I haven't been to church in about fifteen years."

He sent his fifth ball into a pocket. "My point is, sharing a basic religious categorization with someone doesn't make me empathetic to their way of life. I've never been to Saudi Arabia, but I can't imagine anywhere with state-sanctioned beheadings is a particularly nice place to live."

"It's not. What's Sweden like?"

He missed, moved aside for her turn. "It's amazing. Beautiful, safe, good mix of historic and modern. I'm from Gothenburg, which is a university town, so there's always something going on. Sweden's expensive, though."

"And cold?" She pocketed a ball, moved to aim for another.

"I grew up with the weather so I don't feel it, but it's cold compared to Atlanta."

She missed, straightened. "I grew up in Jasper, about fifty miles north of the city. I can't remember the last time I saw snow. A Swedish winter would probably kill me."

"You'd be fine. Couple pints of Falcon, hot plate of reindeer meat and you won't even notice the weather."

"I would be so up for eating reindeer meat." She grinned at him across the table as he took his shot, sinking another ball. She had a pretty smile, and it lit up her face in a way its forced, professional equivalent didn't.

He gave her a quick onceover before focusing on his last ball. She was too tall for him, too likely to match his height in heels. He liked soft and curvy—she was flat and lean. He dated only super-smart, super-successful women, and he doubted Kate had a college degree.

So why did bright white heat pulse deep within his rib cage every time he looked at her?

He sank his final ball, took aim to hit the eight, then changed his mind.

"Have you ever been to a Skyline match?"

She shook her head, then nodded toward the table. "Your turn."

"I know." He propped the cue on the floor. "We're playing Tucson on Saturday. Want to come?"

"Me? Why?" Surprise brightened her eyes and warmed her expression before she resettled into her typically cool composure. "I mean, thank you."

"You're welcome," he replied smoothly, enjoying her momentary bewilderment. "I'll courier the tickets to your office tomorrow."

"Tickets?" she echoed, emphasizing the plural.

"Bring a friend."

Then he angled his cue on the green felt and leaned down, ending the conversation. He looked at the eight ball, squinted at the distance beyond it, but in his mind he saw Kate, eyes crinkled in laughter and then wide with shock.

He didn't like her. He couldn't like her. There was nothing about her to like. Except her laugh. And her smile. And her refusal to take him seriously. And her honesty. And her endearing curiosity about his home country. And, and, and.

And she was being paid to be nice to him, to sweeten him up, to open the door for her employer to provide exclusive security services to Atlanta Skyline.

He would do well to remember that.

He drew his arm back and snapped his shot. The eight ball spun, rolled, and dropped into a corner pocket with a satisfying *thunk*.

He stood, met her gaze. Didn't smile.

"I win."

Chapter 4

"How does this work?" Kate glanced between her ticket and the map showing the various entrances to King Stadium, home of Atlanta Skyline. "This has north, south, east, and west, but our tickets say EB 44. Is that east?"

"No idea. Let's ask." Jared indicated a customer-services desk beside the box office. They walked that way together, and she hustled to keep up with her colleague's long stride.

"We're lost," she told the woman behind the Plexiglas screen. "Can you tell us how to get to these seats?"

The woman examined the tickets, then broke into a smile. "You're in an Executive Box. You can use the VIP entrance by the south gate. Enjoy the match."

"Wow, VIP," Jared remarked as they made their way to the gate. "You sure do set the first-date bar high, Mitchell."

"Funny," she replied, deadpan. She hadn't made too many friends in the few months since she'd moved to Atlanta, so she'd asked one of the Area Managers from Peak Tactical to join her for the Saturday-afternoon match. Jared was a former security guard who'd been promoted into an operations-management role, and he was one of the few men in the company who'd been friendly to her from day one. They were of a similar age, but it hadn't occurred to her that he would read some romantic intent into her invitation.

Now his flirtation got heavier by the hour. She was embarrassed by her utter failure to see this coming and unsure why it was such a turnoff. He was funny, reasonably attractive, a big muscly country boy who should've been right up her alley.

But she kept thinking about that arrogant, uptight, Swedish-Turkish-Muslim nerd who'd beaten her at pool.

No one beat her at pool. She'd never imagined losing could be so sexy.

"Sweet, check this out." Jared recaptured her attention as they took an elevator up to the VIP tier. They walked through the hushed, carpeted hall until they found a door labeled forty-four. A printed sign hung beneath the number: *Reserved—Özkan Terim.*

"What did you say this guy's name was?" Jared squinted at the sheet.

"I think his full name is pronounced *Erz-kan*, but everyone calls him Oz."

"If you say so." He pushed open the door and she followed him inside.

"My God, this is…uh, hi." Kate processed only a glimpse of the plush suite—mini fridge full of drinks, several bottles chilling in a bucket, hot and cold buffet lined up on a ledge against the back wall—before her gaze came to rest on the three men lounging in front of the sliding door that overlooked the pitch.

"Hi," one of them replied, rising and extending his hand. "I'm Glynn."

"I'm Kate and this is Jared." She shook his hand, committing his name to memory. *Glynn is the black guy.*

"Nice to meet you guys. This is Ted and Sean."

Glynn, black. Ted, Asian. Sean, redhead. Got it.

"How do you know Oz?" Ted asked as all three of them rounded the sofa to join her and Jared by the mini fridge.

"I don't, really. My company installed the security in his house earlier this week. Jared and I work together. How do y'all know him?"

The three men exchanged unreadable glances before Sean replied. "Glynn and Oz went to college together. Ted's a video game reviewer and I'm a programmer, and we met Oz at an Outlaw Brigade launch a couple years ago. Do you play?"

She blinked. "Play what?"

"I guess that answers my question." Sean smiled warmly. "Outlaw Brigade is a military-themed, first-person shooter video game. Oz has an endorsement deal with the company who produces it."

She nodded, deciding this probably wasn't the right time to inform them she'd shot someone in real life and it wasn't fun at all.

"Video game reviewer is a job?" Jared asked.

Kate cringed, but Ted didn't seem offended as he explained, "It can be if you're good enough. I started out interning at a newspaper, and now I have columns in magazines here and in Australia."

Jared grunted and turned to the fridge. "Who's ready for a drink?"

Sean and Ted joined him in discussing the multitude of options on offer, while Glynn slid open the glass door. It led to a private stand positioned just above the halfway line, with spectacular, uninterrupted views toward both goals.

"This is amazing," she murmured, joining Glynn outside. The match was due to start in a few minutes, most of the seats were full and the tense, excited atmosphere reached all the way to their sky-high tier.

"Are you a big soccer fan?" he asked.

"Total novice. This is my first match."

"I'll be honest, I wasn't into it until I met Oz. It's a lot easier to take an interest when you know one of the players."

"You said you met in college? I thought he went pro when he was, like, seventeen."

"He made a deal with Roland Carlsson. He would move to the US only if he could study while he was playing. It took him an extra semester to finish, but he did it." He shrugged his admiration. "We actually went to different schools, but it's easier to say we met in college. I went to MIT."

"And where did Oz go?"

Glynn watched her for a second too long, as if he was waiting for the punch line, then he answered, "Harvard."

"Oh. Right," she stammered, her cheeks heating. "I guess I should've known that."

He waved a dismissive hand. "It barely gets a mention in the press. Reporters are much more interested in how many goals he scores than his philosophy degree."

She nodded noncommittally, fighting the urge to turn and run all the way back to her crappy one-bedroom apartment. She was way out of her comfort zone. These were not her people, this was not her sport, and Oz was definitely nothing more than her client.

"For you, fair maiden." Jared appeared at her side and handed her a glass of champagne. Sean and Ted followed him and they all arranged themselves in the hard plastic seats lined up outside the box.

A cheer went up as the two teams filed out of the tunnel and lined up alongside each other while the announcer boomed the names and numbers of the players. The Jumbotron at one end of the stadium showed each player's photo, and an unexpected thrill went through her as a familiar face flashed larger-than-life and the deep voice declared, "Number eighteen, Özkan Terim."

The two teams shook hands, and then the players moved into position. Kate watched as Oz raised cupped hands, lowered his chin and murmured to himself, then brought his palms over his face.

He was praying. In front of seventy thousand people.

No wonder he'd found his way onto Citizens First's list.

The whistle blew and the game began. Kate watched the two teams pass the ball back and forth and back again. No one had scored after ten minutes, and she could tell from Jared's fidgeting that he was as bored as she was.

"I'm going to grab another drink," he said, rising from his seat. "Want anything?"

"I'll take a beer if they've got it."

"Be right back." He pulled his phone from his pocket as he stepped inside. She suspected he might be awhile.

The crowd gasped at something and she returned her attention to the match. Tucson's goalkeeper booted the ball all the way back to the center line and players in brick-red Skyline uniforms raced after it.

Glynn nudged her. "Do you want some play-by-play?"

The crowd sucked in a breath at something else she couldn't see, and she nodded gratefully. "Yes. I have no idea what's going on."

Ted leaned around him. "You've come to the right place. Glynn loves externally processing everything that happens in a match. Pass to Silva, Silva loses possession, Vidal charges up the side, but can he win it back?" He expertly mimicked Glynn's voice.

"Don't forget the facts and stats," Sean added. "Random striker hasn't scored at Skyline's ground in his last five appearances. Oz has never conceded a goal against so-and-so subbed in from the bench. And did you know what's-his-name is from Cameroon and despite its Francophone classification, Cameroon was briefly a German colony?"

Glynn smiled broadly, and she wondered how iceman Oz had managed to round up such a nice group of friends.

"Please ignore these gentlemen, whose love for the game massively exceeds their deeper understanding of its nuances. First, let me set the scene. Skyline had a banging start to the season after finishing in the top four last year. This is Roland's—and Oz's, come to think of it—third year in Atlanta and the Carlsson turnaround is in full swing. The first year he instilled European discipline and sophistication. Last year he attracted a wave of up-and-coming players, and this year Skyline should have a clear run at the title."

"Except." Ted inclined his head knowingly.

"Except their star winger, Rio Vidal, went down with torn ligaments in March, and then one of the center backs, Paulo, was out with a pulled hamstring. Vidal and Paulo are playing again but the last couple of months have been terrible."

"They haven't been that bad," Sean protested. "Oz has kept a clean sheet more often than not, we just aren't scoring goals like we need to."

"Our ginger friend here is an optimist," Ted explained.

"No, I'm just not as cynical as you two," Sean countered. "What's the point of supporting a team if you aren't hoping for them to win every time they kick off?"

"Hang on," she raised a hand to slow them, peripherally noting Jared's return as she accepted a bottle of beer from him. "Rewind. Clean sheet?"

"Oz is a left-back," Glynn replied. "That makes him part of the defense, which means his performance is measured in how many goals he lets in as opposed to how many goals he scores. If your defense keeps the other team from scoring at all, it's called a clean sheet."

"Like a shutout in football."

"Exactly."

"But Oz keeps running up to the other team's half, like right now." She pointed to where all of the Skyline players were clustered near Tucson's goal.

Glynn squinted at the pitch. "He should fall back, actually. They're pretty open and Tucson could easily break out to counter. Anyway, Oz is unique among defenders. He originally trained to be a winger—an up-front, attacking player—because he's super-fast and nimble. Roland moved him to the defense as a wing-back—someone who attacks, but is also quick enough to retreat in time to mark an opposing player and defend the goal."

"There are very few players who can do what he does," Ted added. "He's big enough to make tackles and get in other players' way, but not so big that it slows him down."

"And here I thought it was all about kicking a ball into a net," Jared remarked loudly—too loudly, considering how warmly they'd been welcomed into what was clearly a regular audience in this box.

Then again, no one else seemed bothered. Maybe she was overreacting. Weren't her mother and sister always telling her she was too uptight? Although they could use a little more detail orientation between the two of them, so…

Glynn shrugged. "There's a reason why soccer is the most popular sport in the world. You can enjoy it on a simple level, like kicking a ball into a goal, or on a very complicated, technical level."

"Guess on which level Glynn resides?" Sean grinned.

Kate's interest grew as the match wore on, largely thanks to Glynn's commentary. His friends rolled their eyes but she liked how he explained the stakes of each missed shot, each lost tackle, each yellow card raised by the referee. She enjoyed getting the color of player rivalries and injury bouncebacks, and although she still relied heavily on his technical commentary, by the middle of the second half she understood the basics enough to raise her fist in anger at an unfairly awarded free kick.

"This is called a set piece," Glynn explained as both teams arranged themselves in front of Skyline's goal. "Tucson isn't having a good season, but they've had a lot of goals from set pieces. Skyline is in real danger here."

The scoreboard was still nil-nil, and the crowd held a collective breath as the ref blew the whistle and the Tucson midfielder shot the ball. It arced with seemingly deadly aim, until Oz jumped above the opposition player in front of him and headed it far from the area.

Applause thundered around the stadium as the ball went back into open play, and Ted and Sean high-fived their approval.

Glynn grinned at her. "And that's why sometimes stopping a goal can be just as important as scoring one."

Beside her Jared groaned under his breath, and she turned to him guiltily. She'd invited him, then ignored him most of the afternoon as she got caught up in the game. She forced a smile, determined to give him more attention.

"I'm dying," he muttered. "This is the most boring sport in the world. How much longer does it go on for?"

"Twenty minutes. But Ted said the box stays open for two hours after it ends."

She counted the beer bottles at his feet while he weighed up this information. Good thing she was driving.

He sighed. "Free booze is free booze. I guess I can stand a little more time with the nerd brigade."

She flinched at his last two words, suddenly reminded of too many men, all of them bullies. Her tone hardened as she replied, "I want to stay long enough to say hi to Oz and thank him for the tickets. Maybe I should call you a taxi."

"It's all good, babe." He shot her a seductive smile she bet usually worked like a charm. "I want to hang with you, it doesn't matter where."

Great. She'd invited Jared because she thought they were squarely in the friend zone. He'd read that as romantic, and now she had to reject him, probably losing her one work ally—and by extension his entire division—in the process.

Nice work, Mitchell. One more item for the list of Reasons Kate Will Be Single Forever.

She was still pondering when and how to make her lack of interest clear to Jared when the whistle blew, ending the match. The scoreboard was goalless—a draw.

"All that running and no one even got a point," Jared remarked, stretching as he rose. "One of these days y'all should check out a football game, see how a real sport gets played."

The guys ignored his comment as they filed back into the box, where a fresh dessert buffet had been set out. Jared loaded a plate while she hung back with Sean.

"Does Oz normally stop into the box afterward? Or should I wait for him outside or something? I want to thank him for the tickets before we head out."

He wrinkled his nose. "It depends. If they win he might come up and celebrate, but for a draw… I doubt it. Do you want me to text him? He has to do the press thing, shower and change. You might be waiting awhile."

Her heart sank. "That's okay, I'll call him later."

"Or," he mused before shouting over to Glynn. "Hey, Kate was hoping to see our man. I don't think he'll come up, do you?"

Glynn shook his head, crossing to join them. "Not today."

"But she wants to thank him for the tickets."

Something passed between the two friends, unspoken, inscrutable. Glynn turned to her with a smile. "Why don't you come to my housewarming tonight? He'll be there."

"Tonight? That's really nice but you don't have to—"

"You said you're new to the city, right? Come hang out, meet some new people," Sean suggested.

"I wouldn't ask if I didn't want you there," Glynn added. "You seem cool. And we're always about recruiting new soccer fans."

Heat crawled up her ears. Cool? *Cool?* God, if only they knew. Her idea of a wild night was getting pizza delivered instead of picking it up.

"We'll be there," Jared announced, appearing behind her. He grinned down at her and winked. "Let's show these soccer fans how to party."

* * * *

Oz paused on the landing outside Glynn's apartment, which occupied the entire top floor of a converted warehouse, and tried to shake off his bad mood. It wasn't Glynn's fault Skyline couldn't get a goal today, and it wouldn't be fair to drag this black cloud into his party.

Oz inhaled, exhaled even more slowly. He often struggled to wind down after a match, and this evening was no exception. His mind whirred as he involuntarily reviewed every move he'd made in those ninety minutes, and at intervals his body literally trembled with excess adrenaline.

He wouldn't sleep tonight, that was for sure.

He breathed deeply again. Closed his eyes. Reopened them when all he saw was the zero-zero scoreboard. He debated going home, saving his friends from his bleak mood, but female voices approaching in the stairwell prompted him forward.

He opened the door. *Maybe the love of my life is inside.*

Oz had seen Glynn's apartment before, having accompanied him on one of the walk-throughs when he was deciding whether to buy it. The cavernous, echoing space they'd surveyed that day seemed a lifetime away from the vividly decorated apartment ringing with laughter. Music pumped from the built-in sound system, a bartender tossed bottles into the air, and the space heaved with the best and brightest of the tech world in which Glynn was a major figure.

He smiled, proud of his best friend's success. Glynn spent his first year in Atlanta sleeping in one of Oz's spare bedrooms, investing everything he earned from his IT day job into a startup company. Now he produced and licensed some of the most popular apps in the world while always keeping his eyes open for the next big innovation.

They'd both come a long way from eating cold pizza for breakfast on lazy undergraduate mornings.

Glynn spotted him and raised a bottle of brown liquid in the air as Oz approached.

"Chocolate milk, peanut butter, and half a banana. One Wizard Recovery Special, primed and ready to go." Glynn handed over the smoothie, which Oz accepted with one hand while giving his friend a half-hug with the other.

"You're a king among men, my brother. Too bad your party sucks. Couldn't you get anyone to come?"

"They heard you were here and bolted."

"I have that effect." Oz grinned. "Seriously, the place looks great. And it was a great idea to pay all these people to turn up and pretend to like you."

"You'd be amazed at how cheap it is to buy friends these days. Hey, sorry about the result, but a clean sheet's a clean sheet, right?"

Oz's momentarily lightened mood resettled heavily. "We needed the win today, and we should've walked over Tucson. I don't know what's going on up front, but we have to fix our finishing."

Glynn shrugged. "You've got Boise next week, and they've been in existence for, what, five minutes? You'll win that before you set foot on the pitch. Paulo will get the rest he needs, and Vidal will have a chance to up his tempo without being under too much pressure. It should be a nice turning point in the second half of the season."

Oz grunted, unwilling to let Glynn's logic dent his irritation. "Anyway. Kate texted to say thanks for the tickets. Was she okay in the box?"

"Of course she was okay. She was great. Why wouldn't she be?"

"I don't know her too well."

"She's cool. And she's here."

"She is?" Oz glanced around the crowded room. "You invited her?"

"Sure, she's a budding soccer fan. Can't say the same for the guy she's with, but you can't win 'em all."

Oz stiffened. "She gave the second ticket to a guy?"

"Yeah." Glynn crossed his arms, looked him up and down. "What's up with you? Are you interested in her?"

"No, I just—"

"Because I wouldn't blame you. She's funny, friendly, and she's got that whole girl-next-door thing going on."

He shook his head resolutely. "She's not my type. She works for the security company Roland hired."

For a few seconds Glynn didn't respond, but Oz could read the skepticism in his friend's eyes. Finally he nodded to one end of the room. "Well, if you want to say hi, she's over there with her man friend. Big bodybuilder dude, shaved head, unfortunate T-shirt. Answers to Jared."

"I'll catch you later."

It took only a minute for Oz to spot them. Jared's V-neck was too tight, so instead of showing off his muscles it awkwardly drew attention to the visible outlines of his nipples.

Kate, on the other hand, looked stunning in tight jeans and a slim-fitting, women's-cut Skyline jersey. The smile she flashed as she caught his approach completed the picture.

"Here he is," she beamed. He stopped in front of her, unsure how to greet her. Should he shake her hand? Wave?

She decided for him, leaning in for a quick, friendly hug. It lasted only seconds, yet long enough to give him a vivid impression. Her slim, sturdy body. The crisp scents of strawberry and mint. The soft press of breasts that felt bigger than they looked.

He cleared his throat, shifted his weight. Desperately tried to ignore the hard-on pressing against his fly.

"Check out my souvenir." She spun to show him his name and number printed on the back of the jersey. "What do you think?"

His smile felt as tight as his jeans. "I'm flattered."

"Jared." The owner of the name stuck out his hand, which Oz shook dutifully. "Thanks for the tickets. Interesting sport. What're you drinking?"

Belatedly Oz remembered the smoothie in his hand. "Recovery shake. Mostly chocolate milk, with some peanut butter and banana."

Jared shook his head. "You should never have dairy after an intense workout. Too hard on your stomach. I use this fast-digesting carbohydrate powder. Way better. I'll give you the name."

"Thanks, but—"

"I'm telling you, this stuff's amazing. I barely even bother with recovery days anymore. It's expensive but it's worth it."

His shoulders tensed, but Oz bit back his impulse to inform this moron that he was utterly incorrect. "Okay," he muttered instead.

"Have you thought about bulking up at all? Might help you stay on your feet." The six-foot-three muscle tower had the audacity to wink at him. Oz tightened his fingers on his sports bottle.

"I loved the game," Kate interjected, diverting his attention.

"It wasn't our best performance."

"Could've fooled me. The whole thing was—wait, let me remember my vocab—*box to box.* Wasn't it?"

He smiled. "It was."

"The seats were amazing, and your friends are so nice. This may sound silly, but I loved all the running. You guys never stop! Not like football, where there are a lot of pauses."

Jared snorted derisively. "Good call, Kate. Soccer is definitely not like football."

Oz caught the flash of irritation in Kate's eyes and the already too-taut spring of his temper coiled dangerously tighter.

He had to walk away before he did something stupid. His nerves were too raw, his emotions too amped. He really, really wanted to punch someone, and Jared became more tempting by the minute.

"I'm glad you had fun," he addressed Kate directly. "Hopefully next time you'll get to see us win."

"I'll be repping number eighteen no matter what. Thanks again for inviting me."

"No problem. I need to say hello to a few people, then I'm heading home. Nice to meet you, Jared. Kate, I'm sure we'll be in touch soon."

He exchanged another handshake with Jared, while Kate inclined her head to say goodbye. He raised his drink in salute and bee-lined for the nearest familiar face.

It turned out to be Sean, standing a few feet away.

"Everything okay?" his friend asked.

"Of course. Why wouldn't it be?"

"Because I spent all afternoon with that mass of *musculus* and you're so high-strung you're practically vibrating, so I have trouble imagining you two calmly discussing current affairs."

"I walked away. Are you proud of me?"

Sean lifted a shoulder. "That depends."

"On?"

"What you do when you find out your beefy buddy is getting handsy."

Oz spun in time to see Kate leaning out of Jared's grip, Jared's hands settling on her waist, Kate removing them and stepping backward.

Oz planted his smoothie on a table and steamed in, his rational mind politely stepping aside to give way to a wave of white-hot anger.

"Keep your hands off her," he seethed, shoving Jared with a flattened palm on his bulky chest.

Jared's answering smirk was like a red flag to a bull. "Is that the best you've got, bro? Or should we take this outside?"

Blood pounded in Oz's ears and he saw Tucson's enormous center-back, felt the faint press of the man's cleats against his calf in a borderline illegal tackle, relived the defender's exaggerated effort to haul him back up onto his feet, and the boiling frustration when the referee ignored Oz's appeal and motioned for them to play on.

Jared moved in. Got in his face. Set his jaw. Narrowed his eyes.

Oz stuck his foot behind Jared's ankle, led with his shoulder, knocked the bigger man off-balance and sent him sprawling onto his back.

Jared's head hit the floor with a *thud* and Oz instinctively raised his hands in innocence, fully aware he'd fouled his opponent.

Except he wasn't on the pitch, he was at Glynn's party. Where everyone was staring at him. And Jared lay gasping on the floor.

Too late, he looked at Kate. She glared at him as she knelt beside Jared's supine form.

"Come on," she urged Jared, although her glacial stare was clearly meant for Oz. "You just got the wind knocked out of you. Get up and let's get out of here."

He should apologize. He was out of line. But then he recalled the image of Kate removing Jared's hands from her waist and he decided to follow the two of them out of the apartment instead.

"Kate, hang on, I—"

"Stop," she hissed, spinning to face him just outside the door as Jared limped down the hallway, coughing and spluttering.

"He was bothering you. I was trying to help."

"You were trying to make a scene, and you succeeded. Happy?"

Sheepish. Embarrassed. Maybe even a little guilty. But no, definitely not happy.

Oz's complex discomfort crystallized into a simpler, more readily accessible emotion. Anger.

"You brought him here," he countered. "You brought him to my box, pushed him on my friends. Don't blame me for intervening when your bad decision got out of control, and certainly don't trouble yourself to say thanks."

She rolled her eyes. "The situation *was* under control. I can take care of myself. And if I did need someone to fight my battles for me—which I don't—frankly I'm not sure you'd be the one I'd call."

It stung, because it was so obviously true. Oz shoved his hands into his pockets. Why did every conversation he had with Kate turn into a fight—and why did he always lose?

She sighed, looked down the hall, then back at him. "I have to give Jared a lift home. Thanks again for the tickets. I had fun."

She didn't sound like she had fun, but he offered no reply as she jogged down the hallway and into the stairwell. Within seconds her footsteps echoed to nothing.

For a minute he stood, alone, listening to the dull thump of music through the door. His head throbbed. His shoulder ached. He should go home and try to sleep.

Instead he pushed back into the apartment, into the noise and movement and wide, anticipatory gazes of his friends.

"So," Glynn remarked dryly. "That went well."

Chapter 5

"And that includes installation? And a month's subscription. Wow. No, I can't match that price, but you know with us you get the benefit of—hello?"

Kate sighed, typed a note beside the client's name in the database and dialed the next one. A female voice answered after two rings.

"Hi, this is Kate Mitchell from Peak Tactical. I'm calling to let you know that we've signed a preferred-provider agreement with your neighborhood watch association, and as part of that deal we're offering twenty-five percent off in-home security—"

"No thanks, we have a Rottweiler." The line went dead.

Kate coded the client's name as not interested, dialed the next. Waited. This time a man's voice picked up.

"Hi, this is Kate Mitchell from Peak Tactical. I'm calling to—" Dial tone.

She groaned inwardly. She thought winning the contract with the neighborhood watch would open the door for sales to all the resident members, but after two hours on the phone she'd sold only one response-service subscription, and it was the barest-bones option at that.

Hopefully things would get easier the longer she was in the job as she grew her network and client base. The Skyline account was the only reason she'd reached this month's sales target, but next month already loomed.

And chances were the Skyline account was bust before it ever boomed. She sat back in her chair, staring unseeingly at her computer screen.

Only forty-eight hours had passed since the incident at Glynn's apartment, but she must've replayed it in her mind at least a hundred times.

Jared wasn't exactly on his best behavior, but Oz's response was worse. She hadn't asked for his help—she hadn't needed his help. She was a veteran, a security contractor—she'd spent a year in Saudi Arabia. Did he really think she couldn't hold her own against one tipsy asshole in a room packed with people?

Of course she could. She was strong. Fearless. Tough as any of the men she'd served alongside.

Then why did it give her an illicit, guilty thrill every time she remembered the fury in Oz's eyes? Or the unhesitating purpose in his movements. Or the cool, calm way he'd dumped Jared on the floor.

She shook her head in self-disgust and refocused on the database. For a self-proclaimed pacifist Oz was rude and aggressive, and she shouldn't find that attractive. She didn't need a protector, and this was just one more way her mother's lifelong desperation for male attention had taught her that her own strength wasn't enough, and that her value depended on how much a man liked her, and—

"Those guys are here for you again, Kate." Lorraine leaned into the room she shared with five other sales associates.

Kate frowned at her over the top of her cubicle. "Which guys?"

"They were here the other week. Forgot what it was about."

Maybe you should've asked their names. You're only the freaking receptionist.

"Where are they?"

"Boardroom."

Kate grabbed her notebook, stuck her feet into the high heels under her desk and clomped down the hall. Must be those guys from the cash-in-transit business, she concluded irritably. Because telling them for a third time that Peak Tactical didn't want to form a partnership would really complete her already fantastic afternoon.

She swung open the boardroom door and stopped dead.

"Roland. Oz. Hello."

The two men half-stood in greeting, but she waved them down as she took a seat on the opposite side of the long table. "What can I do for you gentlemen?"

Roland frowned. "Aren't you expecting us? I spoke to your receptionist this morning."

Goddammit, Lorraine. "I'm sorry, the message didn't get through. How can I help?"

Oz wouldn't look at her, focusing instead on the edge of the table. She couldn't tell whether his stony expression veered more toward apology or hostility, and in the end she supposed it didn't matter. His demeanor broadcast that he didn't want to be here, and he didn't want to see her.

Too bad for him, she decided, trying not to notice how exceptionally hot he looked. Black hair perfectly coiffed, cheeks smoothly shaven, T-shirt just tight enough to—

Roland interrupted her thoughts. "Oz says the personal security installation at his house was both sensitively and comprehensively done, so thank you. Unfortunately, we're back."

Had Oz really said that? She glanced at him for confirmation, but he was pokerfaced.

Roland continued, "Skyline is playing away on Friday, at Boise Amity. They're a brand-new club, keen to make an impression, but they have relatively limited funding after one of their sponsors went bust. Their manager called me yesterday to let me know they've received several anonymous calls threatening both teams if Oz is allowed to play."

She winced. "Citizens First?"

"Probably. They've got a pretty substantial following in the area."

"Do the local police think the threats have any credibility?"

"Probably not, but none of us want to take chances. Amity is low on resources and I don't want to embarrass the manager by making demands for personal security, so I wanted to ask whether you—or maybe a wider team from Peak Tactical—can accompany us to Boise."

Kate tried not to grin. *Cha-ching!*

"VIP services are our bread and butter. I recommend we subcontract personnel in Boise once we have a more detailed understanding of the situation. That'll be cheaper for Skyline as it prevents us potentially flying people we don't need across the country."

Roland nodded. "If possible, I'd also like you to attend, and compile a report after the trip that might help us develop a framework for player security going forward. I certainly hope this is a one-off, but in case it's not, we should have a policy we can refer to."

"Absolutely." Sales numbers *and* a trip across the country. She fought the urge to raise her fist in triumph. "Let's consider Boise a test case, after which I'll draw up recommendations for the rest of the season."

"Perfect. I also wanted to—" He pulled his buzzing phone from his pocket and frowned at the screen. "Sorry, this is urgent. I'll be right back."

Roland rounded the table, opened the door as he answered the call and then shut it again, his voice dulling through the wall.

That left her and Oz. Alone.

Silence stretched long and wide. She clasped her hands in her lap. She wouldn't make this comfortable for him. Oh, no. If he had something to say, he could damn well—

"How are you?" He finally looked at her, raising those big eyes to fix her with an inscrutable gaze.

"Fine," she replied primly. "Yourself?"

"Not great."

"I'm sorry to hear that."

"My best friend threw a party on Saturday night. Everyone was having a great time, and then I acted like a little bit of a dick."

One corner of her mouth lifted. "A little bit?"

"I acted like a dick."

"How big are we talking? Five inches? Six?"

He put the edge of his left hand on the table and planted his right hand next to it. Then he slid his right hand over to make the space in between wider. And wider. And even wider.

"I'll believe that when I see it," she told him dryly.

He smiled, flattening his palms on the table. "My point is, I behaved badly and I'm sorry. I'll apologize to Jared if you think it's necessary."

"He's moved on and so have I. I appreciate your apology, though."

"Good." He paused, and the humor in his expression dimmed. "Can I show you something in confidence? I don't want Roland panicking."

Mentally she stumbled at his sudden switch from personal to professional, and it took her a second to shift gears. "Of course, go ahead."

He pulled out his phone, tapped and scrolled, and then handed it over.

"More of these Ausonius comments," she murmured. "Your privacy settings are all locked down?"

"As tightly as anything on the Internet can be. I triple-checked when these comments started appearing. Every time I block this person, a new username pops up with the same content."

She leaned back in her chair, thinking through the problem as he asked, "Do you think I'm overreacting? I don't want to alarm Roland if it's just some stupid fan of a rival team who thinks they're funny. For all we know this person might not even be in America, let alone anywhere near Atlanta."

"It's always good to be overcautious, and I would tell you if it felt completely benign. The persistence, though, raises a red flag for me. This person doesn't seem to be getting bored."

Oz shook his head. "The opposite, if anything."

"Let me talk to our cyber-security guy. We'll keep it off the record for now, and I'll let you know if he suggests we do something Skyline might have to pay for."

"I'll pay for it. It'd be worth it to keep Roland from freaking out any more than he already is."

"I'll give our guy a call and see what he says. Otherwise—Here's Roland."

The manager burst into the room, blatantly preoccupied as he glanced at his watch. "Bad injury news, I'm afraid. I need to get back to the training ground. Are we done here?" Then, softening his tone he added, "I mean, feel free to call me to follow up if you have any other questions."

"I think we're good." Kate smiled brightly. "I'll prepare the invoice."

Chapter 6

"Paulo's ball!"

Oz ducked at the center back's instruction, avoiding an accidental deflection into their own net if they both tried to go for the ball at the same time. Instead Paulo comfortably cleared it with a header, one of their midfielders took possession and within seconds they were all running back toward Amity's goal.

Midfielder Nico Silva made a nicely weighted pass to Rio, who took an audacious shot on goal that went wide. The clock ran down and Oz glanced at the fourth official, who raised a digital board showing the minutes added on for injury time.

Only two, thank God. He was tired, and Skyline's two-nil lead was unlikely to be challenged in only a hundred and twenty seconds.

Skyline's forward players passed the ball between them with deliberate sluggishness, and he vaguely marked an even more exhausted-looking Amity midfielder. Finally the whistle blew full time, ending the match and sealing Skyline's victory.

"Nice one, good match," he told the Amity player as they shook hands. He repeated a similar pleasantry to each player he encountered as he moved toward the away stand, and all of his opponents had similarly sportsmanlike—if slightly breathless—replies.

"Oz, pleasure to play with you today." Boise's captain—an American in his late thirties who'd had a successful career in Europe—spoke enthusiastically as they shook hands. "I know there was some noise around you coming to Boise and I really appreciate that you gave us a chance. We're trying to build a strong franchise out here and the last thing we want is for top-flight players to be put off by the hostility of a couple local idiots."

"It's cool," Oz assured him. "I wish you the best. The more clubs thrive, the better the competition across the league."

They parted and Oz joined his teammates in applauding the away fans, who leapt and screamed and waved red-and-navy scarves to celebrate the decisive victory.

Oz forced a smile as he clapped, his shoulder blades drawing together inadvertently, the space between his eyes tightening. Something was bothering him, something heavy and ominous, compressing his lungs and balling his hands, but he couldn't trace its source. He couldn't shake it, either.

Maybe it was the half-full stadium. The rows and rows of empty seats loomed over the pitch like thousands of hollow eye sockets, and the erratic concentration of spectators made the sound of the crowd echo and fade and swell in strange ways as he moved from one end to the other. He didn't think he'd ever played for the viewing benefit of so few people in such a big space, even as a youth player for the Swedish national team.

Or maybe it was the paranoia pervading so many elements of this trip. Kate's presence at the airport, on the plane, in the hotel, and now in the tunnel was a constant, if not totally unpleasant, reminder that certain people didn't want him in Boise. And although the welcoming hospitality from Amity's staff and players was second to none, it was hard to ignore the black-suited security contractors always on the periphery.

"If the people of Boise didn't hate you before, they certainly do now." Laurent Perrin, Skyline's French central midfielder, slapped him on the back as they started toward the tunnel. "Your goal-line clearance cost them the one chance they had to get on the scoreboard. And it was epic, by the way."

"Thanks." Oz cheered up as he recalled his flat-out sprint to catch the Amity striker who'd burst past Guedes and made a run for goal. Oz caught him on the goal-line and flicked the ball up and over the net. "That was pretty cool, huh?"

"Super cool. But what else could we expect from the Wizard?"

"That goal of yours was helpful, too, Lolo. We already had two on the board, but that's when the Frenchman really excels, producing goals that are late in the match, against a weakened side, and ultimately superfluous."

Laurent rolled his eyes as Oz playfully mimicked comments made by a sports journalist earlier in the week. "A goal is a goal is a goal, *non*?"

"*Oui*, my friend." Oz clapped Laurent on the shoulder as they followed the rest of the team through the tunnel into the changing room.

Oz dropped onto one of the wooden benches running along the walls. He began unlacing his boots as Roland arrived and took his place at one end of the room.

"Nice result today, gentlemen. I know it wasn't our toughest game of the season, but it was good to see everyone playing as if it was and supporting the younger guys in their opportunities to hit the pitch." The manager nodded to the three young substitutes who'd come on in the second half, one of whom had just made his debut.

"I know the bright lights of Boise are tempting," he continued. "But we have an early flight home tomorrow and the bus will be leaving for the airport at nine o'clock sharp. Let's think about sticking to the hotel for once, okay?"

Most of the players were too tired to grumble, and the changing room echoed with cleats clunking to the floor and hangers retrieved from hooks. Oz stared at the toes of his boots, turning over Roland's words in his mind.

They'd had earlier flights out of wilder cities. Roland wasn't worried about them partying and missing the bus. He wanted everyone to stay in the hotel where Peak Tactical's contractors could keep an eye on them.

An eye on *him*.

A wave of weariness washed over him, dragging what was left of his energy with it as it receded. He didn't have enough space in his brain to think about this now. He only cared about showering, changing, and getting back to the hotel.

Laurent's comedy singing in the shower perked him up slightly, and after they boarded the bus Rio twisted around in the seat in front of him, wearing his trademark grin. Oz returned it. It was so infectious he'd have to be dead not to.

"Is nice, boys?" Rio asked.

Oz frowned, trying to decipher Rio's Spanglish. "What boys?"

"Boys." The Chilean tapped the window.

"Oh, Boise."

"Boy-see," the midfielder repeated. "Is good?"

Oz shrugged. "Small."

"Is why the boss, he say, go in the hotel, no clubs?"

"Probably," he lied.

"Is fine. All I will want is the big steak. You will come?"

"To the hotel restaurant?"

Rio nodded.

Oz mustered a smile, knowing full well he'd be ordering room service. "Maybe."

* * * *

Kate pressed her ear against the door before she knocked, alert for any sound that might indicate Oz wasn't alone, any cosmic hint that she should turn around and walk away.

Nothing.

She rapped sharply before she lost her nerve.

"Yeah?" His response was muffled, distracted.

"It's Kate."

"Hold on."

He opened the door looking uncharacteristically scruffy in a loose T-shirt and athletic shorts.

"What?" he asked without preamble.

She held up her palms. "I come in peace. I saw the rest of the team in the restaurant, and someone mentioned you decided to stay up here and eat by yourself. I wanted to make sure everything was all right."

"Everything's fine."

"Great. I'll leave you to it."

She turned to go back to her own room, genuinely pleased with the relatively low level of hostility in that exchange compared to every other time she'd spoken to Oz on this trip. Given their accord at her office she initially wondered if he was putting on a disgruntled spectacle for his manager's benefit, but after his third tirade against bodyguards riding on the team bus she stopped caring. Her job was to keep him safe, not happy.

"Where are you going?"

She glanced over her shoulder at his question. Oz stood in the still-open doorway.

"To my room, for an exciting evening of pizza and HBO. Why?"

His mouth curved in a half-smile. "There's no pizza on the menu. I checked."

"You're kidding." She had her heart set on pepperoni and mushrooms.

"Five-star hotel, five-star menu." He nodded into the room behind him. "We'll order one pan-seared salmon and one chicken and waffles, and the squad nutritionist won't know who ate what."

"She checks your room-service receipts?"

"She's tough. Is it a deal?"

Kate exhaled. Even without pizza, the thought of a long, hot bath, an hour of television and an early bedtime was tempting.

And lonely.

"Sure." She let him hold the door as she crossed into his room.

His room was only slightly larger than hers and equally unmarred by personal items, except his Skyline-branded suit hanging in the open wardrobe and an unzipped sports bag on a chair. The TV was frozen on what she guessed was a video game, with the muzzle of a rifle aimed into a wintry landscape, shown from the shooter's perspective.

Oz gestured toward the screen. "An old version of Outlaw Brigade, set in the Eastern Front during World War II."

"This is your system?" She indicated the tangle of wires and controllers on the floor.

"I bring it with me when we travel. Sometimes I get post-match anxiety and insomnia. It helps me calm down."

She picked up the box for the game and scanned the bloody, violent images on the back. "You find this calming?"

"It's mindless. Distracting. Stupid, over-the-top death and destruction. Like a horror movie."

"I don't like horror movies." She put down the box and picked up the in-room phone. "Pan-seared salmon, you said?"

He nodded, sat down on the floor with his back against the end of the bed and resumed playing. He muted the sound as he said over his shoulder, "Can you double-check there's no pork in the chicken and waffles?"

Kate spoke to the room-service operator and placed their order.

"Twenty minutes," she informed him, dropping onto the end of the bed. "Definitely no pork in the chicken."

"Thanks. I know it sounds paranoid, but pork always seems to find its way into Southern recipes."

"So tattoos and alcohol are fine, but pork is off-limits," she mused aloud.

"If I adhere to two of the Five Pillars in a week I consider it a victory."

"That certainly is a unique brand of Islam."

"No one gives Jewish people a hard time if they aren't Orthodox, and I've met plenty of self-proclaimed bad Catholics. I prefer to think of myself as an imperfect Muslim." He lifted a shoulder.

"Don't get me wrong, I met plenty of so-called Muslims in Saudi Arabia who were far worse than imperfect. What's okay for them is most definitely not okay for their wives, you know? Like, being super devout is fine when it means your wife can't drive or make any decisions, but if you want to stay out all night gambling and drinking illegal booze, no one better dare say anything about it."

He nodded, unmuting the screen. "Using religion as a tool of oppression is never acceptable, no matter what holy book it's based on."

"Yeah. Exactly." She bit her lower lip, mildly embarrassed that he could so easily and eloquently articulate what she struggled to get across.

That's what happens when you go to Harvard instead of scraping through a handful of distance-learning credits.

The video-game soldier hiked up and down snow-covered hills, then wandered into an abandoned village. He peered into doorways, crouched behind burnt-out cars and then ducked behind a semi-destroyed brick wall as gunfire popped from around the corner. Oz's soldier returned fire, manually reloading the rifle.

She wrinkled her nose as red mist filled the air. Why anyone would pay to spend their free time playing games like this was beyond her.

The frame froze and Oz twisted around to look at her.

"Am I being an insensitive asshole?"

She blinked. "What?"

He tossed the controller on the floor. "I'm playing a shoot-'em-up war game with an actual war veteran in the room. Kate, I am so sorry."

"You're fine." She dismissed his concern with a wave. "I was in a transportation battalion—combat support, not combat."

"Still, you were there."

"The game doesn't bother me. Honestly. I'd tell you if it did."

He looked at the screen, then back at her, and tapped the carpet beside him. "Sit with me. We'll run a mission together. A non-gory one."

She joined him on the floor and lifted the spare controller while he scrolled through various screens. She tried her fingers on the unfamiliar buttons, squinting at the options.

"Things have certainly moved on from Super Nintendo," she remarked.

"Hang onto it if you still have yours. Collectors will pay big money for those old systems."

"I'm sure my mom sold it years ago. It belonged to one of her boyfriends. He gave it to me and my sister, mostly to justify buying himself something better."

"Sounds like a great guy."

"On the plus side, he didn't last long."

Oz leaned over and pointed to each button in turn. "These are for movement, so this is to crouch, this is to run, and this one jumps. These two are for your weapon—you can switch, or reload. The ones on the edges…"

His words devolved into a fuzzy hum as every one of her senses homed in on the details of his proximity. The long, slim fingers brushing against hers as he indicated each button. The warm press of his hard triceps against her shoulder. The scent of eucalyptus, sharp and clean and bright and so intoxicating she could barely think.

Tremendous pressure settled on her chest, threatening to collapse her lungs as she fought off overwhelming, alien impulses to touch him. To kiss him. To thread her fingers through his hair and close her lips around his tongue. She tried desperately to swim to the surface, kicking and thrashing at the base instincts clasping at her ankles.

Had she ever been this desperate before? This helpless?

Never. Not once.

"Got it?"

His voice was an unexpectedly cold shower from frozen pipes on a winter morning. She jolted back to herself, shaky and disoriented. "Ready," she lied.

He started the game, and their character-selves roamed the snowy Soviet landscape, apparently hunting an enemy sniper. Kate barely managed to keep her soldier moving, occasionally—and comically—transposing the buttons for running and shooting. Oz was enthusiastic nonetheless, making suggestions, letting her character open the door to a barn where they found a clue the sniper was nearby.

"Nice one." He elbowed her jovially, eyes on the screen. "We should check outside the barn. Maybe he only just left. I'll cover you in case he fires."

"Great," she muttered as her heart sank with an all-too-familiar revelation.

They were just friends. She was one of the guys. Again.

An unwelcome lump rose in her throat as she struggled to maneuver her character to exit the barn. She should be flattered, not on the verge of bawling like a weak, oversensitive baby. A professional athlete with thousands—tens of thousands, probably—of fans wanted to hang out with *her*. She was fun. Easygoing. Friendly. Like a sister. Isn't that what countless numbers of would-be boyfriends had told her, year after year after year?

At least she knew where she stood, and it was comfortable, familiar, easily navigable ground. No pressure. No stress. She could concentrate on being the friend Oz clearly wanted and shelve her silly, fantastical attraction without ever having to face it head-on, or worry about it diverting her focus from rediscovering herself as an independent, self-sufficient woman with no Army safety net beneath her.

She risked nothing, would lose nothing. It was the best possible outcome, really.

And the disappointment dragging down her shoulders—she'd get over it. Eventually.

Their soldiers moved to the door. Oz's crouched in readiness, weapon drawn. She fumbled to get her own rifle more or less in position, then sent her character forward into the wilderness.

Her hand hovered over the button to shoot but suddenly the screen froze. The bare trees on the horizon became odd-looking stalks of pixels and she turned to Oz with a frown.

"Is it broken?"

He shook his head. "I paused it."

"Why? I was about to kick some sniper ass."

He turned to her with a concerned expression. "I think I should kiss you."

Her jaw practically hit her lap. After a second or two of stunned silence she managed to yank it back up, realign her teeth and force her mouth to form words.

"What did you say?"

"Spoiler alert." He raised an apologetic hand. "There's some pretty serious fighting up ahead and I don't want either of us to be distracted."

"So you want to—"

"Kiss you." He smiled and, hot damn, he was delicious. "Maybe I'm wrong, but I think we're both wondering if it's going to happen, when it will happen, should it happen... It's drawing attention away from this mission, which is, frankly, pretty important to the eventual victory of the Allies over the German military forces."

"You want to kiss me," she repeated dumbly, struggling to wade through the shock and disbelief muddying her mind.

"It's up to you. I'm just saying, there are ten million Soviet lives at stake." He shrugged.

"Okay," some distant, detached part of her responded.

And then it happened. He put two fingers beneath her chin, tilted her face toward his and pressed his lips against hers.

She stiffened, her mind and heart vying for the fastest pace.

She shouldn't do this. Getting involved with anyone was the last thing she needed right now, not to mention a client—oh, shit, was this a violation of her terms of employment? Had she even signed terms of employment?

Her boss wouldn't care, surely. She saw Rich, his crew-cut, his oversized belt buckle, his habit of spinning a tobacco tin in his hands during meetings. Would he fire her? Not if her sales figures were good. That's all he cared about. But if they slipped, she bet he wouldn't hesitate to...Mentally she slapped herself. *You're making out with a guy you really like—the first time you've gotten any action in years. Stop thinking about your job. Stop thinking about the bigger picture. Enjoy the goddamn moment for once.*

She wrenched her awareness out of her brain and shoved it into her body, forcing herself to be present, to experience his touch.

God, he tastes good.

Peanut butter. Chocolate. Something else, something hot and sweet and exhilaratingly masculine.

She found the back of his neck, the warm, soft skin, the brush of his hair against the edge of her finger. She raised her other hand to his shoulder, trailed her thumb along his collarbone. The pressure of his mouth was gentle but encouraging. Patient. Confident.

Her breathing quickened as she parted her lips cautiously. Too soon? Too fast? She didn't want him to think—

He hummed his approval low in his throat, pushing his tongue between her teeth.

The intimacy nearly stopped her heart.

Her temporarily silenced brain whirred into motion again. When was the last time she'd been touched like this?

She remembered the last guy she slept with, while she was still in the army. A bored, drunken capitulation to impulses that had left her unfulfilled and annoyed. She'd heard his oblivious snoring, felt the bite in the Midwestern spring air as she crossed the apartment complex to her front door, recalled her limp, drained sense of defeat as she shoved her vibrator back into its box.

She remembered the year in Saudi Arabia. Days spent cloaked in a shapeless *abaya,* drifting around the periphery of her client's life. Nights alone in her room in a house she shared with three male security guards whose opposite schedules meant she barely knew them. At first she'd enjoyed the privacy, the isolation, the absence of romantic pressure. It had taken a month to feel lonely, another to borrow from her client's supply of romance novels as bedtime reading, three more weeks to wake from vivid dreams of sizzling passion, true love and the promise of happily-ever-after. One month after that she'd stopped dreaming altogether.

She thought of her mother. Beautiful. Funny. Desperate. Her bra strap falling unnoticed to her elbow as she wrote her phone number on the back of the car salesman's business card and slid it across the counter.

She thought of her sister. Even more beautiful than their mother. Funnier, sexier, more charming, with even worse taste in men. Her niece's father, his crooked front teeth—

"Hey."

Oz's soft voice jerked her into the present so fiercely she was disoriented. Slowly she put the pieces together. Hotel floor. Video game. His face, brows knitted, eyes questioning.

"Where did you go?"

"Nowhere. I'm here."

He pulled away and she felt his loss keenly, achingly, until she had to dig her fingers into the carpet so she didn't snatch him back.

"Are you okay? Was *that* okay? Because if I crossed a line—"

"No, not at all." She forced a bright smile and tried to ignore the panic drumming in her chest. "I'm fine. We're fine."

"I don't believe you."

"Then I don't know what to tell you."

"Tell me what happened."

"A mistake, clearly." Flustered, guilty, embarrassed, she got to her feet.

"Kate? Hang on." He trailed her to the door and put his hand on hers to stop her from turning the handle.

"I'm going. Don't be annoyed. It's not you. This was just a bad idea."

She could see the *why* forming in his mind, working its way down to his mouth, and then disappearing. He turned the handle and pushed open the door for her.

"If for some reason the nutritionist asks, you ate the waffles," he instructed flatly.

"Fine. Goodnight."

She stepped into the hall, nearly colliding with a handholding couple in formalwear. The door shut behind her without a parting word from Oz. She sighed, waiting for the lovebirds to pass before she started toward the elevator.

She pressed the button too hard, jammed her fingers into too-tight fists, reproaching her foolish disappointment at Oz's failure to chase after her.

What did she expect? She'd seen his house, his car, his job. He could have any woman he wanted.

She squeezed her eyes shut, refusing to acknowledge the hot tears welling behind her lids. *I fucked up, but it's over now. It's done.*

A *ping* announced the elevator's arrival. She stepped aside as the doors slid open to reveal a hotel employee with a room-service cart.

He pushed it past her. The smell of chicken and waffles was unmistakable.

Chapter 7

Oz turned at the tap on his shoulder. A girl in her early twenties stood behind him, her asymmetrical bob dyed bright pink.

"I'm so sorry to bother you, and I know this isn't part of this event, but would you sign this for me?" She pulled a Skyline jersey out of her messenger bag.

He glanced over her head, making sure the video game company's uptight publicist wasn't nearby.

The coast was clear. "Sure. Do you have a pen?"

She produced a black Sharpie. He flattened the shirt on one of the cocktail tables dotted around the martini bar that had been turned into a gaming lounge for the launch. He wrote the two letters of his name with a practiced hand and added his number beneath.

"Thank you so much," she gushed, clutching the shirt to her chest. "Can I ask you one more thing?"

"Go for it."

"Can I take a photo?"

"Of course. Put that away first so the publicist doesn't give you trouble."

She stuffed the shirt in her bag and pulled out her phone.

Ted extended his hand. "Here, I'll take it for you."

She got into position and Oz had his arm across her shoulder when Glynn piped up, "Did you not want my autograph?"

Her expression fell from gleeful to stricken. Oz smirked at Glynn's oft-used joke, which, on a handful of admittedly hilarious occasions, had led the fan to ask him if he was a particular hip-hop artist or basketball player.

This girl was too smart for that, and Oz squeezed her upper arm. "Ignore him, he's not famous."

She recovered her smile for the photo and thanked him profusely. She scrolled vigorously through her phone as she walked away, undoubtedly posting it to her various social-media accounts.

On a hunch, he took out his own phone and checked his notifications. The photo was already on Twitter and Instagram. He tapped to like it on both platforms and watched as the girl spun around across the room and gave him a thumbs-up.

"You were saying?" Ted prompted impatiently.

"Where was I?"

"Anti-sniper mission in Outlaw Brigade: Stalingrad."

"Best edition ever," Glynn added.

"Agreed. Anyway, we were about to leave the barn and obviously things get hectic from that point, so I said I should probably kiss her. You know, to break the tension."

Ted whistled. "Damn, you're smooth. Teach us?"

"Speak for yourself," Glynn retorted. "What did she say?"

"She was up for it. Seemed happy, into it, into me. Then she froze. She didn't say anything, but she didn't need to. I could practically hear her changing her mind."

Ted winced. "Ouch."

"I asked her what happened but first she said it was nothing, then she said we'd made a mistake and walked out."

"And that was it?" Glynn asked.

"That was it. Next morning we flew back to Atlanta and the few times I spoke to her on the trip she was polite, professional, like it never happened."

Ted summed it up. "She rejected you."

"I wouldn't put it—"

"She did," Glynn agreed. "She had a taste, tried a sample. Elected not to proceed. That's rejection."

Oz blinked at his friends. In the couple of days since his encounter with Kate he'd examined it from every angle, trying to put his finger on what stung so sharply. Now he knew.

"She rejected me," he echoed in disbelief.

Ted frowned in genuine bewilderment. "That's never happened to you before, has it?"

"No," Oz replied honestly. "Never."

For a minute they stood in collective silence, contemplating this unusual turn of events.

Glynn spoke first. "Don't take this the wrong way—I like Kate a lot—but she's so different from the women you normally date. What's the attraction?"

"She's funny. She doesn't take shit. She's lived an interesting life.

She's pretty. She's got a great body." He shrugged. "I don't know, it's hard to itemize."

"Maybe it's for the best," Ted offered. "You keep saying you're ready for something serious, something long-term. Someone who fits The Plan. Can Kate be that woman?"

"No," Oz admitted. "I acted on impulse. I saw someone I wanted and made my move."

"Not necessarily the best way to find your real-deal woman," Ted replied, not unkindly.

Oz considered his friend's point. "You're right. If I want something long-term, I need to be deliberate."

"For a guy who's waited as long as you have, you deserve to be discerning." Glynn slapped him on the back.

The publicist appeared then, taking Oz by the elbow. "Excuse me, gentlemen, I need to steal away our special-guest gamer for his big moment."

He waved to his friends. "See you guys later."

"Don't embarrass yourself," Glynn called cheerily as he walked away.

Oz followed the publicist up the steps of a platform at one end of the room, where three short, square leather stools had been set up in front of three televisions. A huge screen covered the wall behind the TVs, cycling clips from the new release of Outlaw Brigade, set in a dystopian future where a cannibalistic gang ruled a post-apocalyptic America.

The other two celebrity players joined him on-stage—a hip-hop artist he'd seen on TV, and a football player he'd met before at a similar event. They all shook hands and exchanged the overly polite small talk that always seemed to accompany product launches like this one.

The publicist took up the microphone. It didn't take more than a second for everyone to crowd around the platform, smartphones at the ready to capture this first glimpse of the highly anticipated new release.

One of the game's writers stepped up to talk about the latest edition, divulging a few details about the plot and characters and offering context for the mission about to be undertaken by the three celebrity gamers. He introduced each of them in turn, instructing them to take their seats.

Oz was on the left. Their backs faced the audience, but the big screen overhead now showed their three characters' video-game perspectives, with an inset of each player's face at the bottom so the crowd could see their reactions.

The game launched to applause and whistling from the crowd, which he could barely hear through his noise-cancelling headphones with an attached microphone. Their characters were futuristic Marines who'd escaped the captivity of the marauding gang to lead the resistance to defeat them and reestablish order. Oz and his fellow players were embarking on a mission to infiltrate one of the gang's strongholds and free another group of soldiers.

The scene opened with an escaped soldier giving them information on the layout and security at the gang's hideout. Oz ran through his weapons options as he followed the other two characters across a barren, midnight landscape to what remained of a blown-up casino.

They searched the ground floor, took out a couple of gang members, and then moved into the emergency stairwell beside empty elevator shafts. The football player took out another enemy and they pressed on to the next floor.

She rejected me. Oz tapped the controller to shoot a couple of bad guys.

They crouched behind busted slot machines as a wave of gunfire erupted in front of them.

"We have to get to the fifth floor," the football player reminded them over the headsets. "Get back to the stairwell, I'll cover."

"No point checking all these floors," the hip-hop artist agreed. "We're wasting time."

"Good with me." *Okay, she rejected me, that's fact. But why? What did I—*"Oh, shit."

"I told you I'd cover," the football player complained. Oz had sent his character out from behind the slot machine too early, without waiting for cover fire, and he'd taken a lethal shot to the head.

Oz tried to stifle his embarrassment as his character regenerated and play continued. Expertise in this game was measured by the ratio of how many characters you killed versus how many times yours died. He was off to a terrible start.

Unfortunately, his kill/death ratio only got worse as the game wore on. Any time he seemed to get into his semi-meditative groove an unsolicited thought of Kate popped up to distract him.

*Crouch, shoot, reload. Maybe I moved too fast. Maybe she wasn't—*His character reeled with the force of an enemy's deadly shot.

*Run, jump left, duck behind the open door. Maybe I shouldn't have let Kate leave. Maybe she wanted me to follow her and I—*Oz dropped his controller into his lap as his character fell five stories, having stepped backward through a glassless window.

"Damn," the hip-hop artist remarked as they all took off their headphones, the mission complete. "I didn't even know a character could die like that. I figured the game would automatically bounce them back into the room if they got too close to an open window."

Oz forced a smile as he shook hands with the other players and accepted the applause of the audience. The game writer made a few more comments into the microphone—kindly refraining from mentioning Oz's specific performance—and then invited the rest of the launch attendees to take turns trying out the mission.

Oz raised his hands in defeat as he rejoined Glynn and Ted. "I know. I don't want to talk about it."

His friends exchanged glances, and Ted pushed a glass across the table.

Oz eyed the clear liquid. "Please tell me that's vodka."

"Water."

He grumbled his disappointment, then downed half of it. Apparently racking up a humiliating K/D ratio in front of sixty onlookers made him thirsty.

Ted's gaze drifted over his shoulder, then his friend snapped his fingers. "Of course, I should've thought of this before. I'm going to introduce you to someone. She's perfect for you—super smart, funny, not a doctor. I'll be right back."

"Not a doctor?" Oz repeated, but Ted was already on his way.

"Your last serious girlfriend was a medical student, as was that girl you went out with a couple weeks ago." Glynn clarified. "Time to branch out."

Oz blinked. "I never even thought about that."

Ted returned, leading a short, curvy brunette with big eyes and a polite but skeptical smile. "Gentlemen, I'd like to introduce you to D. Goldberg."

"The gadget columnist," Oz filled in as the name registered. He extended his hand. "Oz Terim."

"The soccer player," she acknowledged, her smile warming.

"And this is Glynn Washington, app developer," Ted explained.

"I read your column every week," Glynn told her. "Can I say something potentially offensive?"

"You thought I was a guy?" she asked.

Glynn nodded. She shrugged.

"*D* is for Davida. When I first started pitching to magazines, I found I had a better hit rate if I let people assume I was male."

"Very Brontë," Oz remarked.

"That's what I tell myself. So, soccer player, what position do you play?"

"Left-back."

"I played left-wing in high school."

"Were you any good?"

"Regional champions three years running."

Oz caught his friends swapping a knowing glance, then quietly sliding down the table to carry on their own conversation.

"I hope you're better at soccer than at Outlaw Brigade."

His turn to smile. Being called on his shit was definitely one of his turn-ons. Kate did it the first time they met, but he shut down that line of thinking as soon as it fluttered to life.

"I'm having an off day."

"Let me guess, your K/D ratio is usually five-point-eight."

"One-point-five, tops. I'm not very good." He grinned, intent on disarming her. It worked. She peered at him warily, then broke into a broad smile.

"I guess Ted told me the truth when he said you're not another gamer diva."

He shook his head. "Gamer diva, no. Soccer diva, all day long."

"I don't believe you."

He pulled out his phone and opened a video app. "I'll show you the time I swore at a Turkish referee during an international match. He awarded a free kick against me, so I called him a son of a bitch in Turkish. Wait, it's loading."

She laughed. A nice laugh, pretty, musical.

But not as bubbly or delightfully startling as Kate's.

"Okay, I'll buy that you're a soccer diva. I don't need to see your bilingual profanity skills."

"Trilingual," he corrected. "I can be deeply offensive in Swedish as well."

"You win. I've only got a couple of mild French swear words and some Yiddish that's probably fifty years outdated."

"If you've had your fill of gamer divas and Outlaw Brigade groupies, maybe we should get out of here."

Her eyes twinkled. "I know a good place down the street."

"Is it quiet enough for me to teach you an international range of insults?"

"Definitely."

He extended his arm. "Let's go."

She wrapped her fingers around his elbow, he waved goodbye to his smug-looking friends, and they made their way out of the basement-level lounge and up to the sidewalk. The early-summer sun had set while they'd been inside, and the street seemed foreign, fresh, full of potential.

She nodded down the block. "This way."

"I'll follow you." And not spare a thought for that harsh, unyielding, sexy-as-hell woman he kissed in a hotel room, who walked away and didn't look back.

Chapter 8

"Double or nothing."

"You sure?"

"I'm sure."

Kate shrugged, slapped the ten-dollar bill she'd just taken from him onto the side of the pool table. "Cash on the barrel head."

He put a matching bill on top of hers and racked the balls. "My turn to break."

"Be my guest." She propped her cue on the floor and leaned against it, already bored.

Her first mistake, she concluded as he sank a ball, was accepting the date with Jared. She'd agreed because she felt guilty, then dreaded the Friday-night dinner until the moment he buzzed her apartment. She'd spent the entire meal trying to drop hints that they were only ever going to be friends.

Her second mistake was bringing him to her favorite dive bar. She thought she could get support from Carrie, the bartender she was becoming more and more friendly with.

Her third and totally unanticipated mistake, it turned out, was introducing Carrie and Jared. The two of them practically sizzled with instant chemistry, Carrie distracted to the point that she filled Jared's glass until beer poured down the sides and then handed a half-empty one to Kate. She spent nearly an hour waiting for one of them to wake up to how rudely they excluded her before giving up, muttering something about a headache and walking out. Carrie had the decency to look mildly apologetic as she waved goodbye. If Jared even noticed her departure, he gave no sign.

She traded the dive bar for the hipster-looking one down the block. She'd started the evening counting two people as burgeoning friends in her new city, and within hours she was back to zero. The last thing she wanted to do on a Friday night was go home sober.

She sighed, taking up her cue as her opponent missed. She hated fashionable, overpriced bars like this one, not to mention the fashionable people buying the overpriced drinks. Thankfully it had a pool table and plenty of men keen to show off their skills. Jared had paid for dinner, so if she played as well as she knew she could, she would end the night in profit.

Small consolation, but she'd take it.

She eyed up the table, considered her angles. Then she put hours of taxpayer-funded pool games in isolated desert outposts and windswept Midwestern Army posts to good use.

Clack, thunk. Clack, thunk. Clack, thunk. She worked the table methodically, ruthlessly, calling each shot until only the eight ball remained.

"Wait a second," her opponent objected, striding up to the table. "We didn't agree on the rules before we started. In pub pool you have to give the other person their turn to—"

She sank the eight ball mercilessly, swept up his ten-dollar bill and turned to the handful of onlookers who'd gathered to watch the action.

"Who's next?"

As was her experience, almost every man in the room wanted to be the one who finally beat her. She bought a stupidly expensive beer while they jostled to write their names on the chalkboard behind the pool table. Then she flexed her fingers, put resin on her cue and spent the next two hours relieving each one of them of ten, fifteen, or twenty dollars.

Clack, thunk. Ten-dollar bill in her pocket. She watched her opponent wipe his name off the chalkboard and realized he was the last one. She shook his hand. He offered to buy her a drink. He wasn't a bad pool player, nor was he bad looking. She opened her mouth to accept when a voice rumbled behind her.

"Time for one more?"

She spun to face the last person she wanted to see.

"Oz. Hello."

"How've you been?"

"Just fine. Yourself?"

"Couldn't be better. This is Davida. Davida, this is Kate."

She nodded to the short brunette at his side who, to her credit, already glanced between the two of them with a less-than-impressed expression.

"How do you know each other?" Davida asked.

Oz's eyes leveled on hers. From the moment she left his hotel room she'd hoped he wouldn't take her departure personally and somewhat fantastically envisioned them becoming friendly, if strictly professional, acquaintances. Specifically, the sort of acquaintances who offer spots in their VIP box.

Now she was pretty sure she'd never be crossing that VIP threshold again. Ever.

"Kate's a contractor for Atlanta Skyline," he replied icily.

"Speaking of which, don't you have a match tomorrow?"

"Sunday."

She slid her gaze to the glass of water in his hand. "I guess that's why you're keeping *halal* tonight."

Her words came out more acidic than intended, but by the time she registered her tone the damage was done. Davida's eyes widened while Oz's narrowed.

"I'm leaving," Davida announced, placing her untouched cocktail on an empty table.

"Wait, hang on." Unlike Jared had with her, Oz pursued Davida to the door and out of Kate's earshot. She picked up her beer and watched their exchange over the rim of the glass. Oz gestured and leaned in, not quite blocking her exit but not getting out of her way, either. She smiled but shook her head firmly, patted his arm and left.

He watched her walk out and shut the door behind her. Then he turned and fixed Kate with a hard glare.

She raised her glass in salute.

He stormed across the room. She straightened her spine and arched a brow, her eyes never leaving his as he halted in front of her.

"Yes?"

He nodded to the chalkboard. "How much to play?"

"Ten."

"Let's make it worth my while." He counted out five twenty-dollar bills and flattened them on the edge of the pool table. Then he racked the balls and picked up a cue.

He broke without asking permission, and silently pocketed three balls before he missed. He looked at her expectantly.

She took her time. The hundred he'd nonchalantly slapped down would almost double her winnings...or decimate them.

She didn't begrudge him his money, his house, his car. She'd spent her life on the far side of that divide, learning to go without, tiptoeing at the edge of bailiffs' shadows. Poverty didn't scare her—it was too familiar to be frightening—but no matter how far ahead of it she ran, it had hardened her. Made her hungry. Brought everything into focus until she saw exactly what to do and how to do it.

A hundred dollars was half a week's rent. Three tanks of gas. A thrift-store summer wardrobe for her niece.

She would take Oz's money, and she would enjoy doing it.

She walked around the table, examining the balls' positions, gauging her options. He was good, so she wanted to give him as few turns as possible.

She leaned over, lined up. *Clack, thunk.* One down.

He moved into her line of vision and crossed his arms. She almost smiled at his attempt to put her off.

Clack, thunk. Two.

"Davida's a tech columnist," he volunteered. "She writes for a men's magazine. She's hugely influential."

"Interesting." *Clack, thunk.* Three.

"Very."

"Why did she leave?"

"She thought you were an ex-girlfriend."

She smiled, positioning her cue on the felt. "I hope you told her I wasn't the competition."

"I did, but she didn't believe me. I guess it was too obvious."

"What was too obvious?" She squinted, lining up her shot.

"That I think you're fucking hot."

Pain seared across her knuckles as she scraped them against the table's splintery edge, the tip of the cue scratching along the felt. Balls bounced around the table, and Kate cursed under her breath. Oz wore a smug expression as he stepped up for his turn.

She shook out her sore hand, sucking briefly on a place where the skin had split open. She'd let him get to her. Inexcusable. And with an obviously provocative comment that shouldn't feel this good.

She exhaled as he leaned over the table, trying to cool the fever that had settled over her body at his words. He hadn't meant it. Even if he had, it didn't matter. She couldn't learn to stand on her own two feet while she had a man between her legs.

At a push—a drunken, horny, desperate push—she might allow herself a totally anonymous one-night stand, but not with Oz. Not with someone she was guaranteed to see again. Not with someone who could cost her a job.

Not when she knew one night would never be enough.

She shut down that train of thought and recovered her focus. She wanted that hundred dollars, and goddammit, she would do what it took to get it.

Oz pocketed his fourth ball and moved to find his fifth. She watched his dark eyes flicking from one ball to the next. Calculating. Considering.

She glanced down at the outfit she'd chosen for her apology date with

Jared. Purple flip-flops. Tight jeans. A sleeveless pink top selected because it hid the way her fly sat awkwardly on her stomach and gave her a muffin top. No jewelry. No makeup. Certainly no cleavage.

Seduction wasn't her thing. Most of the men she'd slept with had started as friends, a one-of-the-guys situation that eventually bubbled over into the bedroom. She knew how to be buddies with men, how to drink with them, play pool, watch sports, swear, talk trash. She inhabited her body comfortably but practically. Her physicality was functional, not decorative.

Oz bent over the cue. She drifted into his sightline. No matter how unnatural it felt, she knew she had to act quickly.

As he drew back his arm she let her cue drop from her grip and clatter to the floor. He paused, giving her a dark look.

"Slipped. Sorry."

He huffed his annoyance and returned his attention to the table. She edged around the corner in pursuit of her cue until she was—by her calculations—just in his peripheral vision. Then she bent forward from the waist to retrieve it, presenting him with an unimpeded view of her butt.

Wood scratched felt, accompanied by non-English words that she didn't need to be multilingual to know were filthy.

She didn't bother hiding her smile as she informed him cheerily, "My turn."

He moved aside—slightly. Her quick glance found unyielding determination tightening his jaw, narrowing his eyes, flat-lining his mouth.

God, he was gorgeous.

And close. Too close. He propped a hip against the side of the table. The zipper on his jeans was inches from her cheek as she leaned over. She could count the stitches on his pocket. His muscular thigh strained the denim.

Solid red, corner pocket. Her eyes flicked traitorously to Oz's crotch. Jesus Christ, was he hard?

Clack, thunk. She'd gotten lucky, but she might not again. Time to get serious, to play like her life depended on it, to ignore—

He not-at-all-accidentally brushed past her as he stalked to the opposite side. Definitely hard.

Her throat tightened. That wasn't something he could fake. And he wanted her to see it. Know what she did to him.

Her face heated until her vision swam. She gave herself a bolstering shake, sipped her beer, and then tried to turn fresh eyes to the scattered balls.

Four shots away from a hundred dollars. Three solids and the eight ball. She'd been on a winning streak all night. She could do this.

If Oz moved or made a face or did anything intended to distract her, she didn't notice. She found the impenetrable concentration she perfected on the firing range and her next two shots were textbook, rolling neatly into pockets as if tugged by magnets.

Then she made the mistake of looking up as she changed position. Oz moved in parallel, like a snake tracking its prey, barely blinking as he watched her reset her angle.

She thought about the money. The satisfaction of winning. She did her best to ignore him, to shut out his eucalyptus scent, to forget that his lean, trim, unapologetically masculine body showed such an obvious reaction to her nearness.

She drew back her arm and he broke into a sudden, exaggerated yawn, stretching his arms over his head...and pulling up his shirt to expose a perfectly sculpted abdomen at the exact moment she took her shot.

Kate's eyes were on the last solid ball slicing across the table, but all she saw was the faint line of dark hair bisecting the stacked muscles of Oz's stomach. The image was so consuming that she didn't celebrate the ball landing in a pocket, didn't even realize it happened until the owner of that exquisite six-pack spoke up from the other side of the table.

"Last shot. Don't choke."

"I won't."

She would take Oz's money, sure, but her real victory would be walking away from him. Resisting this seductive, insistent, terrifying thing happening between them, because it couldn't end well. Their lives were too different, the distance separating them totally unbridgeable. Even if it wasn't, she had to focus on figuring out who she was—not Kate the dutiful daughter, Kate the sensible sister, Kate the reliable aunt, Kate in the military or Kate in a relationship.

Just Kate.

He stopped at her side, so close she caught the faintest whiff of the shaving cream he'd used on those smooth cheeks.

"Do you mind?" She gestured for him to move away.

"Not at all." He crossed his arms without shifting an inch.

"I'd like a little space to take my winning shot."

"I'm sure you would."

"But you're not going to give it to me," she replied resignedly.

"I have a hundred dollars on the table. I'm taking every advantage."

She picked up the resin block and rubbed it on the tip of her cue. "Sounds like a sore loser."

"Sounds like someone worried about choking."

"Please." She rolled her eyes. "Stand wherever you want. I'll still take your money."

"Do it."

She didn't need to be told twice. As it happened, the final shot was an easy one. The eight ball sat on the edge of a corner pocket, largely unimpeded. If both her arms fell off she could probably sink it with the cue in her mouth. There was no excuse not to win.

Except the tall, dark-haired one hovering at her side.

She leaned over the felt and he leaned over her, near enough for the heat of his body to warm her back. Her nipples tightened inside her bra as she imagined that same heat more intensely, accompanied by the hard press of his bare flesh and the weight of his muscular frame.

What would he be like in bed? So different to the rest, she imagined. Dominant but unselfish. Tender but firm. Admiring, energetic, playful...

She positioned her cue on the table and he traced his finger across the bare skin where her shirt parted from her jeans. She gritted her teeth and clutched the wood beneath her fingers as his touch launched a wave of heat roaring from her ears to her toes.

Had she ever had such an overwhelming, vision-blurring urge to throw a man to the floor and ride him until he begged for mercy? Only in her most private, dead-of-night fantasies.

Which never, ever came true.

Nor would this one. He was trying to put her off, that's all. They would never, could never have a relationship. She barely managed to sustain two or three dates with men she knew as friends, what chance did she have with someone like Oz?

Someone smart, successful, sophisticated. Someone whose future floated higher and higher every day, not tethered close to the ground like hers, not weighted by the burden of a careless mother and a reckless sister and an innocent little niece.

Different worlds. Different people. She slipped out from beneath Oz's hand. He let it fall to his side, maybe wounded at her repeated rejection, maybe bored with their back-and-forth. Maybe indifferent, already thinking about that woman he came in with and how he could convince her to meet him again.

Childish, irrational jealousy spiked in her chest and she popped her shot, sharp and precise. The ball found its pocket comfortably. She slapped her hand over the stack of bills.

Oz placed his hand on top of hers. "Wait."

"Why? You lost, and I'm ready to go home."

"Have a drink with me."

"You're not drinking."

"You know what I mean, Kate." God, her name sounded good when he said it.

"Why?"

"Because I like you."

"You barely know me."

"Change that." He pressed his palm against her knuckles. "Stay."

She wanted to be the woman who would—who *could*—kiss him. Who could toss her hair, soften her expression, let him read all the sultry intention in her eyes. Who could slide her fingers to the back of his neck, press her thighs between his and say all the right things to get him in bed and keep him there.

But she was Kate Mitchell, in flip-flops and ill-fitting jeans. The soldier. The pool shark. The to-be-determined.

She jerked her hand out from under his, pocketed the money and stepped backward.

"You're a smart man, Oz." She spoke without looking at him, picking up her purse and rooting through it for her phone. "Call Davida. I'm sure she'll forgive you."

He said nothing as she walked away, and she didn't glance over her shoulder to check his expression. She hoped it was longing. But she knew it probably wasn't.

At least she was a hundred dollars richer than she'd been a half-hour earlier. She walked down the block as she opened an app to call a taxi, using every bit of her willpower not to run back into the warm glow of the bar, into Oz's waiting arms.

Chapter 9

"Eighteen, take it easy. Don't test me a second time."

Oz rolled his eyes as he turned his back on the referee and walked away. Skyline was up one-nil with twelve minutes to go. He was sick of his opponents hurling themselves all over the pitch as if they'd been mortally wounded, and even sicker of this passive-aggressive ref and his linesmen. If this guy offered one more vague, don't-test-me threat, he was going to—

"Eighteen. *Eighteen.*"

Oz spun on his heel. "What?"

The ref's eyes narrowed in irritation as he reached into his pocket and raised a yellow card.

Oz threw up his hands. "Are you kidding me? For what?"

"Dissent."

"That is an absolute joke. That is a complete fucking—"

"He is sorry." Kojo, Oz's Togolese counterpart on the right wing, stepped in with his palm raised.

"Play on," the referee decreed, and the two defenders jogged toward the midline.

Oz heard his name. Roland gestured angrily from the manager's box, and although the crowd was too loud to make out what he said, it was clear he was unimpressed.

He exhaled, trying to ignore the cramp in his thigh, the free kick awarded against him, the manager swearing at him in Swedish. They were winning, and unless something outrageous happened in the next ten minutes, this home match would end with three points on their score sheet.

Yet he was as pissed off as if he'd personally conceded a goal. Because he couldn't stop thinking about Kate.

It was unlike him to be so fixated on a woman, never mind one who'd made her disinterest so abundantly clear.

Then again, he'd never had to get over a woman who'd turned him down before.

Maybe this was his karmic comeuppance. His turn to feel the sting of the rejection he'd dished out time and time again. Maybe this would be a valuable lesson in humility. Hadn't every woman he'd ever been with eventually told him he was arrogant? And maybe Kate was right, his attraction was misguided, and it was best this whole crazy idea ended before it began.

He'd get back on the dating app, he decided as Skyline's forwards passed the ball slowly between them, letting the clock tick down. Lots of bored, single people spent their Sunday nights flipping through profiles, trying to set up dates for the week. He'd be one of them, and by Wednesday Kate would be a distant memory.

"You better slow down or your thumb's going to fall off. Is it left here?"

"Sorry." Oz looked up from the app to peer through the windscreen of Deon Ellis's super-high-end SUV. With his own car in the shop for a minor repair, he was grateful for the post-match lift. "Yeah, left here."

"What is that, anyway?" The striker stopped at a red light and craned his neck to see Oz's phone.

"Dating app. You swipe left to reject, or right to say you're interested."

Deon winced. "Harsh."

"It's a jungle out there. You're lucky you got to Olivia before she knew better."

"So lucky. At fourteen I only had to compete with the other guys in our high school. No social-media catfishers to intercept my game."

"That's the problem. There are so many profiles you have to be ruthless. Like this one. Amanda. Located five miles away, age twenty-six. Brand and marketing executive. Interested in literature, baseball, wine, and jazz." He held up the phone so Deon could glance at her photo.

"Looks hot. Are you going to swipe right?"

"Left." He moved his thumb across the screen decisively.

"What? Why? She's perfect. You like wine, and you also refer to books as literature."

"I hate jazz."

Deon shook his head. "Picky. Read me the next one."

"Layla. Age twenty-seven, six miles away. She's wearing a ski outfit in her photo." He held up his phone.

"She's cute. What's her profile say?"

"She likes tennis, whiskey, and the Sunday crossword. Recovering corporate lawyer now working for a legal-aid charity. Then she writes, Let's get pizza."

"Dude, swipe right. Swipe right immediately."

He swiped left. "Not for me."

Deon shot him a look of shock. "Are you trying to be single forever?"

"I don't want to waste anyone's time."

"What do you want, then, if not a crossword-completing, whiskey-drinking, public-good-doing lawyer?"

"I don't know." Oz lifted a shoulder. "I'm looking for someone a little more down-to-earth. Someone who'll stick with me after the soccer thing fizzles out. Who can spend a Saturday afternoon in my VIP box and not get conceited about it. Who'll laugh at me and tell me I'm being pretentious. Then beat me at pool."

Someone exactly like Kate Mitchell.

"But you're assuming the women in those photos aren't like that, when there was nothing in their profiles that suggests that."

"True." He pocketed his phone and turned to the striker. "What's the secret to a long and happy relationship?"

Deon smiled and shook his head. "I've got only eleven years of experience. You should ask someone else."

"I'm serious. You and Olivia are the couple everyone wants to be. Steady, drama-free, and so affectionate it makes most of us feel sick, to be honest. What's the magic formula?"

"Compromise," Deon answered promptly. "Adjusting what you want or need—or what you think you need—to suit the other person in a way that respects you both."

Oz waited, and when Deon didn't elaborate he asked, "That's it?"

"That's most of it."

"What's the rest?"

Deon's teeth shone bright white in the dark SUV. "Super-hot sex as often as possible."

A bolt of desire arrowed through him with such force he had to grip the edge of his seat to brace himself as Kate's image lodged in his mind. That inch of skin between her shirt and her jeans. Warm and soft and beckoning. He wanted to know what the rest of her felt like. Wanted to see her, touch her, taste every hill and valley in—

"Here we are." The striker stopped in Oz's driveway. Oz swept up his gym bag from between his feet, hoping his teammate didn't notice his unsteady hands.

"Thanks for the lift. And the advice."

"Swipe right on Layla. I want to hear all about your date at Pizza Hut."

"I'll think about it. See you on Monday."

Oz shut the door behind him and waved as Deon reversed down the driveway.

The noise of the SUV's engine receded as Oz fumbled in his bag for his house keys. He unearthed them from beneath a spare pair of shin pads and made his way up the flagstones to the front porch.

Maybe Deon—and Glynn and Ted and Sean, for that matter—were right. So his last few dates fell flat—how much of that was his fault? He'd let Kate, or the idea of Kate, distract him from the type of woman he'd always been with, the type he'd always sought. The type who would finally make his parents proud.

The busted evening with Davida was one hundred percent at his feet. He didn't give her the respect and attention he should have. He wondered whether she would take his call now if he was sufficiently groveling and apologetic.

Probably not.

He hiked his bag up onto his shoulder and took his phone from his pocket as he climbed the front steps. He'd swiped left on Layla and Amanda, but there were plenty of other profiles to thumb through. He'd make his recovery shake, settle into the study with—

He stopped two steps inside the house, his hand hesitating over the light-switch panel.

He'd just pushed open the door without unlocking it.

Or turning the handle.

He barely breathed as he stepped backward onto the porch, squinting up at the house and around at the lawn, on high alert for any sign that something, or someone, was where it shouldn't be. Moving as quietly as possible toward the road, he unlocked the screen on his phone and typed in 9-1-1—then stopped, his thumb hovering by the call button.

He was being paranoid. As far as he could see nothing was out of place or broken. The security lights were on, the garage door was shut. The mailbox was clean and shiny, free of graffiti.

"What the hell?" he asked himself in Swedish.

Maybe he left it open and never noticed. He normally came in through the garage—when was the last time he even used that door? It could've been hanging open for days. He hadn't bothered to put on the alarm or the beams, as usual, and the keychain with the panic button linked to the security company was on the kitchen counter.

He was definitely being paranoid. He cancelled the 911 call and scrolled to Kate's number instead. She was his security contractor, after all. This was what the team paid for.

She answered on the second ring, sounding exasperated. "Hi, Oz."

"Don't worry, this is a professional call." He mounted the steps again.

"With regard to?"

"I just came home from our match and my front door was open."

"Where are you now?" she demanded, her tone rocketing from casual to urgent. The change made him slightly uneasy, but he pushed through the door a second time and dropped his bag on the floor.

"I'm inside."

"Don't take another step. Turn around and leave. I'll alert our dispatch to send a car, but in the meantime you need to call the police."

"It's really not—"

"Give me two seconds to call dispatch. Get out of the house."

The line crackled as she put him on hold. He flicked on the lights in the entryway and scanned the vast room. Everything looked exactly as he left it. He exhaled in relief.

"Oz? Are you there?"

"I'm here. I probably left the door open by mistake. Everything seems completely normal." He wandered through the big house toward the kitchen, turning on lights as he went.

"The car should be there in less than five minutes, and I'm on my way," she explained. He heard the *whoosh* of wind and the *thud* of her car door. "Did you call the police?"

"I don't think it's necessary. I hardly ever use the front door. It's probably been open for days. Anyway, I'm in the lounge now and all the windows are shut tight, the TV's still here. Nothing's been touched as far as I can tell."

"You're still in the house?" she asked, incredulity shrilling her voice. "Oz, *get out of the house.*"

"Look, I shouldn't have called you. I overreacted. I've checked the whole ground floor. I'm walking into the kitchen now. The back door is shut, everything is—"

He stopped short, his jaw slackening. Words dried up in his mouth. Thoughts slowed to a halt in his brain. All he could do was stare.

Kate's voice squawked his name on the line, but at a lower and lower volume. Eventually he realized it was because his hand was drifting to his side, his fingers barely managing to stay tight around the phone.

"Oz? Are you there? Tell me what's going on. Are you all right? Oz? Hello? For God's sake, will you please say something?"

He couldn't. Couldn't speak. Couldn't move. Couldn't breathe. Couldn't believe this was happening to him.

* * * *

"I arrived approximately fifteen minutes after my patrol-team colleagues and found the scene exactly as you see it."

Detective Hegarty nodded, scribbling in his notebook. "And did Mr. Terim explain why he called you instead of dialing 911?"

"He thought he'd been absent-minded and left the door open," Kate explained.

"Why would he call private security if he'd been absent-minded?"

"My bet is he second-guessed himself. Instinctively he suspected something was wrong, but he didn't want to make a fuss in case it was nothing."

"Got it. Anything else he said, or that you want to share, which you think could be of value to this investigation?"

She bit her lower lip, thinking carefully. "No, I've told you our whole exchange. You have the history and context—the graffiti on the mailbox and all that. But if I remember anything else, I'll let you know."

"I'd appreciate that." He scanned over the page. "I think that's all we need from you."

"You have my number, if not."

"We do. Thank you, Miss Mitchell."

"No problem."

At the other end of the room a police officer wearing rubber gloves shook open a large plastic bag. He used it to scoop up the severed pig's head that had been dumped on Oz's kitchen counter amidst a series of swastikas—finger-painted in animal blood—marring the pristine white cabinets and stainless-steel appliances.

As awful as it was, she hoped ugly hatred was the simple motivation behind the break-in. If the perpetrator knew Oz well enough to understand how deeply he would feel an attack on his beloved house, it made this personal, and gave it potential to happen again.

She turned at the thought of Oz. He sat on a couch in the lounge with his back to the kitchen, elbows on his knees. The policeman walked past with the bagged pig's head, and Oz watched him all the way to the front door.

She stared at Oz for another minute, her lingering irritation receding into sympathy. She wanted to strangle him when she took his call, first for failing to use any of the layers of security in place at his house, and

Rebecca Crowley

then for recklessly barging into what could've been, and turned out to be, a crime scene.

Now, though, he was quiet and alone amid the busy energy of policemen circulating, Peak Tactical personnel guarding the house's perimeter, and the occasional flash through the window from the handful of paparazzi lining the curb.

She bet those photographers were disappointed their police-scanner eavesdropping hadn't led them to a bigger celebrity crime. Served them right.

She crossed the room and dropped into the empty space beside Oz.

"How are you holding up?" On impulse she put her hand on his knee, then ripped it off so quickly she nearly rocked backward.

Boundaries. That he looked sad and isolated and inappropriately broody-sexy didn't make her the right person to rescue him.

"Fine, considering."

"Did you speak to Roland?"

He nodded. "He flipped out, unsurprisingly. He's probably calling the FBI right now. Or buying a gun."

"It's good to have a boss who cares about you."

He shrugged, distracted.

"I had a long conversation with one of the detectives," she began. "The good news is that although you wouldn't let us install surveillance cameras here, one of your neighbors has them on their property. They got a glimpse of a man hurrying down the sidewalk at around the time they think the break-in happened. The picture isn't great, and the guy has the hood up on his sweatshirt, but it's something. The other potential lead could be the pig's head itself. There aren't too many places to buy one intact like that, and they may be able to—"

"Why would someone do this to me?" he interjected.

She paused as he faced her fully. She'd never seen his expression so open, his dark eyes soft and rounded, brow furrowed in confusion. She hadn't realized his icy exterior protected such a sensitive core, and it took everything she had not to wrap comforting arms around his shoulders.

She bit her lower lip. "What do you mean?"

"I'm not from the Middle East. I don't speak Arabic. I'm barely religious. Not that any of those things would justify the crime, but in my case, social media is full of my *haram* transgressions. Drinking, tattoos, not fasting for Ramadan. I'm a legal immigrant, I'm not politically active, I don't even have a beard. I'm fucking Swedish," he finished emphatically.

"I know," she soothed. "Hatred isn't rational."

"I get that, but surely it's at least pragmatic. If I move back to Europe, what changes? My departure wouldn't topple any secret terror cells, or have radical Muslims throwing their Qur'ans into the Mississippi." He dug his fingers into his thighs.

"They're probably too scared to go after anyone who might actually fight back," she offered.

"What, like all those Muslims who are real terrorists? The ones named Ahmed, wearing *taqiyahs*." He rolled his eyes.

"Actually, yes. You and I know those things don't make someone a terrorist, but whoever was in your house tonight doesn't. He or she probably thinks Arabic-speaking men with beards have explosives in their basements. Which is why they chose to come here instead." She shrugged. "Cowardice, pure and simple."

"I'm not convinced breaking into someone's house is the act of a fearful person."

"You'd be surprised what fear can make people do."

The detective she'd spoken to made his way over and perched on the edge of the steel-and-glass coffee table in front of the couch. The table creaked under the detective's weight and she glanced at Oz, whose jaw was tight with obvious displeasure.

"We've got everything we're going to get from the scene," the detective explained. "We'll follow up on a couple of leads and let you know if we find anything."

"Are you treating this as a hate crime?" Kate asked.

"The state of Georgia doesn't have hate-crime laws, but I assure you we're taking this seriously." He hauled himself to his feet. "You've both got my number. Give me a shout anytime."

Oz gave no indication of movement, so Kate took it upon herself to walk the detective to the front door and see him out. The photographers had moved on so she waved away the Peak Tactical team. With the house finally empty of police personnel she shut the door, locked it, and pressed the button to switch on the alarm system.

When she turned Oz stood by the fireplace, lifting a clear, rectangular hunk of plastic with what looked like a medal encased inside.

"They didn't take this," he murmured when she joined him. "CSL Young Player of the Year. This is worth a lot of money."

"The police said the intruder didn't take anything of value."

"So they were motivated purely by bigotry, not greed. Is that good or bad?"

"I'm not sure," she replied honestly.

As he replaced the award on the mantel she noticed his hand trembling, and lightly put steadying fingers to his elbow. "Oz, you're shaking. Do you want to sit down?"

"Low blood sugar. Normally I eat right after a match. Tonight there's been a delay, for obvious reasons."

"I'll make you something. What do you want?"

He shook his head. "It's late. Go home. I'll be fine."

He gave her an out. She should take it. She should ignore the strange comfort of his presence, and her secret elation that he was still speaking to her after their acrimonious game of pool. She should keep this professional, remind him to turn on the motion-sensor beams after she left and give him a follow-up call tomorrow.

She looked at the front door, then past Oz, in the opposite direction toward the kitchen. The wide-open sight lines in the house meant she got a full view of the pig's blood still smeared across the cabinets and floor, and the outlines of swastikas drying on the granite countertop.

She should leave. But she couldn't leave him to this.

"Why don't you chill out in the study? I'll bring something up to you."

Frowning, he followed her line of vision into the kitchen.

He sighed, and it was so bone-deeply weary that Kate wished she could tighten her arms around him and shove all that oxygen back inside until he perked back to his usual, arrogant, contrary self.

"You don't need to stay here and clean that," he told her quietly. "I'll get what I need from the cupboards and call my housekeeper in the morning."

"Let me do it. I owe you."

"For what?"

"Friday night. I know I won fair and square, but I could've been a little more gracious about it."

He shoved his hands into his pockets. "Beating me at pool doesn't oblige you to clean hate symbols drawn in blood."

"No, it doesn't. Which is why you should probably take advantage of my offer before I realize that."

His smile was faint, but it was the first one she'd seen all evening.

"Let's do it together. I'm very particular about which cleaning products are used on which surfaces."

"Of course you are." She rolled her eyes playfully as they moved into the kitchen.

The metallic stench of blood was almost as offensive as the swastikas. Drips and smears stained most of the beautiful space.

Oz reached into a high cupboard and retrieved a series of cleaning products—all unfamiliar eco-friendly brands and probably twice the price of what she used at home. He launched into an explanation of what was to be used where and why, but after a few seconds she held up a palm to silence him.

"Give me a bottle, a cloth, and point me toward something. In the meantime I want you to eat."

"Okay," he agreed. With unprecedented obedience he passed her a microfiber cloth and a purple bottle for the counters, then found a spoon and a jar of peanut butter and settled onto a stool at the island.

Silence hushed the massive house. She sprayed and scrubbed and rinsed and sprayed again, enjoying the way the silvery flecks in the granite sparkled as they picked up the light.

If Oz had any criticism of her technique he kept it to himself, although his eyes never left her. The weight of his gaze grew heavier until she was hyperaware of every movement she made, every slight twist or turn. Her decidedly unsexy cotton T-shirt felt like silk as it shifted against her skin, and her nipples hardened inside her fraying sports bra.

She pressed her back teeth together. A man was watching her clean bloody swastikas off his kitchen counter. There had to be something wrong with her if she was getting aroused.

She stole a glance at Oz. His eyes were charred chunks of wood in a roaring fire—coal-black and dangerously hot. He sucked on the spoon in his mouth, ran his tongue over the back of it, dropped it with a clatter into the empty jar.

Then he was on his feet, snatching up a cloth and a bottle. "I'll help you."

They scrubbed in silence for a while, the kitchen quiet except for squeaks and squirts and the occasional splash. Oz dug out a mop and started on the floor, and she reached above her head to remove splatters from the top of the fridge.

She tried to think of an excuse to indulge her curiosity and open the cabinets or the freezer, wondering what their contents would reveal about this man that their sterile, uncluttered exteriors didn't. Maybe everything was stacked in haphazard piles, half of it expired, most of it unused. Or maybe it was all arranged with the oldest purchases at the front, labels facing outward, alphabetically ordered by brand name.

Maybe most of the cupboards were empty. Maybe he followed one of those crazy celebrity diets and ate only raw, organic fruit and vegetables fresh out of the farmer's field.

Or maybe he went completely the other way. Maybe he hated cooking but burned so many calories he needed to take in whatever he could, so stocked up on pasta, bread, cheese, and cookies.

She stole a glance at him from the corner of her eye, her fingers itching to tug open the refrigerator door. He appeared to be deeply focused on wringing out the mop. Would he notice if she took a quick peek? Would he care? His brow furrowed in concentration. What was he thinking about?

He raised his gaze to meet hers with such sudden intention she wondered if he'd read her mind.

"Why did you leave the army?"

She blinked, expecting a more serious, probing question. "My contract ended and I decided it was a good time to get out. I'd been in for eight years. It was time to make some real money."

"So you took the job in Saudi Arabia."

"The pay was amazing. I pretty much lived off my housing allowance and sent the rest home. My sister and my niece live with my mom, who's usually one rude hand gesture away from losing whatever part-time retail gig she's got. Long story short, in six months I paid off my sister's car, bought my mom a dishwasher and set up a semester of afterschool tutoring for my niece."

He stowed the mop in a tall cabinet, then leaned against the wall. "But Saudi Arabia was too terrible to stick it out for more than a year, even with the money?"

She paused, considering whether or not to tell him the full story.

"I didn't quit my job there. I was fired."

"Really. Why?" He resumed his seat at the kitchen island.

She wrung out her cloth and draped it over the edge of the sink, quickly surveying the kitchen to see what else needed to be cleaned. It was spotless, but she picked up a dry cloth and started buffing the faucet.

"The woman I was supposed to protect, the oil executive's wife, was attacked."

Her back was turned, but she read Oz's silence as his request for her to go on. "The residential compound was out in the desert, but there was a town nearby—a city, really. Maybe a hundred thousand people. For the most part the Americans stayed in the compound, but occasionally my client went into the city to shop, go to a restaurant, attend a doctor's appointment, and I went with her. We wore *abayas* and headscarves and spent most of our time in a chauffeured car, but every so often we walked from one place to another."

She sucked in a breath, smelling the exhaust fumes, hearing the cacophony of SUV engines and beeping horns, blinking away the sand constantly swirling through the air.

"Usually Saudis give foreigners a pass," she explained, turning to prop her hip on the island. "As long as you're making an effort to respect the laws, the *muttaween*—the religious police—don't give you any hassle. That day we were standing outside a shopping mall, waiting for the driver to come around the block and pick us up. We were both covered from head to toe, holding bags from the shops we'd visited. This guy came up to us and started shouting in Arabic, gesturing to the bags. Then another one joined him, and another, and another. It was a crazy, random mob scene, and we were in the middle, unable to understand what we'd done."

She closed her eyes, briefly revisiting the vivid memory she still hoped might fade. Her private-security skills put to the test for the first time and failing as, unarmed, off-guard, she was no match for the ten men crowding around them.

"I tried to move in front of her," she continued, opening her eyes but not able to look at Oz. "I tried to shove her out of the way, but it didn't work. One of the men pushed her down—maybe accidentally, it was hard to tell—and she cut her cheek open on the concrete."

Kate ran her finger across her cheekbone to illustrate the damage. Oz winced.

"The blood freaked the men out, I guess. They didn't want to be responsible for damaging another man's property. They scattered as quickly as they gathered, just in time for the driver to arrive."

"Did you figure out why they were so angry?"

"The driver guessed it was the picture of a woman on the outside of one of the bags. It had been Photoshopped to cover her cleavage, like everything is there, but you could still see her neck and part of her shoulders." She shrugged. "My client needed stitches and a plastic surgeon to fix the scar, and I was thanked for my service and relieved of employment."

She was pleased with her ability to recount the incident with barely any hint of the devastation and deep-seated worthlessness that underpinned that experience. She wasn't over any of it—not the event, not being fired, not her failure to do her job and protect her client.

But she sounded like she was. A step in the right direction, at least.

Oz whistled. "Tough."

"It was probably for the best. I hated the job, but would've struggled to convince myself to quit considering the salary." She smiled bitterly. "I have a tendency to be a victim of—What do you call it? Inactivity? When just nothing happens."

"Inertia?"

She snapped her fingers. "That's it. Inertia. Sums me up in a single word."

"That's not the word I would choose."

She glanced at him sharply but he was on his feet again, his expression closed and inscrutable. He swept up the few bottles of cleaning fluids on the counter and took the cloth from her hand, then stowed everything underneath the sink.

"Thanks for your help tonight. Cleaning up pig's blood is definitely beneath your pay grade."

She waved off his comment. "The least I could do. If anything, I should apologize for going off on a tangent about getting fired."

"No, that was interesting. Sometimes my life is so immaculate it borders on sterile. It's good to be reminded that not everyone's world is quite as tidy."

"I think most people would trade."

"I know." He smiled. "Don't worry, I'm not one of those woe-is-me rich people. I was born lucky. Stable, well-educated parents, natural athletic talent, and the right coaches and mentors to develop it. The greatest trauma I ever endured was getting five stitches after I cut my shin on a diving board in Turkey."

"Until tonight."

"Until tonight," he echoed, his tone darkening. Kate instantly regretted her words, which lowered the mood they'd only just managed to lift.

"I should go." She ducked around him to leave the kitchen, heading for the bag she'd tossed on his dining-room table.

He followed, watching her levelly as she dug through the clutter to produce her car keys. "You can stay if you want."

"Why would I want that?"

She asked the question in jest, but Oz's response was dead serious. "To protect me. In case they come back."

She put down her bag. "Do you want me to stay?"

"I defer to your professional judgment."

She narrowed her eyes, studying his expression and examining his tone for any clue to his intent. Was he making fun of her? Testing her?

Either way, it didn't matter. They couldn't do this. She could lose her job to those big, searching eyes. She could lose her whole self.

"I think you'll be fine," she decided. "Turn on the alarm and the beams. The local tactical team will respond in less than three minutes if anything happens."

He inclined his head, accepting her verdict. She slung her bag over her shoulder.

He followed her to the door and reached around her to open it.

She paused in the doorway, stupidly reluctant to leave, to walk away from this brief, trusting period in which she'd felt so comfortable. Like she was in exactly the right place. "Will you call someone to stay with you tonight? Because I can wait."

He shook his head. "Like you said, I'll be fine."

"Okay." She glanced at the hushed darkness beyond the front lawn, the light from the doorway casting a slanted rectangle on the porch. "The other night in the bar, playing pool, maybe I—"

"You won."

"I know, but—"

"But nothing. It's done. We've moved on."

She shifted her weight. "We have?"

He said nothing, fixing her with that unblinking, inscrutable stare that seemed to be his default. Was this poker face the key to his success on the pitch? The fans did call him the Wizard, so maybe—

His lips were on hers, without warning, without so much as a glance at her mouth or angling of his chin to lessen the surprise. She started, then froze.

And then relaxed. *Exactly the right place.*

This kiss was different from its predecessor. Sincerity replaced coy flirtation; impulse and honesty guided the pace. As she flattened her palm against his chest she thought she'd learned more about Oz in the last ten seconds than in all the time she'd known him.

He raised his fingers to her cheek and her whole body eased, as if someone cut a string that was holding her upright. His arm came around her waist as she pushed against him, the pressure of his mouth increasing to complement the growing softness of her posture.

She didn't know why she was able to let go of her anxieties and enjoy this kiss, as opposed to the one in Boise. Because of the comforting backdrop of crickets chirping in the early-summer evening? The quiet camaraderie between them as they'd cleaned the kitchen? The way the vast house and empty street made it feel like they might be the only two people left in Atlanta.

She didn't know, and she didn't care. She kissed Oz like the end was nigh, like this was her last chance. Like she'd never heard of consequences.

Except she had. And when he withdrew gently, she could think of nothing else.

"Go," he urged, rough-voiced. "Before I do something stupid."

Like sleep with a redneck security contractor who was fired from her last job, and might very well get fired from her current one with this kind of behavior. "Sure. I get it."

"You don't." He squeezed her arm above the elbow. "But you will. Just not tonight."

She frowned, but she was too tired and overwhelmed and still reeling from their kiss to bother trying to figure him out.

Instead, she jangled her car keys and stepped backward onto the porch.

"We'll talk soon."

He nodded.

"Put the alarm on," she reminded him, then turned to make her way to her car. The long rectangle of light on the grass told her he still watched from the doorway, and she marveled that her feet touched the ground when she felt lighter than air.

Chapter 10

"Oz! Over here!"

"This way, Oz!"

"What the—" Oz cut himself off just in time. Kojo was giving him a lift and the West African hated swearing.

Kojo shook his head as he steered the car past the knot of press photographers and reporters at the entrance to Skyline's training complex. "These people, they have no shame," he pronounced in his thick French accent.

His fellow defender parked, and as soon as they got out of the car the frenzy increased.

"Oz, do the police have any leads?"

"Are you afraid to be in your home?"

"Is it true that Citizens First is sending you death threats?"

"Do you plan to fast during Ramadan?"

"What do you think about the growing hostility toward the Muslim community?"

He waved Kojo inside, shouldered his sports bag and walked toward the clamoring crowd. Microphones bobbed and cameras flashed, and one photographer leaned so far over the red-and-white boom pole Oz thought he would fall flat on his face.

"I'm glad to see you're all taking an interest in me," he began, the group hushing as they clicked on their tape recorders. "I've been in Atlanta for a few years now, was a CSL Player of the Year twice, and have scored more goals than any other Skyline defender, but I never seem to hear from any of you. To be honest, I even considered firing my publicist."

He offered them the flash of a smile. A few of the reporters piped up with questions but he continued, "I assume you're all here to discuss my footballing ascendance and Skyline's outstanding season, right? Surely it hasn't taken a hate crime to spark your interest in someone who plays the most popular sport in the world."

"So you're confirming it was a hate crime?" a reporter lobbed back, setting off another wave of shouted questions.

Oz drew breath to launch into a long-winded tirade on the lack of diverse sports reporting in America and its impact on future generations of soccer players, but before he could begin a member of Skyline's PR department arrived at his elbow, breathless from her jog across the parking lot.

"Hi everyone, thank you, but Oz is late for training. Later this morning Skyline's press office will release a statement regarding the act of vandalism carried out against one of our players. Any further questions or requests for interviews should be directed through your normal channel of contact with the team."

She tugged Oz away with her hand on his forearm.

"I know," she acknowledged before he could speak. "I heard you, and I don't disagree. Do you know why I told them that last point about normal channels of contact? Because none of them have any, and I have piles of unused credentials for Skyline press conferences to prove it."

The PR assistant did her best to pacify him, but by the time he entered the dressing room his mood was black. It didn't help that all his teammates abandoned their conversations and rushed up to him the minute he stepped through the door.

"Damn, Oz, I'm so sorry. I should've walked in with you, or at least waited for you to give me the all clear. I went to bed as soon as I got home so it was only this morning—"

Oz raised a hand to halt Deon's verbal gushing. "Don't apologize. Neither of us could've known what was inside the house."

"So it's true. They were all the way inside your house." Normally jovial Laurent shuddered. "Could you sleep there last night?"

Oz shrugged, unwilling to reveal that he'd managed only three hours of uneasy sleep during a night mostly spent pacing from one brightly lit room to the next. "It's still my home. If I'd put the alarm on this probably wouldn't have happened."

"This guy? I find." Guedes, one of Skyline's two Brazilian defenders, smacked his fist into the palm of his other hand to communicate what his limited English apparently couldn't.

"I appreciate that." Oz patted Guedes on one of his enormous arms and moved to his locker, ending the conversation.

His teammates fell into uncharacteristic silence, but his thoughts shouted louder than ever as he changed into his training kit. Was he not taking this seriously enough? He never expected the press would turn up. Maybe it was a slow news day. Or maybe they were jumping on the bandwagon. There had been a few high-profile incidents of anti-Muslim action by Citizens First followers recently, and although technically no one had claimed the break-in at his house, maybe the press hoped they could link this local event to a broader national theme. Just a week ago a handful of self-proclaimed Citizens First members had burned down a Muslim family's house in Michigan. Maybe the Atlanta media outlets were betting on a similar escalation against him and wanted to get on the story early.

Which cycled him back to his first thought. Was he not taking this seriously enough?

The training session was short and light since they'd played a match the day before. After a warm-up they ran a drill designed to quicken their reactions to teammates' instructions. The full squad stood in two parallel lines, facing each other, with small, fluorescent discs on the floor between each pair. Oz found himself opposite Colin Russell, a defensive midfielder who never started but often came on as a substitute. Ross, the head trainer, shouted instructions about where to place their hands—ears, eyes, mouth—before randomly adding *go* as a signal to grab the disc. Whichever player grabbed the disc first won, and moved on to face another winner until the exercise came down to two finalists.

Oz was the reigning champion, a title only occasionally threatened by Uruguayan winger Nico Silva. There was a reason his Fantasy CSL player profile had a full ten points for agility. This drill was made for him.

They crouched in their positions, forearms on their thighs.

Colin winked across the short space between them. "I'm glad I got you. Means I can sit out the rest of this."

"Try to give me some competition. It's lonely at the top."

Ross blew his whistle, then shouted in his Liverpool accent, "Mouth! Nose! Mouth! *Go!*"

Oz snatched at the disc, then sat back in astonishment when his hand came up empty.

Colin leapt up, staring in astonishment at the disc in his hand. "I won. I won! I beat the Wizard!"

Oz stretched his legs in front of him, joining his teammates' applause. Then he made his way to the sideline and, for the first time he could remember, sat out the rest of the drill.

His performance went downhill as the training session progressed, until Ross pulled him aside.

"The boss wants to talk to you, and you look like you could use a week of sleep. Hit the showers, speak to the big man, and then head home."

Oz didn't argue. He trudged into the empty changing room and showered quickly, missing the camaraderie of his teammates. He dressed, made his way to Roland's office, and quickly scrolled through the notifications on his phone while he waited for the manager's PA, Michelle, to give him the nod to go in.

He flicked through the usual series of comments on his Instagram account. Links to porn sites, comments in Arabic, fans imploring him to transfer to one team or another.

His thumb paused above the screen as he read the next one. The username was AU5ONIU5, the comment an address. It took him a second to understand what it meant, and when it did a wave of nausea nearly dropped him to his knees.

The door opened and Roland leaned out, gesturing for him to enter. "Sorry, got stuck on a call."

Oz followed him into the familiar office on shaky legs, then stopped short as he saw the person seated in front of Roland's desk.

"I asked Kate to join us," Roland explained as he took his own seat. "We should make a plan for the away match in Charlotte on Friday."

"Okay." He inclined his head in greeting to Kate as he eased into the other chair. An image of last night's kiss lodged at the front of his mind. He hoped his arousal wasn't as obvious as it felt.

He stole a glance at her, then wished he hadn't. What was it about her? Why did he want to rip off her ill-fitting suit? Why did she threaten twenty-seven years of ironclad self-control so badly?

"Unless you suggest otherwise, Kate, I think we should keep the same protocol as in Boise. We'll leave it to you to subcontract local security personnel, and if at all possible, we'd like you to travel with the team again."

She nodded her agreement. "I don't think last night's incident should change anything, except to remind us to be vigilant at all times."

"Good." Roland turned to him. "Anything from your side?"

"Just this." He opened the AU5ONIU5 comment on his phone and passed it to Roland.

His manager squinted at the screen, frowned, and swore colorfully in Swedish as he passed the phone to Kate.

She looked between the two of them. "What does it mean?"

"It's the address of the hotel the team booked in Charlotte," Roland explained, removing his glasses and rubbing his hand over his eyes. "And the name is a reference to—"

"I told her." Oz shifted in his seat. "It's not the first time I've gotten a message from a similar username."

"And you didn't tell me? Özkan," Roland chided, with more weariness than anger. "We should move the team to a new hotel as discreetly as possible. I'll ask Michelle to work on it this afternoon."

"I'll liaise with her to inform both hotels of the issue, and do what we can to keep the switch confidential," Kate suggested. "In the meantime, Oz, can I borrow your phone for the day? I'd like our cyber security guy to take a look at it, see if he can find out anything."

"I guess, but I'll need it for the next couple of hours. Nico is giving me a lift to the dealership to pick up my car, but he has a physio appointment so if there's any delay I'll need to call someone else to bring me back."

"I'll take you," she offered. "And I'll follow you home. Give the security system another sweep to make sure everything's working as it should."

A twenty-minute drive in her car, after which she would be inside his house. He swallowed hard. "Okay."

"Thanks to you both," Roland said, concluding the meeting. Kate rose and left the office, and as they heard her speak to Michelle, Roland grabbed Oz's arm.

"Don't give her a hard time," his manager instructed.

"I won't," Oz promised. He intended to give her a whole lot more.

* * * *

Kate gritted her teeth and pressed the accelerator, fighting to keep up with Oz on the drive to his house from the dealership. His high-performance car sailed down the highway while her third-hand subcompact shuddered if she pushed the speedometer over sixty. Occasionally he deliberately slowed to wait for her, only to shoot off as soon as she caught up.

Following his sleek, white Mercedes was difficult and annoying—and sexy as hell. He drove as he seemed to live, with precision, control, and a muted impatience that hinted at the full-force wildness that made him so fast and aggressive on the pitch.

She imagined his hand on the gearstick, elegantly yet mercilessly putting the car through its paces. His feet instinctively, smoothly working the pedals. His expression cool and calm, unmoved by the hum and purr and roar of the engine.

They stopped at a light and she pressed her thighs together, desperate for some relief from the pressure that had built between her legs from the moment he slid into her car at the training ground.

He had shoved the seat all the way back but still dominated the small space. Her heart thudded as she maneuvered out of the parking lot and toward the dealership, every breath filling her lungs with his eucalyptus scent.

He said little on the drive, apart from the occasional direction. She was too nervous to carry the conversation. Her fingers stayed tight on the wheel, paranoid she'd say or do something to shatter the strange, sensual harmony that seemed to have settled between them.

"I was surprised when I saw this car at my house last night," he said eventually.

"Really? Why?"

"I assumed you drove a pickup truck."

Her cheeks heated at what she took to be his insinuation that she was some country girl from the sticks, and because she intended to buy a pickup if she ever saved enough money. "What does that mean?"

He glanced over, startled, as if it had only just occurred to him that she might take offense. "I meant you seem practical. And you'd want a useful vehicle, not a pretty one."

"Oh." She put on her blinker, grateful the dealership was in sight. "Well, this is what I can afford."

She winced as she recalled that statement, following Oz through the light and down the street toward his neighborhood. She was so attracted to him, and she let stupid shit like that roll out of her mouth?

She followed him into his driveway. She coached herself as they both waited for the garage door to open.

Go inside, check his alarm system, get the hell out. You cannot be with this man. Don't let your horny-ass heart overrule your head.

Oz pulled into the garage and she parked behind him. She waited while he unlocked the door to the house, then disarmed the alarm that gave a warning squeal as they stepped inside.

"Glad to see you're using the system," she remarked, quickly scrolling through the panel screen to check the history. "Have you had any trouble with—"

He put his hands on her shoulders and pressed her against the wall, his lips finding hers, his kiss hot and impatient.

Well, shit.

Her foolish, horny-ass heart won out as she flung her arms around his neck and drew him closer, his body flat and hard against hers. No beer belly, no exaggerated gym muscles—he was lean and wiry and perfectly proportioned.

He raised his hand to the nape of her neck and threaded his fingers through her hair. She parted her lips and he responded hungrily, his tongue finding hers, retreating, then seeking it again with renewed vigor. He tasted like mint and smelled like eucalyptus and he was so exciting, so different from anyone she'd been with that she moaned in sheer delight.

Ruddy color stained his cheeks when he pulled back. "Over here."

He led her to the white-leather sofa where last night he'd sat with his head in his hands, shocked to silence by the act of hate committed on his property. She pushed that image of him from her mind and focused on this one instead—the sexy tilt of his mouth as he smiled, the evidence of her touch in his slightly mussed hair, the dark shimmer in his eyes as he motioned her down beside him.

She hesitated above the pristine piece of furniture. "I feel like I'm going to get this thing dirty just by looking at it."

"Is that a promise?" He took her hand and tugged her into his lap, then replaced his mouth on hers.

She let her shoes slide off her feet, hiked up her too-big pencil skirt around her thighs and straddled him, steadying herself with her palms flat on his chest.

They both groaned as the bulge in his jeans met the cotton of her panties. Oz shoved her suit coat off her shoulders and ran his thumbs down her arms, which were bare in the sleeveless, fake-silk top she wore underneath. He squeezed her biceps, then broke the kiss so he could study them in greater detail.

"How much do you bench?"

She rolled her eyes to mask a wave of self-consciousness. "If I had a dollar for every time I was asked that in the Army I wouldn't be fighting with professional athletes about where to install their alarm panels."

"Seriously."

"I don't know. A hundred. And ten."

"How much do you weigh? Don't answer that. Sorry, I went into locker-room mode."

"Don't worry, I won't," she replied dryly, but her heart sank. She was becoming one of the guys again. He was probably about to suggest they skip the sex and watch sports instead.

He lowered his head and brushed a kiss over her biceps, then trailed his lips up the inside of her arm, around her shoulder and along her neck.

"I'll have to up my game in the gym," he murmured, his mouth behind her ear. "I can't have you beating me on the pool table and the bench press."

Her eyes drifted shut as he kissed her jaw, her cheek, then found his way back to her mouth. As she opened for him his hand gripped her waist, slid up her ribs and settled below her bra, his thumb daring to brush the underwire.

She pulled back and leveled her eyes on his as she unbuttoned her top and tossed it aside. Quickly she unclasped her bra and let the straps slip down her arms, then dropped it on her discarded shirt.

Oz's eyes widened as his gaze fell to her breasts. "Wow. Okay."

"Okay?" she asked in mock offense. She knew she wasn't exactly voluptuous, but what she had was perky and well-shaped.

"Good. Great. Excellent. Amazing. I'm running out of English words."

"Save the Swedish for later." She grabbed his wrists and brought his hands to her breasts, unable to stifle a moan as his warm palms covered her taut nipples.

He lowered his left hand and replaced it with his mouth. She squeezed her eyes shut as the tip of his tongue teased her sensitive flesh and she ground against him, desperate to relieve the ache between her legs.

She moved out of his reach and put her hand between them, slowly lowering the zipper of his jeans. He gripped her hips, his eyes never leaving her face.

She shoved aside denim and cotton to find hot, rigid flesh. He was bigger than she expected. Thicker. Longer. She purred her approval, pushing her fist down his shaft.

He groaned, an unbidden, rough sound, as he shifted on the couch. She repeated the motion and he pressed his hand over his eyes, baring his teeth.

She smiled, enjoying her control over this tightly self-controlled man. She stroked him again, and again, and again, until he arched forward and stopped her with a hand on her wrist.

"You're destroying me," he told her gruffly, angling to press a kiss to her neck.

"You're doing some damage, too." She guided his hand between her thighs. He slipped his fingers beneath her panties and exhaled raggedly.

"Fuck," he muttered, his middle finger gently probing her slick sex. "It's not even lunchtime."

"I'll make you a sandwich afterward." She propped her hands on his shoulders as she kissed his forehead. "Go, get protection. I promise I'll be naked on this fancy-pants couch by the time you're back."

He shook his head. "I can't."

"Really? I figured you'd have plenty. Let me check my purse, I may have—"

"Wait." He pulled her against him, settling his hands at the small of her back. "I mean, we can't have sex. Not today."

Uncertainty drew her brows together. "Why not?"

"Because I don't."

"Don't what?"

"Have sex."

The pieces slowly came together in her mind. "Like, you're celibate?"

"Not exactly."

She sighed, growing more exasperated and uncomfortable by the minute. "Explain."

"I've never had sex."

It took her a few seconds to realize her mouth hung open. She snapped it closed. "Ever?"

"Never ever."

Comprehension staggered and struggled through her thickening haze of emotions. Self-consciousness. Humiliation. Unbearable, painful awkwardness.

She snatched up her suit jacket from the arm of the couch and pulled it over her shoulders, holding it together over her breasts.

"Don't," he began, then stopped himself. His expression shifted from reluctance to resignation, and she knew she had to leave.

"It's not a religious thing, or a hang-up, or anything like that," he explained, his tone increasingly defensive. "I decided to wait until I was ready. I'm not ready. And I won't apologize for that."

"I'm not asking you to apologize. I wish you'd spelled out your expectations a little earlier, though."

"I'm not sure either of us saw this going so far, so fast."

"Letting a woman strip half-naked and grind on your lap is usually a pretty good sign that sex is in the cards," she replied testily. She climbed off the couch and gathered up her clothes.

"Excuse me for not presuming your consent," he shot back, zipping his jeans and rising to his feet. "As far as I'm aware, the only signal that gives the go-ahead for sex is saying so."

She bit her lip to cover a surge of tenderness. She'd never been with a man who said something like that. Hell, she'd rarely been with a man sober. Now she'd found one who was respectful and thoughtful and he was a goddamn *virgin*. "I have to go," she muttered, shoving her feet into her shoes and stumbling to the front door.

Oz was right behind her. "Kate, stop. Please," he implored, his tone softening. "I'm sorry I didn't tell you sooner, okay? You don't have to go."

She shook her head. "I really should get back to the office."

He slid his forefinger beneath her chin, prompting her to meet his gaze. "What changed? We were having fun."

"I'm embarrassed," she admitted, heat crawling up her cheeks. "I threw myself at you, and if I'd known—"

"I threw myself at you first," he reminded her, his hands linking

Rebecca Crowley

around her waist.

"I guess." But his attempt to console her only made her feel worse. She'd been proud of her lack of inhibition and her sexual confidence—two things she'd always struggled with. She wanted Oz to know her as a self-assured, sensual dynamo. Instead, she was back in the all-too-familiar territory of uncertainty, anxiety and regret.

"Stay. Have lunch. We'll talk." His thumb swept over her stomach, bare beneath her hastily pulled-on suit jacket. "Or not."

She hesitated. He looked so good. And she was starving.

But the moment was gone. She'd be awkward and stiff if she stayed. She needed time to collect herself. If he'd waited this long, he probably wanted to wait for a relationship, and that was so far from what she could offer it was in another galaxy.

"I'm going," she decided.

"Dressed like this?" He touched her top button. It sat high on her stomach. The jacket lapels barely covered her nipples.

"Yes." Quickly she did up the other two buttons. It made no difference.

"I'll enjoy imagining your drive back to the office. And hope you don't get pulled over."

"Thanks," she replied, then cringed at the rigidity in her voice.

He reached around her, unlocked the door and pushed it open. "I guess I'll see you on Thursday."

"Sure. Sounds good." She nearly stuck out her hand to shake before she caught herself. Jesus, this wasn't a business meeting.

"I'd tell you to call me if you want to get together before then, but you've got my phone."

"Right. Of course. I'll make sure our cyber-security guy couriers it back to you as soon as he's done with it."

"I'd appreciate that," he said neutrally.

She narrowed her eyes. Was he making fun of her? He wore his characteristically indecipherable expression, though it was slightly undermined by his passion-mussed hair and still-unbuttoned fly.

Whatever. She tossed an excessively upbeat farewell over her shoulder as she hurried down the porch steps and around to her car, praying none of the neighbors spotted her daring take on business attire.

She tucked into the driver's seat, reversed down his driveway and sped along the street without noticing in which direction she'd gone. She turned the corner and pulled over halfway down the next block. Then she cut the engine and rested her forehead on the steering wheel.

Regret, disappointment, humiliation, and unfulfilled lust competed for attention in her swirling thoughts. She exhaled, forcing herself to take each one in turn.

Regret. She wished she'd slowed down and presented a calmer, more contained version of herself. But would she feel the same if Oz hadn't stopped her and they'd had sex? He certainly hadn't minded her forward, even brazen style. She had no reason to regret. Cross that one off the list.

Disappointment. That was fair enough, frankly. She wanted to have sex with Oz, looked forward to having sex with Oz, bad idea though it was, and now it would never happen. She winced as disappointment bit even more sharply. Ouch.

Humiliation. Again, this was all down to her. Oz gave her no reason to feel embarrassed. On the contrary, he'd insinuated she could stay and get up to even more frisky behavior. She sighed. It was hard—really hard—but she had to push away the humiliation. Its roots were planted firmly in her mind and nowhere else.

Last but certainly not least, the hot pressure that still thudded between her legs. With a quick glance out of the car windows to double-check that the residential street was empty, she slipped her hand inside her suit jacket and teased her bare nipple.

Yes, just like that.

She settled back in her seat. Let her hand drop between her thighs. She thought of Oz, his clean scent, his hard body. She slipped her fingers beneath the damp fabric of her panties and rubbed slow, lingering circles against her clit.

Her eyes fell shut, her vision filling with images of him. His thick, soft, midnight-black hair. His eyes—large, hungry, shining with appreciation as he watched her. She imagined his hand in place of hers, his skillful, unhurried fingers instead of hers, his expression shifting from playful to intensely serious as he watched her breathing hasten, her mouth open, her head fall back...

She came suddenly, sharply, too briefly. She moaned her dissatisfaction as the pleasure subsided, jerked her hand up and started the engine.

She put trembling hands on the steering wheel and checked her mirrors before pulling out onto the road. That hadn't been enough. Not nearly enough. And she wouldn't get anything more.

Chapter 11

"Number twenty-four, Kojo Agassa. Number eighteen, Özkan Terim."

Oz barely registered the applause of the away fans. He swept his hands down his face to complete his prayer, then studied the team lined up on the other side of the pitch.

Charlotte was one of Skyline's fiercest competitors this season. Their striker was big and powerful, but he was getting older and slowing down. The midfielders were clever, creative and agile but struggled with finishing, and relied on the striker to convert their elegant assists. Skyline's job would be to intercept those long passes, or even better, to beat the midfielders off the ball.

The whistle blew and the match started tentatively. Laurent made the first move for Skyline, darting forward to win the ball. Charlotte's right-back chased him to the sideline, then kicked the ball out of play, giving Skyline a throw-in.

Oz exhaled. Tried to get his head in the game. Tried to remember that fans had traveled and spent money and waited to see this match, and that he was paid a princely sum to perform to their expectations.

He couldn't think about the unspoken, unresolved sexual tension that settled heavily on his shoulders whenever Kate entered a room.

He couldn't think about the way her eyes widened in disbelief when he'd told her he was a virgin, or about her decisive, sudden departure, or about his sulky disappointment.

He definitely couldn't think about her total silence from the moment she left his house until they met again at the stadium before the team's departure for Charlotte, or her detached, professional manner when she did speak to him.

And, on that note he most certainly couldn't think about the embarrassing level of personal security he'd endured on this trip, from having to wait alone in the lobby so his room could be inspected to the bouncer-looking guy who'd preceded him on and off the team bus. Although his teammates knew he wasn't the prima donna his security presence suggested, he hated the thought of a fan or an opposing player coming to a different conclusion.

He shook his head as he jogged to mark a midfielder, imagining he was shaking out thoughts about anything except this match.

Soccer. Listen, react, run. Nothing else.

He spent the next ninety minutes in constant motion. Precise, controlled, relentless. He executed tackle after perfect tackle, neatly winning possession and sailing the ball up the midfield. He chased Charlotte's forwards, leapt to defeat their stylish passes and cleared the striker's best, squarest shot of the match, a breath away from the goal line.

He was at his best, playing with exactly the combination of ruthless aggression and clinical self-control that made him stand out in his youth-league team when he was ten years old. He was faster now, sharper, better trained, but at times he still found himself reaching back to the raw instinct discovered in his childhood, the relentless determination and brutal efficiency he'd learned from watching his uncle.

The scoreboard read nil-nil when the final whistle blew. Skyline's forwards' shoulders slumped in disappointment, but Oz smiled. That zero was hard earned and he was proud of it.

He slapped backs to celebrate with his fellow defenders and shook the hands of the opposing players. He bantered with one of the Charlotte midfielders, traded a joke with their goalkeeper and accepted wry praise from their famed striker.

He grinned as he left the pitch, exhausted, relaxed, pleased.

"Very nice." Roland nodded his approval and spoke in Swedish as Oz walked past. "Stunning work today."

Oz stuck up his thumb to show he'd heard, following his teammates toward the dressing room. One of Charlotte's media coordinators waved at him from a bend in the hallway, beckoning him over.

"Number eighteen, you've been named Skyline's man of the match," she announced brightly. "Can we grab you for a five-minute interview?"

"Of course," he replied, delighted. Man of the match was rarely awarded to defenders, and he hadn't been given the honor since he unexpectedly scored a winner at the beginning of the season. He followed her to the pressroom, where tall boards showing the sponsors' logos were set up to form a corner.

Pavel Kovar, Skyline's goalkeeper, was already in place. As the team's captain he gave a short interview after most of the matches, and his comfort in front of the cameras was evident in his easy posture.

"Good work today." The Czech slapped Oz on the back as he took his position in front of the boards. "Especially that last clearance."

"I'm sure you would've saved it if I hadn't."

The older man smiled. "I wasn't going to say it, but since you did…"

The correspondent from the major sports channel which aired CSL matches hurried in, microphone and cameraman at the ready.

"Good to go?" he asked without preamble, and the two players nodded.

He motioned for the cameraman to start rolling. "Pavel, Oz, thanks so much for joining us after what appeared to be a punishing draw against Charlotte. The match was truly box-to-box and a real credit to both defensive sides that neither team was able to create an opportunity to score. Pavel, how important is communication for you with pacesetters like Oz and Kojo Agassa on your end?"

"Communication is absolutely fundamental to keeping a clean sheet," Pavel explained. "We know where we all are at all times, to avoid mistakes and maximize our strengths."

The reporter pivoted. "Oz, stats show us that you run more than the average left-back, but in this match you clocked a whopping eight miles of distance covered, more than anyone else on the pitch. Do you see your position as being more than a defender?"

"Much more," Oz replied. "I have my defensive duties, of course, and I can't neglect them, but where possible I love to chase up the pitch and get involved. My aim is always to assist the team from wherever, whenever."

"And I know you must be tired, but tell us, Oz, you consistently hit top marks in speed and distance. Would you say you're in the shape of your life?"

Oz smiled, envisioning the headline the reporter clearly wanted. *I'm in the shape of my life, reports Skyline's man of the match Oz Terim.* He supposed it wouldn't hurt to do the guy a favor.

"Yes, absolutely," Oz affirmed. "I'm twenty-seven and at a physical peak, but I'm also settled at Skyline, settled in Atlanta, and surrounded by some of the best players in the CSL."

The reporter signaled for the cameraman to cut, then nodded to the media assistant. She produced a soccer ball-shaped statuette and handed it to Pavel.

"We'll just get a shot of you receiving your award, Oz, and then we're done."

A few minutes later Oz entered the dressing room with his statuette in hand, to the warm applause of his teammates. He accepted high fives and fist bumps and although everyone was clearly tired, their smiles and well wishes were genuine. Oz undressed and showered with a sense of relief, glad to have proof that no one judged him for his new bodyguard.

He dressed in his Skyline tracksuit and joined the rest of his team in the lobby to board the bus back to the hotel. When Kate appeared from around a corner he forgot the awkwardness between them, pushed aside her rejection and launched into unapologetic flirt mode.

"Hey, do you think we'll need a bigger bus so I can get this back to the hotel?" he joked, holding up the statuette and beaming at her as she approached. "I don't know what the load limit on these things is, and I'm pretty sure this is one hundred percent solid plastic, so—"

His words died at her grim expression.

"We have a problem," she told him soberly. "A self-proclaimed *jihadi* opened fire on a shopping center in Decatur. He wounded three people and killed a mall security officer before turning the gun on himself."

It took him a few moments to process her statement and form his response. "That's terrible, but I don't understand what that has to do with me."

"Citizens First called for its Atlanta supporters to speak out against people they consider to be *jihadi* sympathizers." Her lips thinned into a line. "Fifty people are picketing outside your house."

Chapter 12

"Got it. Will do." Kate thanked her boss and pressed the red button to end the call. Hard. "Undermining prick."

She rapped on the hotel-room door behind her. The last remaining contract bodyguard opened it, his colleagues having been dismissed in waves that afternoon.

"I spoke to Rich, he wants you to escort Oz to Atlanta. Does that work for you? All on the clock, including the drive back tomorrow, but not double time."

The beefy guy shrugged. "Fine by me. Can I go home and pack a bag?"

"Take your time. We'll hit the road at eighteen hundred."

As the guard set off down the hallway, she moved into the room and let the door shut behind her. It slammed loudly into the frame but Oz didn't flinch. He sat motionless by the window, a book overturned on his knee.

She perched on the edge of the bed. This was the first time they'd been alone together since—well, since everything.

"I talked to my boss," she told him, plunging headfirst into the silence. "He wants us to wait until six."

Oz sighed, dragging his gaze away from the window to meet hers. "That's another two hours. The rest of the team has been back since noon. If anyone was hanging around the training ground to see if I arrived with them, they'd know I didn't."

"There's still a crowd outside your house. Smaller, but not by much. Hopefully they'll start to disperse once it gets dark."

"Some of them camped out last night," he countered.

"And if that's the case again, we'll have to put you in a hotel."

He shook his head. "I'm not going to a hotel in the city where I own a house. I want to go home."

they'll give up."

The headlights of another car briefly illuminated his tight jaw, but he turned around without speaking.

She watched the vehicles around them as they approached the deserted training complex, while loosely memorizing makes and colors so she could hopefully recognize any that reappeared on their way out. The security guard waved them in and Zach parked next to a car she recognized as Roland's.

As if on cue, the manager appeared at the door of the building.

"What are you doing here?" Oz called, tugging his bag out of the back of the SUV. "Go home to your wife."

"I couldn't stop thinking about those racist assholes outside your house. It was either drive over there and put the hose on them or come here and wait with you."

Oz smiled, patting his manager on the back. "I'm not sure you made the right choice, but I appreciate the company."

The two men fell into conversation in Swedish as the four of them proceeded into the complex. Rich was also waiting for them, and Kate seethed inwardly as she imagined her boss sweet-talking Roland. She didn't even want to think about how he planned to calculate his percentage now that he was elbowing into her account.

He didn't have good news, either. "The group is down to fifteen people, but that's still too many for us to risk bringing you in, not to mention leaving you there. We can wait, or we can find you a hotel for the night."

Oz shook his head decisively. "I spent all day in a hotel. I'll wait."

And so they did, with the exception of Zach, who was released to a motel for a night's sleep before driving the SUV back to Charlotte. For the next several hours the four of them drifted around the enormous building. Roland worked on his tablet in the lobby. Rich checked out the gym. Kate wandered outside to chat to the security guard, and when she came back Oz was asleep on the floor behind the reception desk.

"I told him to at least use one of the physiotherapy tables, but he ignored me as usual," Roland remarked without looking up from his screen.

She crossed her arms and tilted her head, surveying Oz's prone form. Stretched out on his stomach, his shoes arranged neatly beneath the receptionist's chair, with what looked like a lumbar-support cushion under his head.

"I thought being in the Army taught me to sleep anywhere, but that is impressive." She returned to sit on a hard-backed chair opposite Roland's.

"What's that expression about sleep being easy when you have a clear conscience? It's obviously not true." He shot her a joking grin, and she smiled

"Why do you do that?" he asked.

"Do what?"

"Hide from me."

"I don't. I don't even know what you mean." She half-stood, but he tugged her back down with a hand on her wrist. A hand he didn't remove.

"I'm interested, okay?" He edged closer. "I'm here because I'm interested in you. Attracted to you. What else do I have to say before you'll believe me?"

His words hit her like a sucker punch—just as hard, just as sore. She inhaled, readying herself to be brutally honest. "You said yourself that you'll know your Miss Right when you find her. Clearly she's not me."

"I'm not trying to marry you, Kate. I just want to spend time with you. Figure out this thing between us and enjoy it."

"You barely know me," she protested, but her grip on her objection was slipping. His eyes were so bright, his tone so earnest, and it had been so long since anyone had made her feel so important…

He took her by the shoulders, his voice dropping to a low rumble. "Let me know you. I'm telling you I want to."

Fear constricted her throat and stalled her breath. She shook her head tightly, and when she spoke the words were short, hard, barely above a whisper. "I don't know how."

He pulled her to his chest and wrapped his arms around her. She let herself soften against him, relaxing into his firm body.

"You know I won't have sex with you tonight, so trust me when I say that's not what this is about," he murmured into her temple. "I will touch you, though. Touch you, and taste you, and open you up until you're ready to show me who you are."

She shuddered, pulling back just enough to link her hands behind his neck and nod. "Do it."

His dark eyes flashed with hunger in the second before he captured her mouth, his tongue instantly demanding access, his hand rising to grip her nape. Mentally, she gathered all her self-consciousness, her self-doubt, her lingering wariness, squeezed them into a ball and hurled it to the farthest reaches of her mind.

She wasn't going to be that Kate, tonight, the one who worried and fumbled and woke up embarrassed and full of regret, who was complex and withdrawn and hard to know. She would be the strong, confident, desirable woman she knew she could be. The woman Oz wanted—the woman he saw despite all her attempts to hide.

She reached between them and found the hem of his T-shirt, and slid it up over his ribs. He drew back and took over, yanking it off and tossing it aside.

He moved to kiss her but she planted a hand on his chest, taking him in. He was as lean as she'd expected, with a light dusting of dark hair between his pecs and a smooth, hard stomach.

She traced a line in the tattoo that wrapped his arm from his shoulder to his elbow, an intricate, complicated matrix of shapes and colors. "What does this mean?"

"It's a tessellation. Sacred geometry. If you look at the way mathematics is rooted in nature... I'll explain later." He dragged her into his lap so quickly she had to clamp her hands on his shoulders to steady herself. He brought his lips to hers again and she flattened her palms on his bare chest, murmuring in satisfaction as he moved her legs apart, arranging her thighs on either side of his hips.

He released her mouth and tugged on her olive-green T-shirt. "Take this off."

She obeyed, pulling it over her head. He ran his forefinger along the underwire of the bra she wore beneath. "This too."

She reached behind her back to undo the clasp, and then her bra joined their shirts on the floor.

Oz didn't hesitate. He leaned forward and closed his lips on her nipple, teasing the tip with his tongue. She arched into him and he shifted to give her other breast the same treatment, his thumb rising to fill the absence of his mouth.

She moaned huskily, digging her fingers into his hair, sliding her hands down his chest to grip the thick ridge of his erection through his jeans.

He echoed her moan, then unceremoniously shoved her off his lap and got to his feet. She had only a second to stare up at him, bewildered, before his hands were on her again, tilting her onto her back and unbuttoning her jeans.

He tugged off her sneakers, then her socks, then peeled her jeans down her legs. She reached for his zipper but he paid no attention, mercilessly yanking her panties over her ankles. He knelt on the floor in front of the pull-out bed, parted her knees and pressed his mouth to her core.

Immediately she cried out, a primal, ultra-female sound that would've startled her if she'd had any space left in her brain to acknowledge it. Instead she was consumed with sensation and the delicious torture of his steady, insistent rhythm. She dug her fingers into his shoulders, alternately urging him faster and pushing him to slow down, all of which he ignored. His pace was unyielding and controlled, and within minutes Kate's eyes slammed shut and her back arched and her fists clenched with the shuddering force of her climax.

When her breathing steadied and her heart rate regained some semblance

Rebecca Crowley

of normalcy, she looked between her splayed legs to see Oz's smug smile.

"You okay?" he asked.

She rolled her eyes in mock irritation. "Don't look so pleased with yourself."

"I bet I don't look as pleased as you do."

"Shut up and get undressed." She planted her foot in the center of his chest and pushed him back onto his haunches.

He stood, shucking off his shoes and undoing his fly. She leaned back on the bare mattress and slipped her hand between her legs, letting him know she was enjoying the view. His eyes flashed with heat as he followed the movement of her fingers, and the rise and fall of his shoulders betrayed the quickening of his breath.

He stepped out of his jeans, revealing boxer briefs with a designer logo and long, thickly muscled legs. He paused for a second, giving her a chance to take in the view, then hooked his thumbs beneath the elastic and sent the briefs to the floor.

Kate purred her approval. She crooked her forefinger at him, inviting him to join her on the bed.

He climbed on top of her, and she felt the heat radiating off his trim form as he ducked his head to lick each of her nipples in turn. She wished she could feel his full weight on her. His length inside her. She shivered at the thought.

She guided him to a sitting position and straddled him, nothing between them now. His erection pressed against her clit and she reached between them to cup him, bringing him tight against her folds.

He swore under his breath, gripping her hips as she rocked against him, simultaneously stroking him with her hand and the edge of her sex. "Fuck, you're so wet."

"I am," she agreed, moving faster, her own desire simmering hotter and higher, on the verge of boiling over a second time.

Oz's shoulders heaved with his rapid breathing, his gaze flicking between hers and the place they came together. He brought one hand around and pressed his thumb to her clit, doubling the friction and nearly sending her over the edge. She groaned his name and he yanked her closer, her nipples grazing his chest with every movement.

"Do you have anything?" he asked, his voice rough with urgency.

"Any what?"

"Condoms."

She froze, and touched his chin so he looked into her eyes. "I do. But are you sure you want me to get them?"

He nodded. Then shook his head. "No. I don't know."

"It's okay," she soothed, resuming the rhythm. "This is good. I like this."

"So do I. I like you, Kate."

"I like you, too."

"Do you like this?" He drew a slow circle with his thumb, counterclockwise to the movement of her hips.

She couldn't speak. She couldn't think. She pitched forward as she unraveled for a second time, waves of pleasure tightening and loosening, tightening and loosening, over and over until Oz pressed his forehead against hers and made a helpless, guttural sound. She wrapped her arms around him, feeling his liquid warmth spill against her abdomen, his body stiff with release.

They clung to each other for another minute, and then Oz suddenly pulled back.

"Did you hear that?"

"Hear what?" But as soon as the words left her mouth she heard the strange, metallic creak.

"What was that?"

"I don't know." She glanced around the apartment, trying to identify the source. "It almost sounds like—"

With another creak, a clang, and then an almighty thump, one of the legs of the pull-out mattress folded inward, dumping them unceremoniously on the floor.

"Oh my God." She stuck out her hands to stay upright, glancing at Oz in alarm. "I think we broke it. Are you all right?"

"Fine." He grinned. "Naked. Sweaty. On your floor."

Then he did something she hadn't seen before.

He laughed.

Not the wry chuckle she'd heard occasionally, or the vaguely bemused exhalation he used in interviews. A real, honest-to-God laugh. It lit up his eyes, exposed his back teeth and softened every angle in his face.

She couldn't help it—she started laughing, too. She'd just humped a professional athlete to climax—the evidence of which still glistened on her stomach—with such vigor that they'd broken her landlady's sofa bed.

Soon they both had tears in their eyes as they gasped for breath. She flopped down on her back and he lay down beside her, briefly mopping her stomach with his briefs before tucking one arm behind his head and drawing her into his side with the other. She rested her cheek against his warm skin and closed her eyes, listening to the rumble of his laugh and wondering if she'd ever heard a more beautiful sound in her life.

Chapter 13

Oz plugged in his phone to charge and lay down on the tilted pull-out bed, flipping onto his back and crossing his arms behind his head. It was just after six o'clock in the morning and he'd been awake for half an hour. He'd scrolled through all his social-media accounts, skimming past the Islamophobic comments that had become par for the course and focusing on the positive notes from fans, pleased to see the reactions to his performance on Saturday.

He'd replied to a couple of goading messages from Glynn asking about his whereabouts, quickly thumb-typed an e-mail to his worried agent, and stared unseeingly at an article about a bombing in Pakistan before he put the phone aside and gave in to his clamoring thoughts.

Last night had been one of the best and worst he could remember. Seeing those protesters in front of his house was like walking in to find the pig's head all over again. He felt violated, outraged, impotent. Part of him wanted to get out of the car and confront them, show them how their actions affected a real, living, breathing person, prove to them that he was a good person who paid taxes and bought groceries and watched TV, not some America-hating, caricature terrorist with a suicide vest hidden in the basement.

Another part of him wanted Kate to drive away as fast as she could and never turn back. The thought of his neighbors seeing this spectacle, and of his name being forever affiliated with it in the annals of internet news sites, was beyond humiliating. He saw the bodyguards trailing him in Boise and Charlotte and cringed. Is this how he would be remembered? Not as an agile, impenetrable left-back but as the pitiable victim of hate crime. Would Citizens First ring louder in his legacy than anything he ever achieved? What if someone added an *Islamophobic Incidents* section to his Wikipedia page and he went down in history as a link from the article on xenophobia?

He turned onto his stomach, forcing his mind to the opposite direction. Kate.

He closed his eyes, reliving the taste of her, the weight of her muscular body in his lap, her rare openness as bald emotion flashed across her face. He couldn't remember the last time he'd enjoyed such a strong, hot connection with a woman. Maybe at the beginning of his relationship with his girlfriend in college, but even then he'd been only seventy-five, maybe eighty-percent confident they belonged together.

Kate had been a different person after their antics on the couch. No, not different—more. She'd been *more* of the Kate he kept seeing in snapshots, with the full picture still a long way off. Relaxed, joking, unself-conscious. She'd slipped into his T-shirt, he'd tugged on his briefs and they'd rigged the pull-out back into some semblance of working order. He'd helped her put on the sheets and gotten instructions on how to use the shower, but when he'd made a wry remark about their sleeping arrangements she'd balked. Hesitation had moved like a shadow across her sunny mood and then she was gone, back inside the shell from which he'd only briefly coaxed her out.

He wasn't sure what his comment triggered. Would sharing a bed be too much like they were a couple? Was she worried about her job? His house? Maybe it was something else entirely, something that would never occur to him.

On paper they were oil and water. Yet in person they became kerosene and a lit match.

Because she stood up to him, called him out, didn't let his wealth or fame or talent buy him any latitude. And because as much as he enjoyed and respected her tough exterior, he had to know what lay beneath. He'd seen glimpses of the soft, vulnerable core she was dead-set on concealing, and he'd seen her refusal to allow herself to be weak. She was so hard on herself. Unforgiving, demanding. He wanted to still her self-punishing hands and comfort her instead. Show her how unique and precious and beautiful she really was.

A floorboard squeaked. Light illuminated the edges of Kate's bedroom door and he heard her voice, low and muffled. Dawn warmed the thinly curtained windows in the main part of the apartment as he mapped her movements. The gentle swish and thud of drawers, bare feet padding on a creaky floor, the uniquely feminine sound of a brush clattering against a vanity. He imagined her efficiently clasping her bra, yanking jeans over her long thighs, and shifted onto his side to make room for his burgeoning erection.

The light clicked off and a second later the door opened slowly. Kate edged out, then paused, probably listening to make sure he was still asleep.

"I'm awake." He pushed up on his elbow.

Her loose hair framed her face, and he'd been wrong. She clearly wasn't wearing a bra under that thin T-shirt.

"I'd ask how you slept, but I guess I know the answer if you're already up." She perched on the arm of the sofa, but he reached over and tugged on the hem of her jeans.

"Come here."

She hesitated. He wrapped his hand around her ankle. "I said, come here."

She sank down beside him so slowly that he grew impatient. He pulled her the last inch to the mattress and drew her against him, sliding his bare leg between hers so she could feel what she did to him, finding her mouth so she knew how much he liked it.

She eased into his arms, trailing her tongue lightly over his lower lip before pulling back with a smile. "Good morning."

"Hi." He tapped her nose. "How are you?"

"Tired. And the bearer of bad news." She winced. "The patrol guys from your neighborhood called at six for their shift-change update. Protesters still in place."

"I figured. It's a public holiday. Hopefully they have to work tomorrow so they'll go home tonight."

"Let's keep our fingers crossed. Do you have plans today?"

He shrugged. "Sean is having a barbecue this afternoon. He gets a good view of the Centennial Park fireworks from his balcony. I have training tomorrow morning, though, so I won't stay late. And you?"

"Driving out to Jasper to see my mom, sister, and niece."

"You don't sound too excited."

"I'm not." She sighed. "They're fine—they're a handful. Anyway I need to hit the road by eight so I'm in time to see my niece's Brownie troop in the Independence Day parade. I'll take you out to the training complex to get your car. I hope Glynn won't mind you turning up to his place so early?"

The image of the queen-size guest bed in Glynn's loft was instantly appealing, and the recollection that his friend had bought the same high-end coffeemaker he had in his own house was a triumph.

But the notion of spending his day off without Kate was...disappointing.

"Do you want me to come with you?" he asked.

Her brows shot up. "Beg pardon?"

"I'm at a loose end. I can't go home, and I'm not in the mood to answer my friends' questions about the last couple of days. I want to spend time with you. Or is it too early for me to be introduced to your family?"

She narrowed her eyes. "Too early in what? This was just a casual thing, right?"

"Of course," he assured her—and himself—as he quickly pulled tight the loose reins of his self-discipline. He hadn't wanted to say so at the time, but Kate had been on the money when she'd said she wasn't his Miss Right. He was on the lookout for something serious, something forever—he'd told himself as much a thousand times in the last few weeks. She could be his Miss Right Now, but that was it.

"Fair enough." He held up placatory palms. "I take it back."

"I don't mean to be rude, it's just—"

"We're keeping this casual. I get it."

She nodded eagerly. "Casual. Exactly."

"And discreet, obviously. I wouldn't want you to get in trouble at work."

"I appreciate that."

"No problem."

She was quiet for a few seconds, her expression thoughtful. When she raised her gaze to his it was brighter. "Actually, no. I like you, Oz. I like you a lot. Let's do this. Not coming to Jasper with me—it's too soon—but the rest of this. *Us*."

Concern that he was about to have to deliver another letting-her-down gently speech stiffened his shoulders. He really wasn't up for that right now.

"Not long-term," she clarified before he could respond. "That's not what I'm looking for."

"Neither am I," he interjected quickly, and her smile showed her relief.

"Perfect, we're on the same page."

"Spell out to me what's on that page," he urged, still unconvinced.

"I don't think I'll offend you if I say we both know that we're not going to be together forever. You have a plan, I need to make a plan, and I seriously doubt they'll end up in the same place. I won't be able to map out my future if I'm being pulled off course by a relationship, but if I know this is only short-term, I can work around it. Does that make sense?"

"I think so." He frowned, digesting what she said. "You're saying this won't be the end for either of us, but we should enjoy it while it lasts."

She snapped her fingers. "Exactly. I guess those Harvard degrees are worth something after all."

"You're the one who came up with the idea. It's a good one. No expectations, nothing heavy. We'll take advantage of this spark until it burns out."

"Because it will," she reminded him, and although he nodded, his heart seemed to drop slightly lower in his chest.

　　　　　　　Rebecca Crowley

He brushed it aside. Kate was right. They had to be pragmatic, fit this warm, bright thing around their plans instead of changing them to suit it. Physical satisfaction, short-term emotional connection, and when Miss Right finally appeared, no hard feelings.

"I'm willing to give it a shot," he agreed.

She grinned. "We'll make it work."

"We will," he promised, drawing her in for another kiss.

Chapter 14

She missed the parade.

Oz looked so good with his rumpled hair and bare torso, and then he kissed her, and one thing led to another, and then they both fell asleep for two much-needed hours.

They woke at nine, by which time her niece was probably just beginning her march down West Church Street. While Oz showered she scrolled through a series of increasingly angry texts from her mom and sister, both of whom ignored her call when she tried their numbers. She texted something about oversleeping and turned her phone facedown on the vanity.

She heard the shower cut and shook her shoulders to loosen the familiar tension that always seemed to accompany her drives out to Jasper.

She was flattered by Oz's offer to join her, but agreeing would've been an act of bravery unparalleled even in her long military career. There was no greater test of manhood than spending a day with the Mitchell succubi. Short-term agreement or not, she wasn't ready to risk that he might run a mile when he saw the mound of dirt she came from.

She reflected on the previous night as she pulled clean clothes out of her dresser. He said he wanted her to open up, to show him who she was. Too bad she didn't know who she was from one day to the next.

On one hand, she was glad they'd given in to whatever it was between them last night—glad everything was out in the open. She hoped they could grow closer, that he helped her define this new, post-Army version of herself.

On the other, who knew how he'd feel when the pressure of the last couple days subsided? Maybe this was all down to stress and hormones. Maybe the next time she saw him, he'd end this brief episode with a sentence from his arsenal of polite break-up lines.

And if that happened, she'd deal with it. She'd be disappointed that it came so early, maybe even a little heartbroken, but she'd been through worse before and would go through worse again. He wouldn't be the first guy who wanted her sexually but withdrew from anything too emotional. She was used to it. In fact she expected it.

She liked Oz. She liked him so much it was beginning to stress her out, because she'd reached the point where it mattered whether he liked her, too, and whether he liked her to the same degree, with the same intentions, for the same length of time.

Foreign territory for a woman who'd spent so long in the no-strings-attached zone that she'd almost forgotten how to tie a knot. Exciting, unpredictable, but also scary. And despite laying out that she knew this would end eventually, an unlikeable, nervous part of her thought it might be easier if he simply walked away right now.

So she would roll with things, try not to censor herself or smooth anything over. She'd show herself to him, as much as she knew herself to be. If Oz's interest survived, so be it. If not, she'd get out before she got deep enough to care.

Too late, a mutinous voice whispered in the back of her mind. She blinked it away, snatched up her comb and towel and hurried into the shower, where she tried to focus on the task ahead and not on the sharp, masculine scent of Oz's shampoo that lingered in the tiny bathroom.

Kate ignored the incessant buzzing of her phone as she turned right onto a gravel road demarcated by two mailboxes on the corner. She passed a house on the left—Mr. and Mrs. Keener, retired poultry farmers who'd been old her whole life—and continued for another few minutes until she reached the rundown, two-bedroom ranch house where she'd been born and raised.

The property was as rough and shabby as always. Recent wet weather meant the lawn was overgrown and unkempt. A box air conditioner sat crookedly in one of the front windows, bracketed by pieces of cardboard. Toys littered the porch, a stack of unopened mail sat atop a lawn chair, and her mother had apparently converted a cracked lemonade jug into an outdoor ashtray. Judging by the level of cigarette butts piled inside, that e-cigarette system Kate bought her for Christmas was a big waste of money.

She parked behind her sister's Sentra. The front door opened as she killed the engine and three generations of the Mitchell women of Jasper, Georgia appeared on the porch, lining up like they were in the opening credits of a dated and decidedly unfunny sitcom. Her mother, the fading beauty. Her sister, Emily, the beauty in bloom. And her niece, Dallas, innocence personified.

"Here we go," she braced herself, stepping out of the car.

"You missed the parade," Emily reminded her needlessly as she approached.

"I know. I'm sorry, baby." She directed her apology to her niece, who wrapped her arms around her waist in greeting. "Did you have fun?"

Dallas shrugged. "It was okay."

"She looked gorgeous." Emily smoothed the little girl's hair off her forehead, then raised her eyes. "So where were you?"

Kate smiled to herself, anticipating her mother's and sister's reaction. With anyone else she'd have to lie. But she knew they'd be delighted with the truth.

"With a man."

Both of them erupted into whoops of delight, clapping their hands.

"This calls for a celebration," her mother announced, gesturing for Kate to follow her inside. "Come help me carry out the drinks, then we want to hear the whole story."

Fifteen minutes later they were lined up in matching rocking chairs, occasionally plucking fresh drinks out of a cooler filled with cans of beer, and juice boxes for Dallas, who turned cartwheels on the overgrown lawn.

"Sweden," her mother repeated. "I never met anyone from there."

"The women are supposed to be hot," Emily supplied. "Not sure about the men though."

"I can show you a picture," Kate offered.

Her sister snapped her fingers. "We should've thought of that, of course you can—he's famous?"

"Not, like, *famous* famous," she clarified, pulling up Oz's Instagram and passing over her phone. "Not like a football player."

Emily made a thoughtful noise, squinting at the screen. She handed the phone to their mother, who also frowned at what she saw.

The porch was silent except for the creaking of the chairs as the three women rocked. Finally Kate asked, "So?"

"He's definitely good-looking," Emily decided, taking the phone.

"But he's not your type, Katie," their mother said. "He's sort of…dark. Exotic."

"*European*," Emily added, looking pleased to have found that word.

"A fancy, big-city boy," her mother elaborated. "I think we're a little surprised, is all."

"I was surprised, too." Kate retrieved her phone, glanced fondly at the snapshot of Oz giving a thumbs-up in the changing room after a match, then switched off the screen.

Emily propped up her feet on the railing and stretched her long legs, bare beneath her super-short shorts. "So what's the shape of this thing? Just for fun? Or are you guys getting serious?"

"And what about your job?" her mother chimed in.

"That is a potential complication," she admitted, grimly realizing that with Rich muscling in on the account she'd have to work even harder to keep the affair hidden. She reached down and opened another beer, parking that stressful line of thinking for now. "As for the future, who the hell knows? We lead very different lives. We're very different people. I don't think it'll go anywhere, but that doesn't mean we can't have fun in the meantime."

Her mom raised her beer can. "I'll drink to that."

"Me, too." Emily raised hers.

The three of them clinked beer cans, in silent agreement that when it came to men, anything could happen.

"Dallas! How many times have I told you to put these damn Barbies away?" Emily slurred her words as she chucked two of the dolls into a plastic tub. On the other side of the room her mother thumped the silent air conditioner, muttering profanities under her breath.

Kate scrubbed a hand over her eyes and shut off the television, which was blaring a movie she didn't think was appropriate for Dallas anyway.

"Enough," she declared, drawing the attention of her mother, sister and niece. "Everyone outside. The fireworks will start in a minute."

Dallas happily skipped through the front door. Her mother and sister followed, giving her dark glares as they went. As usual the day had devolved into a mess of drunkenness and hostility, and Kate's head pounded from the last several hours of heat, bickering and raised voices.

For a moment she paused in the empty house, gathering her strength. No matter how well her visits started, or how optimistic she felt for the first couple of hours, inevitably they always ended the same way: with a hangover.

At least they were all still on speaking terms, although it was only eight o'clock. Too early to get her hopes up.

Outside her mother fumbled with a lighter, attempting to fire up a sparkler for Dallas. Emily rocked rapidly in one of the chairs, shouting instructions.

Kate eased down beside her sister, cringing as their mother nearly caught the sleeve of her shirt with the flame.

"Can you write your name, honey?" she prompted Dallas, who waved her sparkler through the air. The little girl nodded eagerly, then moved the sparkler to trace a backward *d*.

When Dallas moved out of earshot Kate looked at her sister. "How are the extra reading lessons going?"

Emily shrugged. "All right, I guess."

"Have you been taking her every week?"

"When I get into town."

Kate exhaled her exasperation. "Those lessons aren't free, you know—I paid for them. And you have to buy the whole session of eight, so I don't get anything back for the ones you miss."

"Get off my case," her sister shot back. "You try holding down a job—"

"A part-time job."

"Holding down *a job* and looking after mom and Dallas. We don't all live the high life down in Atlanta, Katie. Some of us are just doing what we can to get by."

Kate bit her lower lip, stifling a wave of useless anger. She'd had this argument at least twenty times and it never went anywhere. Emily always fell back on her story of the hard-working single mother, Kate countered by itemizing everything she paid for, and her sister and mother ganged up on her with their accusations that she mistreated them, was embarrassed by them, abandoned them out here on their own, both of them in tears, screaming and pointing fingers.

She didn't have the energy for all that, not tonight. In fact every time she visited she found herself caring a little bit less whether their lives improved or even changed. Dallas was the exception, of course, but as for her mother and sister? The older she got, the less responsible she felt for their sorry-ass existences.

She was about to reach for another beer when her phone buzzed in her pocket. She pulled it out and looked at the screen, then hurried off the porch and around the side of the house as she answered.

"Hello?"

"Hello."

"How are you?"

"Missing you."

She smiled, Oz's voice was sweet and warm in her ears. "Too bad, I'm having a great time without you."

"Really?"

"No."

"How's the family?"

Kate peered around the side of the house. Her mom was in the middle of the lawn smoking a cigarette, Dallas waved a sparkler in each hand, and Emily's face was lit up by the square of light from her phone, probably drunk texting her ex.

"They're a mess," she answered honestly.

He laughed, and she caught the faint strains of music in the background.

"Are you at Sean's?"

"Yeah."

"Having a good time?"

"I am. You would be too, if you were here."

"What makes you so sure?"

"Well, I'm here."

She grinned into the darkness. "Someone's confident."

Background noise clouded the line, and when he spoke again his voice was low and conspiratorial, suggesting he'd moved somewhere more private.

"I've been thinking about last night," he began, and she steeled herself for the rejection. As she suspected, he'd had some time and space and sleep and he'd decided this was just sexual, just chemistry.

"I'm in, Kate," he told her firmly. "I'm into you, into us. Into this, as long as it runs."

"I'm all in, too." The words rushed from her mouth so quickly that she clamped it shut as soon as they escaped, terrified at what other secrets might pour out.

But she couldn't take back those four words, and the warmth in Oz's voice showed he heard every single one.

"Then I—"

Fireworks exploded overhead, bathing the property in multicolored light. She heard her sister, mother and niece cheering and squealing on the front lawn, and then Dallas called her name, summoning her to watch with them.

"Coming," she shouted back. She pressed the phone against her heart and stared up at the lights bursting and fading in the sky, bright but ethereal, beautiful but so very far away.

Chapter 15

"Oz's ball!" he shouted as the free kick arced into the line of players protecting Skyline's goal. Laurent obediently ducked in front of him as Oz jumped, stopping the shot with his chest and controlling it down to his feet.

His lungs burned and his breath faltered from the impact, and he sucked in air as he passed to Nico. They were up one-nil in their home fixture, but Miami's manager must have given a rousing half-time talk because the opposition had come back from the break in full-on attack mode. Skyline's defense had held up thus far, but the pressure increased every minute as Miami took chance after chance.

Kojo missed a pass from Laurent and one of Miami's forwards snapped up the loose ball, then pivoted to drive hard into Skyline's half. Oz raced to track back.

Instinct took over as he focused on catching his opponent. He chased the forward with ruthless precision, swiveling, confounding the Miami player's attempts to shake him off. The forward veered toward the sideline, trying to force Oz to kick out any interception he managed, but Oz saw through him. He made his tackle carefully but forcefully, neatly stealing the ball from the forward's feet and booting it to Guedes. Guedes passed to Nico, who passed to Laurent, who sailed it in a beautiful arc to Rio.

Oz was level with Rio when he crossed the ball to Deon. It had the shape of a perfect assist, and Oz held his breath as he looked to see whether Deon was about to raise the score to two-nil.

Except Deon frowned in the direction of the crowd, then turned wide eyes on Oz. The ball curved unheeded behind Deon's back.

"Fuck's sake, what are you doing?" Oz shouted, slapping his palm against his forehead. Deon's response was to run straight toward him.

Bewilderment rooted Oz to the spot as he watched his teammate hurtling toward him, his brow furrowed in determination. Had he missed something?

He turned a questioning gaze to Roland only to find the manager sprinting onto the pitch. He frowned, trying to imagine what could possibly be going on, when Deon ran into him side-on, accidentally shoving him to the ground.

"Move," the striker urged him, desperation in his voice as he yanked hard on Oz's arm, the scents of soil and grass filling his senses as he struggled up from the earth. "There's a bomb, we have to run."

Oz's heartbeat stalled, then resumed in triple time. "What?"

Roland reached them before Deon could answer, frantically pulling Oz the rest of the way up. "Hurry, we have to evacuate the pitch, go for the tunnel and—"

"It's okay," Miami's goalkeeper called as he ran up to them. Oz swayed on his feet. One minute he was on the ground, now he stood, he hadn't even seen anything happen. What the hell was going on?

"Road flares," the goalkeeper told them breathlessly. "Fucking road flares taped to look like dynamite."

Still getting his bearings, Oz followed the sound of a commotion to the stands behind Miami's goal. Rio and Guedes were scaling the rows of seats—with several security guards on their heels—apparently in pursuit of a man wearing a camo hat and a fishing vest over his Miami T-shirt. Then he followed the line of fans' pointing fingers to find what looked very much like a bundle of dynamite with a lit fuse on the bright green grass of the pitch, barely three feet from where he stood.

The afternoon was sunny and hot, but he shivered.

The referee joined their group and put his hand on Oz's shoulder. "You okay?"

"Fine," he answered automatically. In fact he was numb, confused, and totally unsure what else to say.

"Are you okay to continue?" the referee asked.

Oz nodded, then looked around at the four sets of eyes keenly trained on him as realization dawned. "Do you all think this was about me? He's probably just some lunatic who wanted to disrupt the game for attention, like a streaker."

"He threw it right at you, Oz," Deon told him gently.

"I was so focused on the game, I didn't even…" He trailed off, lost in astonishment.

Deon winced. "He called you a—"

"I'll get my other players out of the stands so we can carry on," Roland interrupted, but Oz held up his hand.

"He called me what?"

Deon's expression darkened. *"Haji* bastard."

Oz could've sworn he felt the ground shift beneath his feet. His heart seemed to drop into his stomach and then spring back into place, leaving him dizzy and nauseous.

"Let's bring you off," Roland said quietly. "No one will think less of you."

Oz's thoughts lurched and swam as he struggled to process what had happened—what was still happening. Through the haze, he found himself shaking his head, and his voice sounded thick and far away. "No. I want to finish."

"Good man," the referee decreed with a firm slap on his back. "Mr. Carlsson, round up your players and we'll resume."

Roland's expression was uncertain, but he said nothing as he moved back to the sideline. A security guard scooped the fake bomb into a plastic bag and carried it away. Deon remained at his side while Guedes, Rio, and a Miami defender who'd evidently decided to join their vigilante cause climbed back over the siding. Oz stood limply while the referee gave them each a verbal caution but no yellow cards and the crowd applauded his decision.

"I respect you wanting to see out this half," Deon said quietly. "Show these racist fuckers they can't touch you. You're strong, Wizard. Stronger than any of them."

Oz nodded, but as the referee blew his whistle and the game resumed he didn't feel strong. On the contrary, with every minute that passed the incident sank in a little more and awareness cut more sharply through the receding numbness.

It wasn't bad enough these people attacked his home—now they had to interfere in his career, too? And in front of his teammates, his competitors—in front of all the viewers of that match in person and on TV.

He didn't like to use the word hate. It was a concept he associated with wasted energy and small-mindedness. But as he jogged listlessly behind the action on the pitch he decided he hated the people who were targeting him. Unfamiliar heat seared through his chest. He *hated* them.

But that made him no better, he reminded himself, trying to calm his breathing and regain some semblance of cool, detached logic. He couldn't let them get to him. That was what they wanted. He had to stay aloof. Rise above. Get on with his life and wait for all this bullshit to die down.

Unless it didn't. Unless it got worse. Unless it escalated to something none of them could predict or prevent.

He thought about the pig head in his kitchen, the utter violation of knowing a stranger had been inside his home. He thought about the massive levels of organization that must've gone into coordinating the protest at his house. Imagined the mindset of a man who'd spent the time and money to attend today's match solely for the purpose of tossing a fake bomb onto the pitch. The Ausonius messages that still hit his social-media accounts multiple times per day.

He shuddered. He wished for Kate. He should've offered her tickets in his box. Then he could stagger off the pitch and find strength in her calm voice, her levelheaded response, her practical, pragmatic suggestions for tightening his security.

He wanted to see her so much he ached.

He drifted through the last half hour of the game, his performance embarrassingly bad, but all of the players gave him such a wide berth it hardly mattered. At times the way they played around him, almost apologetically, was more humiliating than his own terrible quality. Their forwards didn't press him, their midfielders loosely marked him, and every Miami player shot him a sympathetic, encouraging smile at least once.

He appreciated their support—he did. He just wished to hell they had no reason to offer it.

Late in the match Pavel Kovar was taken off with a suspected head injury, and Oz's sense of defeat was so heavy he nearly sank to the ground as the final whistle blew. He wanted nothing more than to duck into the tunnel and escape the TV cameras, but as the two teams shook hands on the result, their striker—a high-profile star of the American national squad—insisted on swapping jerseys, then turned his back to the nearest camera so Oz's number was clearly visible, and then he led the stadium in thunderous applause with his arms raised.

Shirtless and wanting to be anywhere else, Oz hoped his smile didn't look as tight and unnatural as it felt. He waved to thank the fans until the cheering finally died down.

Once inside the tunnel, his name echoed off the concrete walls as everyone tried to talk to him at once. He pushed through the cacophony, pausing at the spot where the tunnel split into several corridors. He should turn right toward the locker room, but he also wanted to go straight out to the parking lot, get in his car and drive straight home.

The second option was impossible—he needed to shower, hand in his kit to be washed and pick up his stuff from his locker, including his car keys. But it was so tempting that it swelled hugely in his thoughts, crowding out everything else until he found himself wondering whether he could hotwire his car to avoid getting his keys.

He blinked and the world came back into some semblance of coherent focus, and with a couple of deep breaths he gathered the wherewithal to proceed to the locker room.

Except most of the full Skyline squad, coaching and security staff, and seemingly all of the press office were in his way. Too many questions, too many intense stares, too many concerned expressions. He saw two uniformed police officers approaching from his left and that was it. He was done.

His knees buckled, a fact he realized just in time to brace his back against the wall before he thudded onto the floor. He propped his elbows on his thighs and covered his face with his hands.

Voices grew louder, his name resounded more frequently and he was dimly aware of a rush of movement as people moved closer and crouched down beside him. Hands were on his shoulders but his brain seemed to be shutting down section by section. Within seconds he couldn't remember how to speak English, wasn't sure what day it was, couldn't have found his way home even if he'd managed to stumble to his car.

He balled his hands into fists and pressed them into his forehead as his whole body began to shake, his cleats clicking against the concrete floor with the force of his trembling.

"Oz, you're okay. Look at me. You're fine."

Kate's voice was a hook that snagged in his mind and yanked him up and out of the pitch-black whirlpool he was drowning in.

He moved his hands and opened his eyes, and his slow-moving thoughts caught up with the present in a dizzying fast-forward rush. He registered Kate kneeling in front of him, her expression calm and unfazed. His awareness widened until he found Roland, pale behind his glasses, and Skyline's medic, Tony, watching him keenly.

He exhaled, gratefully comprehending that what had felt like fifteen minutes of bizarre, frightening displacement could've been only a few seconds. He could pull this back. He'd say his legs gave out from muscle fatigue. No one had to know what really happened.

"Sorry everyone, that match really took it out of me." He forced a weak smile. Kate rose and backed up, and he took Tony's hands and let the medic pull him to his feet.

"Let's get you checked out," Tony told him quietly. Oz opened his mouth to argue but Roland shook his head curtly, ending the argument before he could start it.

He caught Kate's gaze and rolled his eyes, shrugging as if to say they were worrying over nothing. She regarded him steadily, blatantly unconvinced.

He set his shoulders as he followed Roland and Tony into one of the medical treatment rooms, leaving Kate and the rest of the crowd behind. His gratitude at her unexpected appearance gave way to concern and regret.

Someone must have called her here in a professional capacity when the guy threw the road flares. He was her helpless client again, and worse, she'd seen him at his weakest and most overwhelmed.

He tightened his jaw. He was strong, impenetrable, in control. That's how he wanted her to know him.

Tony nodded to the exam table. "Sit."

"I'm fine, just exhausted," he insisted as Roland shut the door.

"Sit," the medic commanded, and this time Oz obeyed.

Roland studied him with narrowed eyes as Tony checked his blood pressure, listened to his heart and shined a pen light into his pupils.

"All clear," the medic pronounced. "No signs of shock."

Oz turned to his manager. "You heard him, I'm fine."

Roland tilted his head from one side to the other and crossed his arms. "Do you want to talk about what happened? During the match or after it?"

"I want to take a shower and go home," he replied honestly.

Roland looked at Tony, who shrugged.

"Okay," the manager acceded reluctantly. "I'll call you later."

"I know you will." Oz attempted a teasing smile, but he could tell from their unmoved expressions that he'd failed pretty miserably. Growing more tired by the minute, he slid from the table and let himself out of the exam room. Then he walked down the hall, hoping they hadn't seen his hand shaking as he reached for the doorknob.

Chapter 16

"It's not over." Kate shook her head, motioning for Oz to pass into her apartment ahead of her and then locking the door. "But it's good news. The guy they caught today is a linchpin in the local Citizens First group. The police aren't sure they can charge him with much more than disorderly conduct, but hopefully this arrest will put him on notice and scare the rest of the group into submission."

Oz looked unconvinced as he dropped onto her sofa. She didn't blame him—she wasn't nearly as optimistic as she tried to sound. The man who'd thrown the road flares had been identified as Wayne Seibert, one of the area's key spokesmen for Citizens First. Although the attack was vicious and clearly motivated by hate, Wayne knew his rights and conducted himself carefully so as to avoid anything more than a misdemeanor charge, according to Detective Hegarty. As much as she hoped the group's activities declined from today, in all honesty she doubted they would.

She dropped her purse on the kitchen counter and stole a glance out the window. The wedding shop was closed, but sometimes her landlady came in on Sunday evenings to do paperwork. There was no sign of her yet, and hopefully she'd stay away, otherwise Kate had no doubt she'd be at the door asking who owned the Mercedes in the parking lot.

She opened and closed a kitchen cabinet distractedly. "Can I get you something? Water, coffee, tea? Or are you hungry? It's after six, do you want dinner? I'm not sure what I have, I meant to go to the grocery store this afternoon but then—"

"But then you had to rush over to the stadium," he supplied. "I didn't think about how much I've disrupted your day already when I asked to come back with you. Don't worry about dinner, we'll order something. I'll pay for it."

"You didn't disrupt my day. And I'm glad you're here. You're welcome anytime." She crossed the room and sat down beside him, sliding a comforting hand over his thigh. He'd changed into jeans and a T-shirt and still smelled fresh and clean from his post-match shower. She wanted to kiss him. She wanted to straddle him and unzip his fly. But his weary expression reminded her to be gentle.

An image of the way she'd found him in the tunnel flashed in her mind, and she tightened her grip on his leg. They'd spent most nights together over the last week, and she'd gotten to know more of his relaxed, funny, charming side every day. It made seeing him in pain even worse, his powerful body trembling from the force of his distress.

He smiled weakly and covered her hand with his own. "What were you doing when you got the call to come down to the stadium?"

"I was at work. I'm really struggling to meet my sales targets. The Skyline account is just about keeping me afloat, but Rich is trying his best to horn in on my commission. I don't know what I'll do if he succeeds." She exhaled and flopped back against the cushion.

"Roland knows only to call you, not Rich. Anyway, he doesn't like Rich, thinks he's too pushy. Do you want me to talk to someone in accounts? I can make sure they only put your name on the invoice payments."

She shook her head. "Thanks, but there's no point. Rich is the boss, and if he decides that he deserves some sales allocation from the Skyline account, I can't stop him. Maybe I should start looking for a new job anyway. I suck at sales."

"It's a tough market. On my street alone there must be four different security providers' signs on people's lawns."

"I'm better on the implementation side. Setting out the actual security strategies, not selling the idea of them. There's less money in it, but I could live with that."

He stretched his long legs and leaned back, crossing his arms. "Was it your plan to get into private security when you left the Army?"

"No. I heard about the job in Saudi from someone else who ETSed the same time I did and took it for the paycheck. Then a recruiting agency for veterans pointed me toward Peak Tactical. I had no plan—still don't."

"I couldn't live with that kind of ambiguity. That's where you and I differ."

He smiled, but she couldn't return it. The point at which they differed was a hell of a lot wider than whether or not she had a plan. Never mind the big things like education and money, he had a whole system for rotating which socks he wore and she spent most mornings rooting through the clothes on her bedroom floor to pick whatever was least wrinkled.

His phone buzzed in his pocket and he pulled it out, checking the screen. "My parents want to have a video call. I texted them about what happened at the stadium, now they're worrying. Do you mind if I speak to them quickly?"

"Of course not. I'll go in the bedroom. Call me when you're done."

She half-stood but he grabbed her arm and pulled her back down.

"I'm not talking to your parents," she protested.

"Why not?"

"Because I'm not—We're not—"

He arched a brow. "Aren't we? I think we are, for now at least."

She bit her lower lip, caught between excitement and disbelief. No matter what Oz had said or done over the last week, on some level she always braced for the letdown that was so familiar. Whether it was an afterthought clarification that by short-term he meant strictly sexual, a pretend-sincere insistence that they remain friends or preferably friends with benefits, or a flat-out line about not seeing other again, she was pretty sure she'd heard them all. She'd long ago learned not to get her hopes up, and as a result she didn't get her heart broken, either.

Meeting Oz's parents—even if for only a few minutes on a blurry video chat—implied a degree of commitment she'd given up on years ago. She wasn't sure whether to be delighted or terrified.

Oz tapped his parents' number with his thumb. "I'll just introduce you. They know who you are, but only in a professional capacity."

She wanted to ask why—because they weren't serious enough to tell them, or because they wouldn't like her? Then again, maybe she didn't want to know the answer.

He looked up at her as if something had suddenly occurred to him. "Have you told your family about me?"

She pursed her lips. "Yes."

"The whole story?"

She nodded. "But you haven't met my mom and sister. Telling them anything is like telling—" She clamped her mouth shut as the sound of ringing resonated from the phone. After a couple of seconds the screen lit up and two faces appeared.

Kate smiled nervously as Oz began speaking in what she assumed was Turkish, since it sounded nothing like the language he spoke with Roland. She tried not to stare, but a brief glance told her Oz's good looks were genetic. His father looked like a slightly swarthier, more angular version of George Clooney, and his mother had the same large, dark eyes, and thick black hair. They were seated in front of shelves packed with books and Oz's mother wore one of those little silk scarves Kate imagined sophisticated European women were born knowing how to tie exactly right.

She thought of the video calls she'd had with her family while she was in Saudi Arabia. The TV blaring in the background, her sister screeching at Dallas to quit whatever she was doing, her mom standing up mid-sentence to refill her wine glass.

For a second she closed her eyes and took a deep breath. She wasn't like them. She could do this. She could live up to the commitment this moment promised. She could be the woman Oz wanted.

Hell, apparently she already was.

"Kate, these are my parents, Murat and Alara. This is Kate," he said in English, snapping her to attention. She waved feebly. Hopefully his parents didn't speak much English and they could get this over with quickly.

"Hello Kate," his parents said in unison, and his father added, "Such a pleasure to meet you. We've heard all about the great job you've done on Özkan's house."

"Oh, okay," she replied, feeling more awkward by the second. His parents' accents were thicker than his, but clearly they both spoke perfect English. Probably better than she did.

"We know how particular Oz is about his house—and his clothes, and his car, and his food—so that can't have been an easy task for you." His mother's smile was encouraging in a conspiratorial, woman-to-woman way.

"We got there in the end," she said breezily, trying to remain neutral and not read judgment into every nuance of their expressions.

"Özkan says you're from Georgia originally?" His father asked.

"Yup, a small town north of Atlanta."

"Everyone tells us we should see Georgia in the spring, but for some reason we always find ourselves visiting at the beginning of the soccer season in February or toward the end in the autumn." Alara rolled her eyes self-effacingly as if admitting to something idiotic. If she knew that yesterday Kate's mom had absentmindedly put the garage-door opener through the slot in a post-office drop box she might have a different perspective. "One of these days we'll get there in time to see the azaleas and dogwoods blooming."

"You must find your way to Sweden," Murat said with a warm smile. "Summer is the most beautiful time here, and we have a wonderful cottage on Faro, a little island up north. It takes a while to get there because it's so remote, and requires changing planes, then—"

"Okay, Baba, she doesn't need to know the full logistics right now," Oz interrupted. "Everything's fine. We need to get dinner and the two of you need to go to bed."

Alara smirked at her husband and said something in Turkish that made him laugh. From Oz's narrowed eyes Kate suspected it was at his expense.

The three of them spoke in Turkish for another minute, then Oz said in English, "Goodnight, talk to you later."

Kate waved and his parents waved back, reiterating how pleased they were to meet her. She blushed and mumbled something approximating agreement, then Oz cut the call.

She started to say something about how nice his parents were when he pulled one of her legs over his and kissed her, his hands on her cheeks, his mouth soft and warm.

She crossed her wrists behind his neck, exhaling contentedly. This was the proof that they worked, when on paper they made no sense at all.

She wasted so much energy on anxious will-he, won't-he thoughts, lost hours of sleep tossing and turning and mentally inventorying all the incompatibilities that would eventually doom them. She had to stop. She had to learn to stifle every one of her doubtful instincts and trust him.

"Thank you for that," he murmured against her temple. "I know I ambushed you."

"It's okay. Your parents seem great. And they speak English."

"Most Swedes do. Swedish isn't a language that gets you very far in the rest of the world."

"But were you speaking to your parents in Turkish?"

He nodded. "Turkish at home, Swedish in school."

"Wow. That seems so fancy. Very different to my family," she admitted.

He stretched one arm along the back of the couch. "You haven't told me much about them."

She raised a shoulder. "Not much to tell. I've got my mom, my sister and my niece, all crammed into our little house in Jasper. They don't go anywhere, don't do much of anything, so there's not a lot to say about them."

"Say something anyway."

She sighed. "Well, being a serial dater is the closest thing my mom's had to a career. She drinks too much, smokes too much, spends too much energy on too many men. My sister's slightly better off, but only because she's hung up on her ex. Between the two of them there's usually one part-time job, but it always ends with one of them not turning up because they're hung over or quitting because the latest man has promised he's going to take care of them."

"And your niece?"

"Who knows." Kate threw up her hands. "She's having a real hard time in school, and I've paid for a whole bunch of extra help, plus all sorts of hobbies and activities that will hopefully keep her out of trouble and eventually get her out of Jasper. But she's only six—there's a lot of years left for her to fall into the same pattern as her mom and grandma."

"Sounds stressful."

"It is. I'm not Dallas's mother, but I feel like her whole future is my responsibility." She sighed.

"Do you have a picture of your family?"

"Yup." She pulled her phone from her pocket and scrolled to a photo of them in a line on the couch on the Fourth of July. "My mom, my sister Emily, and my sister's daughter, Dallas. The Mitchell women. Three generations."

He studied the photo. "Your niece is cute."

"And Emily's the pretty sister. Go on, you can say it."

"Don't be ridiculous," he told her dismissively, handing back the phone. "What's the story with your dad?"

"Nothing original. Mom had me when she was seventeen. They were both in high school, he tried to be involved for the first year or so, then lost interest. He moved to Nevada when I was three, haven't heard from him since. Emily has a different father. He's still around in Jasper, used to take us places on the weekends and stuff. He's a nice enough guy."

"And Dallas's father?"

She rolled her eyes. "Also still around. He and my sister only speak when they want to fight with someone, then they have make-up sex and ignore each other for another few weeks. He does pay child support, and my sister was out of high school when she got pregnant, so I guess that's our version of social mobility."

"I'd say you've raised the bar a little higher than that."

"Maybe." She shrugged.

"You're so hard on yourself," he chided, shaking his head. "You've traveled, served in the military, transitioned to the private sector and supported your family the whole time. What else do you want to achieve before you'll give yourself credit?"

His question shot straight through to her core, momentarily robbing her of words. She'd never asked herself that before. Just assumed she was second-best, would always be second-best. What, specifically, did she think would finally satisfy her? A college degree wouldn't hurt, nor would a higher salary or owning a house, but those were things everyone wanted. They were materialistic—they wouldn't fundamentally define her.

Then what would?

Oz. If a man like him loved me—if he *loved me—that would be enough.*

"I don't know," she lied.

"Then you should figure it out. You'll never win if you don't know what you're playing for."

"Thanks, professor." She stood and stretched. "Are you hungry?"

"Very. But we're not done here." He leaned forward, took her hands and tugged her back down beside him. She widened her eyes inquiringly.

"Next weekend's match is in Boston."

"I know. Roland asked me to travel to all the away fixtures until this Citizens First nonsense is resolved."

"You remember I went to college in Boston?"

"Of course."

"I still have a big group of friends there. Two of them are getting married on Saturday, the day after the match. It's last-minute, but I'm sure they'll give me a plus-one if I ask."

She arched a brow. "Are you asking me to go with you?"

"Yes."

She hadn't been to a wedding since her cousin got married when she was fourteen. They'd had a civil ceremony followed by a buffet dinner in a small function room at the VFW. The groom got drunk and the bride snagged her dress on a nail in the floor. The marriage ended in divorce two years later.

All of his friends would be there—his smart, Harvard-educated, successful friends. But she'd held her own with his friends here, plus he'd be by her side. She had to trust that he wouldn't put her in a situation she couldn't handle. And she had to trust herself to handle pretty much anything.

She exhaled. "I'll need a new dress."

"Take my credit card." He slid his hand into his pocket and she shook her head to stop him.

"I'll get my landlady to fix me up with something from downstairs. She's always reminding me she'll give me a great discount."

"Tell her to send me the bill."

"I can pay for my own damn dress, Oz."

"Fine. I'm sure I can find another way to repay you." He ran his hand up her leg, lingering at the apex of her thighs.

She scooted closer, finding the smooth skin on his back beneath his shirt. "I'll let you do that for free."

He growled his approval and pulled her against him, lowering his lips to her neck.

She laughed in delight at his touch, tilting her head to give him better access. "I thought you said you were hungry."

"Starving," he murmured, and proceeded to show her just how delicious she was.

Chapter 17

Oz unbuttoned his collar and loosened his tie, then turned to embrace another two college friends he hadn't seen in years. The sun beat mercilessly on the parking lot behind the church. He'd sweated through his shirt beneath his jacket and his carefully gelled coif was probably deflating in the heat.

He couldn't remember the last time he'd had so much fun.

"Cameron," he greeted yet another old friend with a slap on the back. "How are you? How's Melissa?"

"Due in about three weeks, so she stayed home in Los Angeles. She'll be sorry she missed you, though."

"I'll let you know the next time I have an away fixture in southern California, we'll get dinner."

"We totally should. Caught the second half of the match yesterday, by the way—fantastic goal."

Oz raised a shoulder dismissively, but inside he'd been turning somersaults ever since he grabbed an unexpected and ultimately winning goal toward the end of the match against Boston Liberty. "You know how it goes when you play defense, every so often you happen to knock one in by accident. If I'd missed it, all the pundits would be shouting at me for being so far forward."

"Says the highest-scoring defender in the league," Glynn interjected as he reappeared with Kate.

Kate. Oz's grin broadened as he took her in.

His heart had almost stopped when he'd stepped out of the shower in their hotel room and seen her in her dress. Tight and lacy, it was the color of the ocean in Florida and twice as enticing on this hot day. She'd shyly tucked her hair behind one ear, drawing attention to the fact she was wearing makeup for the first time since he'd known her.

Not that she needed to. She was utterly and naturally gorgeous, from her long lashes to her even longer legs. He couldn't believe he'd ever written her off as not his type.

"Did you find the water fountain?" he asked, sliding his arm around her waist.

She nodded. "We ran into someone who knew Glynn, and asked if you were here. She was right behind us, she must've stopped to talk to someone—never mind, here she is."

His ex-girlfriend approached them, wearing a big, friendly smile.

He watched her, waiting to be dazzled. Waiting for the flash of unsteadiness he used to feel when they were first dating, the momentary sense of tilting and unbalance.

Nothing.

Nedda looked good—as good as he remembered, if not better. Her hair was thick and black, her eyes still big and dark, her breasts just as generous. He'd gotten to know every inch of her body in the two years they were together, and there was a time when all she had to do was flutter her lashes and lick her lips and he'd drag her into the nearest supply closet or backseat he could find.

But they never had sex. It never felt right. He never felt ready. Looking at her now, he was glad. She wasn't the woman he was waiting for.

The long, lean beauty by his side, though, was another story.

"So the rumors are true. You decided to grace us with your presence," Nedda teased, reaching up to give him a hug.

"Caitlin waited eight years for Jack to pop the question. I thought I should be here to chase him down if he gets cold feet."

"Chivalrous as always." She released him, looking expectantly at Kate.

"Nedda, this is my girlfriend, Kate." He replaced his arm around Kate's waist, feeling her instantly stiffen as he used the word *girlfriend*.

He'd wanted to say it all weekend—now he had. He knew he'd face endless questions about it later, probably a long, drawn-out conversation to calm Kate's anxieties. He didn't care. For now she was his, and he wanted everyone to know, especially the woman currently sizing her up.

"I'm Nedda." She extended her hand. "The ex."

Oz clenched his jaw as Kate shook Nedda's hand and stumblingly replied, "Oh, uh, hi, nice to meet you."

"Ignore her," he told Kate jovially, but his light tone was laced with threat for Nedda's benefit. "She thinks she's funny."

"Not funny—factual." Nedda winked.

"Nedda just finished medical school at Johns Hopkins. She's about to start her residency at…" He turned to her questioningly, unable to remember where she'd matched.

"I'm coming back to Boston," she reminded him. "Anesthesiology at Massachusetts General. What do you do, Kate?"

"Private security," Kate replied in her country-Georgia accent. "I left the Army a little over a year ago."

"Oh, wow. And were you deployed or—"

"It's fine, I didn't want you to notice me anyway," Glynn interjected coolly.

"I already said hi to you," Nedda shot back, then seemed to rethink her curt reply and gave Glynn a quick hug. A second later the best man appeared in the church doorway and asked everyone to take their seats inside.

Glynn and Kate turned to file into the church. Oz paused to button his collar and tighten his tie. Nedda put her hand on his arm.

"It's good to see you," she said quietly as the parking lot emptied around them. "Sorry if I freaked out Kate with that ex thing. It was just a joke."

"Don't worry, it takes a lot more than that to freak her out."

He followed Glynn and Kate inside and slid into a pew. Nedda wedged into the space beside him.

"No air conditioning," Kate observed, fanning herself with the program.

"There is, it just sucks." Glynn nodded to a portable air conditioning unit pushed against the wall.

Oz flapped the hem of his jacket. "Good thing we booked a room in the same hotel as the reception. I need to change my shirt."

Kate craned her neck, squinting at the A/C unit. "I see the problem."

She stood and sidled past him and Nedda, then hooked around the back of the crowded church to reach the unit. Muscles stood out in her thighs as she half-squatted, grabbing either side of it and jerking it away from the wall. She peered behind it and adjusted the big plastic hose that ran out the window.

Within seconds the air conditioner shifted from grunting to humming and a wave of cool air washed over the room.

The rows nearest the unit gave Kate a round of applause, and she executed a joking curtsey before making her way back to her seat.

"What sorcery was that?" Glynn asked as Kate squeezed in between him and Oz.

"We used to have one of those things in post housing when I was stationed in Alabama. If it's too close to the wall the tube gets kinked and it can't vent the hot air, so it slows down the cold air."

"Roomful of Harvard and MIT graduates and Kate saves us all from heat exhaustion," Oz remarked proudly.

The crowd hushed as the groom and his party entered from a side door to line up at the altar. The string quartet began playing the wedding march and the audience stood as the doors at the back of the church opened and the bridesmaids filed in, followed by the bride on her father's arm.

They resumed their seats as the bride's father delivered her to her waiting groom and the priest began the ceremony.

Oz smiled as he watched Caitlin and Jack turn affectionate, excited eyes on each other. He remembered when they were all wide-eyed freshmen playing pool and Jack shot Caitlin longing looks down his cue. They finally got together over a bottle of peach schnapps smuggled into Caitlin's dorm room, and that summer Caitlin spent the earnings from her campus job on a flight from her home in Maryland to meet Jack's family in Minneapolis.

Nearly a decade later Caitlin was a lawyer, Jack was an architect, and they'd just bought a fixer-upper in Wellesley with big plans for renovations.

He looked around the church at his former classmates, considering all the different journeys they'd undertaken since they graduated five years earlier. Law degrees, medical degrees, PhDs. Moves across states, across countries, and others who'd stayed put right there in Boston. Relationships forged and broken, and soon Cameron and Melissa would become the first parents among them.

And him—what had he done? His career meant it took him an extra semester to finish his degree. He and Nedda attempted a long-distance relationship during her first year of medical school, but by Thanksgiving he'd signed for Skyline and they called it quits. Then he moved from Boston to Atlanta, following Roland from a mid-tier club to one of the best in the league. He bought a luxury loft apartment, sold it, bought the house of his dreams and perfected it. Averaged five goals per season, kept more clean sheets than he could count, and consistently excelled for club and country.

But through it all he'd been alone. He had his friends, and he dated constantly, but he'd spent every night in his big bed in his big house by himself.

Until now.

He slid his hand onto Kate's thigh. Last night she'd had her own room in the hotel with the team, but tonight they had only one booking. Unless he counted the uncomfortable few hours he spent on her pull-out couch—which he didn't—they hadn't spent the night together yet.

He shifted in his seat, the realization that he'd be waking up beside Kate tomorrow morning suddenly making him wish this wedding—this whole day—would hurry up and end.

He glanced over at her and she gave him a small smile before returning her attention to the ceremony.

He turned unseeing eyes toward the priest. The obsessiveness that drove him to keep his house immaculate, his car in mint condition and his athletic performance at its peak reared in his affection for her, too. He thought about her all the time, re-read even their most neutral text message exchanges over and over, could barely take his eyes off her when they were together.

He worried about her, too. Wondered how she was, if she was tired or bored or stressed and how he could help. He hated knowing that he could fix so many of her financial problems with the painless signing of a check, but at the same time he respected her refusal to accept anything more than letting him pay for dinner.

Seeing Nedda again brought a lot into focus. Until now, she was his most serious relationship. He'd taken her to Sweden to meet his parents, flown to California to meet hers, sat through months of his friends hinting they should get married, insisting they were perfect for each other.

But no matter how hard he tried, he never loved her. She never drove him to distraction. And she never tested his willpower like the woman at his side.

Kate was proud. She was strong and levelheaded and secretly so very vulnerable. She was everything he never imagined he wanted, and all he couldn't imagine living without.

This was the real deal. He was falling for her.

Short-term, long-term, it didn't matter. He knew what he wanted. It wasn't what he expected, or planned, but it was certain.

He flattened his feet on the floor and made a decision.

He tightened the hand on Kate's thigh, prompting her to toss him a teasing, chiding look. He couldn't wait to tell her.

* * * *

"It took a whole day to get back from Faro, but it was so worth it. Then we spent another couple of days in Gothenburg with Murat and Alara, and I met Yusuf, who was visiting for the weekend with his fiancée. Wife, now, I guess." Nedda paused to take a sip of her wine, then replaced her glass on the table. "Anyway, I loved Sweden. Have you been?"

Kate shook her head. "No."

"Oh. Well, it's beautiful."

"I'm sure," she repeated distractedly, glancing over Nedda's shoulder to look for Oz. He and Glynn had gone to the bar for more drinks, but they'd run into so many people they knew—or people who'd heard of Oz and wanted to meet him—the five-minute errand had taken nearly half an hour.

"So do you have any more vacation plans for the summer?"

"Hm? Oh, no, not really." Kate found another smile, although she was worried she'd run out any minute. When Oz left for the bar Nedda had launched an effort to make conversation. To be fair to her, she was nice. Faultlessly nice. Friendly, chatty, sincere.

And still hopelessly in love with Oz.

On one hand Kate couldn't wait to get him alone and find out what happened to end his relationship with Nedda. On the other she wasn't sure she wanted to know, for her own sake. If a stunning, smart, successful woman like Nedda couldn't hang on to him, what chance did she have?

She'd enjoyed the wedding so far, and everyone had been kind and welcoming, but she couldn't shake the nagging feeling that she didn't belong—not among these people, and not in Oz's life.

It wasn't that she didn't think she was good enough for them. Sure, most of them were more educated, had more money and better careers, but that wasn't what bothered her. The most jarring difference, as far as she could articulate it, was cultural. And she found it as surprising as she did unnerving.

She understood the topics around which the conversation had ranged over dinner. Politics, art, theater, politics again. She got it. She got all of it. She just didn't care.

Who were these people, and how much free time did they have, to spend so much energy on trivial issues? Okay, not trivial, but definitely removed from real life. They had so much outrage about things that didn't affect them, from state-by-state disparities in the minimum wage none of them worked for or whether the right play won a Pulitzer and what it said about American values when it didn't. It took everything she had not to roll her eyes right out of her head when one of the other guests went on a rant about public schools failing to provide organic meals and teach students about growing their own produce. She doubted Dallas's kindergarten teacher had ever seen a zucchini, let alone grown one, but that didn't make her any less good at her job.

Until now she'd laughed off most of what she perceived as Oz's frivolous fixations. She shrugged at his super left-wing political leanings, changed the subject when he went on a tangent about a particular filmmaker whose work she *had* to see, and when he began to discuss the design integrity of his house she straight-up told him to get over himself.

He seemed to like her straight-talking, bullshit-reducing perspective. But maybe that was part of her short-term appeal and would become her long-term downfall.

Then again, he'd used the G-word: girlfriend. The last person to call her that was her ninth-grade boyfriend Alan, who was sweet and earnest and never dared past first base.

Her inner cynic argued he'd said it only to keep Nedda at bay, but her heart knew Oz chose his words as thoughtfully and deliberately as he did everything else. As much as she wanted to dismiss that moment as careless and without meaning, blood rushed to her head whenever she remembered it.

He knew what tossing that term out in front of his friends meant to her, and the emotional response it would yield. If he intended to anchor her, to strengthen her tie to him ahead of a chaotic and overwhelming day, it worked. She wanted him more than ever.

Kate searched the room for Oz again as Nedda detailed the difficulties she'd had finding a decent vacation rental in the Adirondacks, but he appeared to be signing cocktail napkins for the groom's young cousins. She sighed inwardly, taking a long sip of beer to steel herself to be appropriately sympathetic to Nedda's hotel-booking woes.

"Mind if I join you? I seem to have lost my seat to the bride's great-aunt." A tall, ruggedly handsome man with a blond crew cut motioned to the empty chair next to her.

"Actually, someone's sitting there." Nedda smiled apologetically.

The guy's face fell and Kate motioned for him to sit. "It's fine. We have extra places."

"Whose seat am I stealing?" he asked, dropping into the chair. "Should I be worried?"

Kate felt Nedda's keen stare. "It's my—my boyfriend's," she managed, forcing out the unfamiliar, slightly terrifying word.

"Damn," he said ruefully.

"Don't worry, he's very civilized. Most of the time."

He peered around the room. "Which one is he?"

Kate pointed and the man's brows rose. "The famous one. Double damn. Well, since I don't stand a chance against a professional hockey player—"

"Soccer," Nedda corrected sharply.

"*Soccer* player, I guess I can give up trying to impress you and focus on having a good time instead." He extended his hand. "Jake O'Malley, cousin of the bride."

Kate returned his handshake. "Kate Mitchell, plus-one of a friend of the bride and groom."

"Nedda Jalil," she piped up from the seat on Kate's other side. "I went to Harvard with the bride and groom."

"Gotcha." He turned back to Kate. "Do you live in Boston?"

"Atlanta. But I was going to be up here anyway for Oz's game yesterday. What do you do, Jake?"

He grinned. "I'm a cop. Quincy PD."

"Nice. I work in private security."

"No kidding." He took a swig from his beer bottle and shifted on his chair, getting comfortable. "Are you ex-law enforcement?"

"Army. Eight years."

"Wow. Did you deploy?"

"Three tours. Iraq and Afghanistan."

"Shit." He whistled. "Did you see much action?"

"I was in combat support, so I guess I saw as much as any enlisted woman could."

"If you stuck it out for eight years you must've liked it."

She shrugged. "The contracts seem to renew themselves sometimes, but yeah, overall I'm glad I enlisted. Only problem is you reach a point where if you don't leave, you'll never leave, and I didn't want to be in the military forever."

He nodded. "Makes total sense. What kind of private security are you in now?"

"Mostly residential. Some VIP. I manage the account for Oz's soccer team. That's how we met."

"Tough job. I know a guy who does security for a bunch of the Sox players, and he—"

"Sorry, that took forever." Oz arrived behind her and put his hands on her shoulders. Glynn set a tray of shots on the table.

Jake shot to his feet and shook Oz's hand as he introduced himself. "I'm going to be straight up with you, man, you've got yourself a pretty awesome lady here."

"I know." Oz's mouth quirked in amusement. Jake moved to vacate the chair but Oz waved him away. "Sit. I'm planning to drag my awesome lady onto the dance floor as soon as she finishes her tequila."

"Really." Kate eyed the glass Glynn slid in front of her. "And where is yours?"

He shook his head. "I'm behaving."

She arched a brow but said nothing. He'd stayed sober all night, which wasn't unusual, but given it was a big party with all his old friends, she expected he'd allow himself at least one drink.

"I never say no to tequila," she declared. She downed the shot, let it burn all the way through her ribs to her stomach, then declined the lime wedge Glynn offered.

"That's hardcore," Jake remarked approvingly. Oz took her hand and tugged her to her feet, then led her along the edge of the ballroom toward the dance floor.

He stopped a few steps short, pulled her into his chest and lowered his mouth to hers. His kiss was possessive, insistent, and she obeyed it gladly. She parted her lips, hummed her enjoyment as his tongue swept over hers, stifled a shudder as he hardened against her hip.

He swore softly as he pulled away and brushed his thumb over her cheekbone.

"You really are an awesome lady."

"Awesome girlfriend, you mean."

He smiled slyly. "That's exactly what I mean."

Before she could say anything else he pulled her into the mass of people swaying and bopping on the dance floor. The live band played a mix of cheesy classics and pop hits, and the night was late enough—and alcoholic enough—that most dancers cheered and sang along and didn't seem to care how ridiculous they looked.

She watched in delight as the intense, serious man she knew transformed into an air guitar-playing college kid. Glynn appeared and the two of them embarked on what was clearly a long-standing air guitar partnership, both of them goading her until she made a feeble effort to accompany them on an invisible drum set.

As the night wore on and the music got cheesier, she tried and failed to remember the last time she'd felt so silly, or so unspeakably, unimaginably happy.

"Oh my God, I never want to see these torture tools again." Kate flung the high-heeled sandals her landlady had talked her into in the general vicinity of her open suitcase. She missed, and they fell on the floor six inches to the left.

"You look so good tonight. You always look good." Oz dropped his tie on the desk and unbuttoned the top of his shirt, then yanked her against him, his hands encircling her waist.

"I've been waiting all day to get you alone," he told her. She was tired and dehydrated and her ears rang with all of the small talk she'd endured for the last twelve hours. She wanted quiet and a huge glass of ice water and about a day's worth of sleep. But the intent in Oz's tone made her want him more than anything.

"Did you have a nice time?" she asked mildly, slowly unbuttoning the rest of his shirt.

"I did. Did you?"

"It was an exhausting day but yeah, I had fun. Glynn is such a good guy. He made sure I was never alone for too long."

"Except when we left you and Nedda together and got stuck at the bar." He tilted his head apologetically. "I don't know why Caitlin and Jack decided to put me and her at the same table. She and Caitlin are best friends, so I would've thought—"

"Then she probably asked to be at your table and her best friend obliged."

"You think so?"

"How can a man as smart as you be so oblivious?" she asked, only half-joking. "Nedda's still crazy in love with you."

"No, she's not," he said firmly. "She recently broke up with someone she'd been with for a long time—longer than we were together—so she may be a little sensitive but she's not in love with me." His gaze sharpened. "Did she give you a hard time when I was at the bar?"

"No, nothing like that. She was sweet. She really made an effort to be friendly." *And she's as in love with you as the day is long, but if you don't want to hear it I'm not going to repeat it.*

"Good."

"Why did the two of you break up?"

He groaned, sliding his hands to cup her backside. "I don't want to talk about her anymore."

"Give me the thirty-second version. I've been wondering all night."

"I've been thinking about why, after seeing her again tonight. On paper we were a perfect match, and everyone else seemed to think so too. But there wasn't enough between us to hold us together."

"Enough what?"

He shrugged. "Enough anything. Passion, commitment, dreams in common—none of it. We were good in college, but never great. Never amazing. She left for medical school halfway through my last season with Boston Liberty and without even proximity to tie us to each other, we fizzled out."

An alarm rang somewhere deep inside Kate's consciousness, but she muffled it before she could detect its source. "And you never slept with her?"

"No."

"When we talked about it in Charlotte, you said you didn't want to fall for the wrong woman. Someone who wanted Oz the soccer player, not Oz the man."

"Exactly."

"Were you worried about that with Nedda?"

He pursed his lips, his expression thoughtful. "Yes and no. On some level I think Nedda was excited to be with a professional athlete. That mattered to her. Does that mean her feelings for me weren't genuine? No, I don't think so. To be honest, I didn't sleep with her because it didn't feel right. I just didn't want to. Not with her."

Kate bit her lower lip, absorbing his words, and as she processed what he said she located the source of her discomfort.

If there wasn't enough common ground between him and Nedda to last, there was no way in hell he had any more of a future with her.

"Enough about Nedda. That was then, this is now." He reached around and pulled down the zipper of her dress, his middle finger trailing along her bare spine as he exposed it.

She slid her hands beneath his open shirt and flattened her palms against his warm skin. Tomorrow worried her more than now, and she didn't even care about then, but that wouldn't get her anywhere tonight. Like him, she'd waited all day for this, and she intended to enjoy it.

"This dress is beautiful, but every time I looked at you it made me think about how much lovelier you are underneath." He shoved one strap off her shoulder and lowered his lips to her collarbone, then repeated the movement on the other side. Then he tugged down the bodice so it gathered at her waist, revealing her sheer, lace-trimmed black bra.

"It's a good thing I didn't know you were wearing this or we wouldn't have made it to the reception." He swept his thumbs over her nipples, visible through the material and already tightened into peaks.

"You haven't seen the bottom half yet." She felt the same smile that had come over her mouth when she'd picked up the set from the clearance rack.

His eyes darkened and he pushed the dress over her hips, down her thighs and onto the floor. She stepped out of it, turned her back on him, then bent from the waist to pick it up, parting her legs to give him the full view the sheer panties allowed.

"Be careful with this. It was expensive," she reminded him with teasing tartness as she straightened and laid the dress out on the desk.

She turned to look at Oz, whose face was tight with hunger. For several seconds they stared at each other in silence, then he grabbed her by the waist and tossed her on the bed.

"Are you in a hurry?" she asked sweetly, propping up on one elbow as he shucked off his shirt and raced to unbutton his trousers with trembling hands, nearly tripping as he stripped down. She took one look at the bulge in his tight briefs and moaned aloud as hot, urgent need thudded between her legs.

He climbed on top of her and jerked the cups of her bra down over her breasts, teasing each nipple with his tongue—left, then right, then left and back again until she grabbed a fistful of his hair and yanked up his head to end the torment.

"I want you so much," she told him breathlessly as he roughly took off her bra and closed warm fingers over her breasts. "I don't think I can wait."

"I won't make you. We have all night."

The thought of all those hours of Oz's body made her even wetter than his touch. She pressed her thighs together, desperate to ease the ache between her legs, but he sat up and skimmed her panties down and off, then pried her knees apart.

She pushed up on her elbows and watched him lick his lips, then drag his tongue along her swollen core. Her head fell back and she shuddered, the ceiling blurring in her vision.

"Fuck, Kate, five minutes of foreplay and you're as wet as a week of rain," he said huskily, running a testing finger between her folds.

"I've been wet for you all night, boy."

His eyes flashed and his jaw clenched and he assailed her with his tongue, his lips, his teeth, his thumb. She groaned and bucked and arched off the bed, incoherent with pleasure, inhuman with hammering need. She fisted her hands in the sheets and at the last second she gathered herself enough to peer down the length of her body at him, at this sexy, smart, successful man devoting all of his energy to making her come.

Their eyes met and something jolted between them, more powerful than lust, more durable than passion. Then he swirled the tip of his tongue around her clit and she lost herself, every muscle stiffening, her teeth clenching, her ears roaring with the unstoppable force of her orgasm.

When the world regained its normal proportions Oz lay next to her, his fingers tracing lazy patterns on her stomach.

She took a deep breath, knowing he watched the way her breasts heaved up and down. "You're wicked, Terim. Wicked and evil."

"I'm not wicked. I'm the Wizard." He grinned.

"You're trouble, is what you are." She reached for the waistband of his briefs, already plotting her revenge, but he moved her hand away.

She rolled over to face him, immediately concerned. "Is something wrong?"

He shook his head, running a comforting hand down her arm. "Are you good? That felt good?"

"Mind-blowing. That's why it's my turn to—"

"No more turns," he told her quietly. "I want to make love to you, Kate."

Her breath stalled in her throat, then left her lungs in a dizzying whoosh. "You mean, like…"

"Have sex. With you. Now."

Her heart beat wildly as she tried to reconcile the two warring forces pulling in opposite directions inside her head. One was her hot, demanding desire. The other was her instinct to protect him, to protect both of them, from making a decision they might regret.

"Hold on." She put her hand over his on the bed and lifted her chin to meet his eyes. "Are you sure about this? Have you definitely thought this through? Weddings can do funny things to people, and seeing your friends—"

"I've been thinking about this for a while," he interrupted.

"And?"

"I bought condoms."

She bit her lower lip. "Since we've been in Boston? Because sometimes when you're away from home things can seem—"

"Before we left. I packed them in my suitcase."

She blinked, racking the shrinking part of her brain that wanted to convince him not to go ahead with this for another reason before it was completely drowned out by her loud, lustful thoughts.

"I'm sober and I'm certain," he said seriously, his eyes never leaving hers. "It's not about the wedding or my friends or anything but you. *You*, Kate. I want this to happen with you. I don't care how long this lasts, or what happens tomorrow. I want to give you something I've never given anyone else. Right now."

Then came the tears, spilling hot and unbidden from the corners of her eyes. No one had ever trusted her with anything so significant, seen her as anything more than a diversion. That Oz wanted to share with her what he hadn't shared with the scores of other women who would've gladly taken it… She could barely comprehend the magnitude of his choice.

He murmured her name and took her in his arms, brushing the tears from her cheeks as he kissed her slowly and sweetly. "What's wrong?"

She took a shaky breath. "I don't want you to make a mistake."

"I won't," he said firmly. "Remember, I told you I'd know when I met her? I know. I want this."

She touched his face, traced its handsome angles, then moved her hands to his hips and slid her fingers under the band of his briefs.

He shivered as she touched him, tracing his smooth, straight length. She kissed him again, indulging in one more grip of his shaft, then pulled back and met his gaze.

"You're sure?"

He nodded.

He stood and tugged off his briefs, then crossed the room to his suitcase, digging through the immaculately folded clothes to produce a small cardboard box. Kate watched him walk back to the bed, her nipples puckering and her mouth watering as she took in his erection. She'd fantasized about having him inside her so many times, but even in her wildest imaginings she never thought it would actually happen.

He sat beside her. She took the box from his hand and removed a foil square. She tore it open and leaned over, ducking her head to run her tongue up his shaft before pinching the top of the condom and sliding it on.

Oz's expression was a mix of trepidation and excitement. The combination aroused her even more. This strong, confident man whose body was his career had chosen her to take him over the final threshold of his sexuality.

She wouldn't let him down. She'd show him she deserved him. All of him.

"Are you okay to… I mean…are you ready…for me?"

She smiled, guiding his hand between her legs so he could feel her slickness. "I want you inside me. Just the thought is soaking me all over again."

He growled and she eased onto her back as he moved over her. She reached between them and found his erection, and stroked the head against her core.

He watched her spread her legs, bring his tip just inside her and then withdraw it, the condom glistening with her arousal. She brought the tip back to her entrance and met his eyes with a question in her own.

"Yes," he managed raggedly. She put her other hand on his hip and urged him inside, slowly, slowly sheathing every inch of him.

She couldn't stifle a primal, guttural moan at the tantalizing pressure of his body within hers. He stretched her, filled her, and she clung to every scrap of self-control to stay still when every instinct screamed at her to wrap her legs around his waist and fuck him as hard and fast as she could.

He trembled above her and throbbed inside her. He breathed heavily, harshly, and she could feel the tension suffusing his body.

She almost laughed when she realized what he was doing, and smoothed a reassuring hand down his cheek. "Come in me. I don't care how quickly it happens. We have all night, remember?"

He grunted in response, every muscle in his arms standing out.

She began to rock beneath him, pressing her palm against his rear to encourage him to move with her. Slowly he loosened up, dropping more closely against her and bringing his hand to her thigh. She murmured her pleasure, savoring his thickness, the smooth rhythm of his chest grazing her nipples, and the lower part of his abdomen brushing against her clit.

He groaned against her temple, a telltale sign that he was close, and she increased the pace. She wouldn't come this time—he was nearly there, she could tell—but she didn't care. Squeezing him tightly, knowing she was the first woman to possess him like this, the first one he'd stroke from within and spill his completion inside, was more satisfying than a lifetime of climaxes. He chose her. She was unique. Special. Unparalleled in his life so far.

As he was unparalleled in hers.

Tears welled again as he clenched her leg and bared his teeth against her forehead, swearing and then holding his breath as his thrusts became frantic, messy, giving way as his body froze and he held himself deep inside her.

"Just like that," she encouraged him, ignoring the tears of pride and love that spilled over her cheeks.

He said her name desperately, pleadingly as he obeyed, digging his fingers into her hair, holding her tightly against him. She clung to him as he arched and stiffened, until his climax receded and he quivered, until his arms gave out and he flopped down beside her.

"Fuck," he roared. He pulled out, disposed of the condom and collapsed on the bed next to her.

"Was it how you expected it would be?"

"No." He stroked an affectionate finger under her chin. "Ten thousand times better. A million times better. A hundred billion times better."

"Do you wish you'd done it earlier?"

"No. It was good because of you. It wouldn't have been the same with anyone else."

She kissed his forehead, his nose, his lips as her heart quietly thrilled. "You have no idea, Terim. Wait 'til I get on top."

Chapter 18

Oz woke to his phone buzzing against the side table. He fumbled in the pitch-dark hotel room to sweep it up, squinting at the text on the screen.

Downstairs @ bfast, coming?

On way he replied to Glynn, replaced his phone and rolled over to wrap his arm around Kate. She didn't stir, her breathing quiet and even.

He pressed his face into her hair, inhaling her sweet, strawberry scent. She was warm and soft in his arms, and he wanted nothing more than to close his eyes and go back to sleep. But he told Glynn last night he'd meet him for breakfast and he couldn't leave him waiting downstairs.

With tremendous effort he slid out of bed, stretching languidly. He yanked on shorts and a T-shirt and shoved his feet into a pair of sneakers.

He glanced at Kate's sleeping form, then found a pen and notepad with the hotel's logo and wrote on the blank page.

Went downstairs for breakfast, come join me! :-)

He tore off that sheet of paper, crumpled it and tossed it into the bin. Too eager.

Downstairs. See you soon.

He shook his head as that note joined its predecessor in the trash. Too unemotional.

Downstairs at breakfast w/ Glynn, will save you a seat.

Satisfied, he signed it *Ö* and slid it onto the table next to her side of the bed. He shoved a key card into his pocket and quietly let himself out of the room.

When Oz turned the corner into the lobby, Glynn stood by the two steps leading to the sunken dining area where breakfast was served. He looked up from his phone as Oz approached.

"Sorry, forgot to set my alarm," Oz explained, then gave his room number to the staff member at the entrance.

Glynn mumbled something unintelligible in response and Oz looked more closely at his friend. "A little worse for wear this morning? Too much air guitar?"

"Too much wine, beer, champagne, tequila—I drank everything in sight." Glynn scrubbed a hand over his eyes. "I need so much bacon and coffee, and I need it yesterday."

"I'm here now. You're in a safe place. We're going to get you through this."

Together they walked to the end of the long buffet table. Oz loaded his plate with fresh fruit and yogurt while Glynn selected two chocolate muffins from a large basket. Eventually they came to the omelet station, where Glynn scowled at Oz's order of egg whites with spinach and tomato, then asked for cheese, chorizo, and bacon in his.

"You're unusually chipper this morning," Glynn remarked as they waited for their omelets.

Oz shrugged. "I stayed off the booze last night. International friendly coming up."

"You know you're never going to get to the World Cup with Sweden," Glynn grumbled, not for the first time. "You're eligible to play for Turkey and they're in an easier group. I don't know why—"

"Because I'm Swedish, that's why. Plus you can't switch once you've declared."

"Anyway." His friend peered at him. "That's not it. You're happy. Like, disturbingly happy."

"I don't think I am."

"You're grinning."

Oh shit, he was. "No, I'm not," he disagreed, forcing his mouth into a line.

Glynn stared at him as they collected their omelets and found an empty table. His friend narrowed his eyes, then widened them in comprehension.

"Oh my God. You had sex with Kate."

Oz froze, uncertain whether to confirm or deny. He planned to tell Glynn eventually, and frankly it took all his self-control not to shout it joyfully across the dining room, but since the three of them had to travel back to Atlanta together today, he'd planned to wait and save Kate any potential awkwardness on the journey.

"Silence implies consent, Terim. Speak now or forever hold your peace."

Dammit. He couldn't lie, but at the same time he didn't—

Glynn snapped his fingers in triumph. "I knew it. One look at your face this morning and I fucking knew it."

"It's not a big deal," Oz replied, hushed.

"Not a big deal? It took you twenty-seven years to decide and now you're wearing a grin the size of Boston Harbor. It is a big deal, my friend, a very big deal."

"What's a big deal?"

Oz had sudden, sharp empathy for deer finding themselves face-to-face with oncoming headlights as he turned at the sound of Nedda's voice.

She looked between the two of them. "What? What happened?"

They turned to each other, then back to her. She frowned, then her eyes rounded much like Glynn's had moments earlier.

"You had sex with Kate," she whispered, her tone harsh with incredulity.

Oz caught Glynn's muttered curse at his side, then watched in horror as Nedda burst into tears.

Oz shoved his plate at his friend and slid his arm around Nedda's shoulders, ushering her out of the dining room and up the steps to the back of the lobby. He found a quiet corner along the railing that looked into the restaurant and stood with his back facing out, trying to give them some degree of privacy.

"Come on, Neds, don't do this," he urged. She pressed her face into his chest and he wrapped his arms around her, shaking his head at how quickly his morning had gone wrong.

Last night had been one of the best of his life. Kate was beautiful, skillful, and unbelievably passionate. She moved as fast or as slowly as he wanted and treated the situation sensitively without ever embarrassing him or making him feel inexperienced.

Most importantly, making love to her turned out to be more of an emotional milestone than a physical one. They connected on a level he couldn't articulate, and which he'd never experienced before. It was so much more than friction, or pleasure. When he was inside her and their eyes met, he knew he'd never be the same. He didn't *want* to be the same.

Just thinking about Kate had blood pumping to his groin and he broke away from Nedda before she got a very wrong idea.

"Tell me it's not true," she said, sniffing. "You were fibbing to impress Glynn. You didn't really sleep with her."

He exhaled, irritated. Since when was this anyone's business but his? But Nedda was having a rough time, she was on the rebound, and he still cared about her as a friend. Telling her to get her nose out of his life and move on was the worst approach he could take.

"I did," he confirmed.

"Last night? For the first time?"

He nodded.

Her face crumpled with fresh tears. "Why?"

"Why do you think?" he asked shortly, fighting to contain his exasperation.

"You're not in love with her," she insisted. When he didn't reply she continued, "Oz, please, be serious."

"I am serious," he replied, and she shook her head.

"You're not thinking," she countered, her voice rising in volume. "We were together for two years. You slept with her after, what, a few weeks?"

"This is different, we're—"

"Damn right it's different," she shot back, ignoring his gesture for her to quiet down. "As women we're *completely* different. I get that she's sweet, has a cute accent, and nice legs. She's also probably emotionally and intellectually uncomplicated. I get that. I see the appeal. But I'm amazed that you don't see what else I see: the complete absence of any future between you two."

Until that second her tirade had slipped over him like a satin sheet, but it snagged on her last sentence.

"She works in private security. She gets paid on commission." Nedda practically spat the word. "Do you really think she's going to move to Istanbul and watch happily while you spend two glory years at Galatasaray? Or live in a flat in Gothenburg and support you through graduate school? Or has your plan changed?" she asked tartly.

It hadn't. Same plan he'd had for almost ten years. Kate was the only new variable.

For a second he could only stare. He held her at arm's length, his hands tight, his stomach tighter.

Having sex with Kate had been an uncharacteristic choice. He'd selected the reality of today instead of the idea of tomorrow.

He hoped it wasn't the wrong decision.

He refocused on Nedda with fresh impatience, even more ready to move on from her. "What does any of this have to do with you?"

"Because it should have been me," she informed him shakily. "I loved you for two years. I put in the work, traveled with you, met your parents, made time for God knows how many soccer games in between exams, essays, MCATs, interviews, everything. I earned your love. I deserved it. But instead, you tell me we're on different paths, we don't have enough holding us together. So spell it out for me. Where does Kate's path join yours in a way that mine didn't?"

It doesn't, he realized ominously, then shoved that thought aside the same way he did whenever his doubts about Kate bubbled up to the surface.

"Look, Neds, I'm sorry it didn't work out with…uh, with—"

"Ryan."

"I know you guys got really serious and you thought he was going to be it. You and I broke up a long time ago—almost five years now—and we've both changed a lot since then. I get that when things aren't going well it's easy to look back on the past and think—"

"Stop." She held up a palm. "Is this the part when you get all patronizing and tiptoe around my delicate mental state to pacify me while simultaneously telling me to fuck off? Because I'd rather skip to the end."

He set his jaw. Apparently some things never changed. "Then I don't know what else to tell you."

"I know. Which is why I'm going to tell you, instead. She's wrong for you, Oz. You were wrong to sleep with her, and you'll be wrong every time you do it again. It won't last—it *can't* last—and you're setting yourself up for a world of heartbreak. You made the wrong choice and you'll regret it. And now you can't say no one ever warned you."

"Great seeing you, Nedda." He stepped back to give her space to leave. "Let's do it again sometime, preferably under different circumstances and without your unsolicited judgment on my life choices."

She took two steps away, then glanced at him over her shoulder. He could swear he saw a flash of regret in her lovely eyes, but then her posture stiffened, her face hardened, and she stalked toward the elevator bank without another word.

He propped his forearms on the railing she'd been leaning against, tilting his face up to the ceiling. He wasn't making a mistake with Kate. Nedda didn't know him anymore. He wasn't sure she'd ever known him at all. She sure as hell didn't know him well enough to make such an unforgiving call on his relationship.

And his uncertainty about the future, his hesitation about how Kate would fit into his plan, his inflexibility about changing that plan—he'd deal with all that later. Maybe.

He closed his eyes and dropped his chin, exhaling in exhaustion. Then he opened his eyes, and instantly wished he hadn't.

Kate and Glynn sat at a table directly below where he and Nedda had stood. The two of them stared in silence at their uneaten breakfasts, both clutching empty coffee mugs like talismans.

"Fuck my life," he said in Swedish, pushing off the railing and starting toward the stairs into the dining room. "Fuck my fucking life."

* * * *

"I'm not an expert, but I believe this is the point in most romantic comedies where it turns out you've misheard my conversation with my ex in a way that makes you decide to dump me. Am I right?"

Kate smiled tightly, wrapping her hands around her third cup of coffee. Glynn had retreated to his room after the three of them had set a record for the world's most awkward breakfast, and now it was time for her and Oz to face the huge, Nedda-shaped elephant in the room.

"I didn't mishear anything," she assured him.

"No?"

She shook her head. "I heard every word loud and clear."

He cringed. She reached across the table and gripped his wrist.

"I'm teasing. You didn't say anything I don't think you would've wanted me to hear. Nedda came off looking pretty bad, but that's all. You're fine."

"Are we fine, too?"

"Definitely," she lied. In truth, she'd never felt less fine than she did at that moment.

It was a steep, hard drop from the bubbly mood she'd woken in. She'd practically floated down to breakfast, buoyant on physical fulfillment and the high of knowing Oz had chosen her, that he'd placed her above all the other women he'd been with. She felt cherished and special and elated when she sat down across from Glynn.

Then she registered his bleak expression. And heard Nedda's voice ringing above them, shrill and severe.

She couldn't fault the way Oz handled what was clearly a painful conversation, the way he defended her, or the heart-stopping pause when he didn't object to Nedda's accusation that he was in love with her. Far more distressing was the way Nedda managed to articulate all her own reservations about their relationship. They seemed even more insurmountable spoken aloud than in her head.

Nedda was right. Their lives were different, maybe irreconcilably, and Nedda was by far the better choice. She couldn't argue with any of that.

But she was falling for Oz. She was falling for him so hard it was difficult to imagine life without him. She wanted to fight for him—for them—but she was scared. The harder she fought, the more losing would hurt. She'd never been afraid of pain before, but the stakes had never been this high, either.

Oz sat back in his chair on the other side of the table. "This has certainly killed my good mood this morning."

She didn't reply, taking a sip of coffee.

He leaned forward again, propping his elbows on the table. "I don't want you to worry about any of that shit Nedda came out with."

"I'm not worrying."

"You are. I can see it."

She bit her lower lip. "It would be hard not to after hearing that."

"She spoke from a place of complete ignorance and massive self-interest."

"She knows you, though, and—"

He cut her off with a shake of his head. "Let's forget about her, okay? Let's focus on the facts we woke up to this morning. Did you have a good time last night?"

She couldn't stop her smile. "Of course."

"So did I. And did last night make you feel more or less confident about our relationship?"

"More. Way more."

"Exactly." He laced his fingers through hers. "So ignore Nedda and her opinions. Focus on what we both know."

"Which is?"

"That we're happy." His self-assured smile faltered slightly. "Aren't we?"

She nodded, then looked away. She shouldn't ask, shouldn't give voice to this question, but she had to. She wanted to see his reaction and hear his response.

What if Nedda is right?

The words were perched on the tip of her tongue, ready to take flight when two boys approached their table with a man she assumed was their dad. He had one hand on each of their shoulders.

"I'm so sorry to interrupt your breakfast, but I had to ask—you're Oz Terim, aren't you?"

Kate sat back and finished her coffee as Oz posed for a series of photos with the two boys. By the time they finished, their interaction had drawn attention from the rest of the dining room, and more and more people were taking out their phones to snap covert, and not so covert, photos.

"I think it's time to go," he muttered as the man and his kids walked away. They both stood, and he led her to the elevator with a hand on the small of her back.

"I hate when people do that," he said as soon as the elevator doors closed. "They blatantly don't know who I am, just that I'm apparently famous enough for one person to recognize me. Then they go crazy filling up their phones with a thousand pictures of someone they can't even identify. What are they going to do with those? Run a reverse image search to figure out how to tag their Tweeted photo of their big celeb spot? Pathetic."

"Are you getting riled? You're so cute when you get riled." She flattened her hands on his chest and smiled up at him, glad to have a reason to back out from asking him whether Nedda could've been right. She was grateful she hadn't asked him. She didn't want to know. Didn't want to face the answer, not yet.

Not yet.

"I'm not getting riled. I'm calmly identifying a major privacy issue," he insisted, but his eyes softened self-effacingly.

"Gotcha. You don't get riled."

"Never."

"So when we get back I can rearrange all the books on all your shelves and it won't bother you."

"Now that's a question of logical organization and I think it's totally reasonable to object to any disruption of that system." He put his hands on her waist and pulled her in tightly.

She ground her hips against him, pleased with the erection she found. "You wouldn't be riled if I did that."

"Not at all."

"You'd merely be objecting."

"Absolutely." He slid his hands to her rear and cupped it, pushing her up onto her toes.

"Too bad. Like I said, you're cute when you're riled."

He lowered his face to hers, trailed his lips along her jawline. "For you, maybe I'll get riled. Just this once."

"Promises, promises," she teased, and kissed him like the morning had never happened, like she'd never met stupid Nedda, like she had every confidence they would work for as long as both of them wanted.

Chapter 19

"Kate?" Lorraine leaned into the room housing the handful of cubicles that constituted the Peak Tactical sales department. "Rich wants to see you."

Kate groaned inwardly as she got up and shoved her feet into her high heels. This couldn't be good. The month-end results had been issued the day before and she'd just hit her target, but she doubted Rich wanted to congratulate her on a job well done.

As she followed Lorraine down the hall, the fear of failure that had always driven her to success before washed over her in a wave, and for a second she teetered where she stood. When it receded she felt stronger, firmer. Ready to face her boss.

It probably wasn't the healthiest form of self-motivation, but it worked. Nothing made her study harder or run faster or shoot straighter than the stress of speculating what might happen if she didn't.

In some ways, getting fired from this job would be worse than failing at any of those things. Her means were stretched more than ever with rent, utilities, gas, and her mom called yesterday to say her doctor switched her to a new blood pressure medication that cost a third more than the old one.

But she also knew he had no reason to fire her. She'd hit her targets this month, despite the slow summer season. Roland was happy with her, and working for Skyline had given Peak Tactical entry into a whole new industry.

Lorraine knocked briskly and then opened the door to Rich's office. He wasn't going to fire her, she told herself sharply. He was probably going to lecture her on sales tactics and make some empty threats and suggest he check in on her pipeline at the end of the week.

"Have a seat." Rich gestured to the chair on the opposite side of his desk. Kate dropped into it as Lorraine closed the door and left the two of them alone.

He laced his fingers over the belly that stretched his button-down shirt. "You saw the month-end results yesterday."

She nodded.

"Matt pointed out an issue with his allocation," he said, referring to one of her sales-department colleagues. "As a result I had a second look at the figures last night and realized I needed to make some adjustments to your allocations as well."

She arched a brow. "Adjustments?"

"On the Skyline account. I did a hell of a lot of work on that last month, Kate, and I think it's only fair that we split it fifty-fifty."

She didn't think that was fair at all, but she said nothing, waiting to see where this was going.

"The revised numbers show you didn't hit your target for July. Not even close, in fact. You've struggled with your sales since you got here, and unfortunately I think it's time for us to let you go."

She blinked, unable to believe what she'd heard. "Excuse me?"

"I'm sorry to have to get to this point. We're always excited to hire veterans, especially females. But I have to put food on the table, too, and you just aren't hitting the numbers."

"The numbers you decided to reallocate last night."

He nodded, and she could swear he almost smirked.

She paused, waiting to feel devastation. Or disappointment. She'd failed—shouldn't this hurt more?

Maybe three nights in a row of hot, satisfying sex with Oz had done her more good than she realized. Or maybe she was flat-out sick and tired of self-important men telling her what to do. Because the only thing she felt was pissed off.

"Let me stop you there." She held up a hand. "Let's schedule a formal meeting to discuss this, maybe tomorrow, to give me a chance to arrange for an attorney to be present. Can you send me the revised figures in the meantime so I can understand the basis for this dismissal?"

"Now, I don't want this to get hostile." He leaned forward. "I know this is disappointing, but let's finish our time together on a positive note."

"I don't really care whether it's positive. I want it to be fair and legal."

"Are you suggesting I'm being unfair or acting illegally?" His tone sharpened, his eyes narrowed.

"I'm not suggesting anything. Just protecting myself."

They stared at each other in mutual dislike for a moment. Rich swiveled toward his computer and poked at the keyboard.

"You want to protect yourself," he muttered. "Have you ever heard about these Internet alerts you can set up? You get a little notification every time someone or something you're interested gets mentioned."

"I've heard of it," she said carefully.

He typed, clicked, broke into a smug smile. Then he turned the screen so she could see it.

She gritted her teeth and clutched the arm of the chair when she saw the photo.

"I set an alert for our friend, Oz Terim. Found this nice article about him going to Boston. Apparently he was playing against his old team, and he even scored a goal. Then I scroll on down and see this."

He tapped the screen needlessly. As if she couldn't see herself in the corner of the photo, waiting patiently while Oz posed for a picture with the two boys in the hotel. As if she didn't want to find whoever had taken the photo let the air out of their tires. As if what should have been a harmless, happy moment wouldn't be burned into her mind forever now.

"I had my suspicions there might be something going on between the two of you, and I think I can safely say I have proof." He full-on smirked. "Two words: gross misconduct."

"How?" She'd re-read her contract before leaving for Boston. Because Oz wasn't the one paying the company's fees, she knew there was no way he could get her on this except emotional blackmail.

"Your contract says you have to act with the highest ethics. Do you think sleeping with a client is ethical?"

"First, Skyline is our client, not Oz. Second, you have no proof that we're sleeping together. Third, you couldn't get me on gross misconduct if you did because the contract isn't that explicit."

He rolled his eyes. "Are you a lawyer now?"

"No. I'm a woman being told I'm losing my job due to a discretionary reallocation of my sales figures."

"Please don't make this a political correctness thing." He sighed exaggeratedly. "It has nothing to do with you being a woman. I treat all my employees the same. If you can't meet the targets that are set the same for everyone, that's no one's fault but your own. Pull yourself together, take your two weeks' notice, and start looking for a job that's a better fit."

She looked away, her anger simmering into calm, lethal determination.

She was out of the military. She was out of Saudi Arabia. She was done taking orders. She had a man in her life who respected her more than anyone else ever had, and no one was going to tell her what to do anymore.

"You treat all your employees the same?" she echoed.

He nodded vigorously. "Of course."

"You definitely don't give preferential allocations to Matt because the two of you spend the day trading links to porn clips."

The color drained from Rich's ruddy face.

Gotcha, fucker.

"I don't know what you're talking about," he said tightly.

"Really? I'm sure I saved that e-mail somewhere. And you might want to talk to Matt about the Reply All function in his next review, by the way."

"Let's not play this game, Kate. Let's be adults about this."

"Agreed," she told him firmly. "I'll pack up and leave the office today. You'll pay me two weeks' salary and the quarterly bonus I would've received if my numbers hadn't been"—she raised her fingers in air quotes—"adjusted."

"Then we both walk away."

"Yes."

"Fine."

It was over. She won. She got what she wanted.

She was numb. So shocked she didn't know what to do.

"Goodbye," Rich said pointedly and she jerked up from her chair. She gave him a curt nod in farewell and strode out of the room.

Safely outside his door she flopped against the wall, exhaling heavily. She wanted to feel triumphant, victorious. Instead she found herself fighting back tears.

No matter the terms, he fired her. She was unemployed.

Just like her mom and sister.

She held it together as she packed her few possessions. The other sales reps looked on but no one spoke. She was sure the situation was obvious, and that she wasn't the first woman to come and go from this macho-man pit. As she walked out with her cardboard box under her arm she imagined all of them sprinting down the hall, trying to be the first into Rich's office to take her place on the Skyline account.

She smiled at that image, chucking the box in her trunk and slamming it shut. Rich thought he could get rid of her and hold onto Skyline. Good fucking luck, buddy.

On that note she pulled out her phone but stopped with her finger hovering over Oz's number. She was seeing him later that night, anyway. She'd tell him then, when she'd had a chance to process exactly what happened, and send out a few resumes.

* * * *

"There you are." Oz appeared at the head of the line leading into the nightclub and tugged Kate out of it, yanking her to his chest and giving her a quick, tight hug.

She savored the firm planes of his body for a second, then broke away and turned a disapproving face to the bouncer. "I told you I was on the VIP list."

Oz's tone was less forgiving. "What the hell, man? You better have an outstanding reason why I had to come all the way out here to get her."

The bouncer ran his eyes up Kate's body, toes to head, blatantly taking in her flat shoes, figure-hugging jeans and plain purple T-shirt. Then he looked past her at the long line of men and women dressed to the nines in designer clothes.

"It's such a common name, I thought maybe I had the wrong Kate Mitchell," the bouncer offered mildly.

"Sure." Oz rolled his eyes and slung his arm around Kate's shoulders, leading her into the nightclub.

He took a sharp right turn just inside the door to climb a set of stairs, and as they made their way along a crowded balcony toward an area labeled VIP she got a glimpse of the glamorous partiers who'd turned out to hear tonight's DJ.

"The website said no flip-flops or sneakers, but I didn't realize it was going to be this fancy."

"You look great," he told her firmly. The VIP-area bouncer unclipped the velvet rope for them to enter and as the handful of people inside got to their feet Oz announced, "I found her."

"Did you get lost? We should've told you the entrance is on a side street." Ted gave her a quick hug in greeting.

"The bouncer was giving her a hard time," Oz said as she embraced Glynn and Sean in turn.

"He was a douche to me, too," Sean assured her. "Guess we won't be back."

She smiled gratefully at Sean, doubtful his slick outfit would've been given a second glance at the door. He was trying to make her feel better, and she liked him all the more for it.

"And this is DJ Balboa, better known to us as Jonas, and his girlfriend, Ella," Oz introduced them.

Kate smiled at the Swedish DJ, the reason they were here tonight. "Nice to meet you."

They chatted as a group for a bit, but when Jonas and his entourage kept falling into Swedish Kate decided to leave Oz to his native language for a while. She joined Glynn, Ted and Sean on a couch at the other end of the area, beside the velvet rope.

"What can I make for you, hon?" A server in a teeny miniskirt arrived in front of the couch.

"Bottle service," Glynn explained. "Vodka and mixers."

Kate wrinkled her nose. "Just a club soda, please."

"You're not drinking?" Ted asked.

"I don't like vodka."

"We can get a different bottle. It's all on the record label's tab. We're only having vodka because we're surrounded by Scandinavians."

"I'm good. I drove here, so." She lifted a shoulder.

Ella joined them, starting up a conversation about visiting Atlanta for the first time. Kate contributed when she could, but she didn't have much to offer about high-end shopping or trendy restaurants. After a few minutes she went quiet, taking in her surroundings and sipping her club soda.

She gathered that Jonas would go on last as the headliner, but another DJ was playing in the main section downstairs and she could see the crowd heaving in front of the stage. Those closest to the DJ seemed like genuine fans of the music, but the further back she looked the more the club appeared to be a meat market. The women hovering near the bar certainly hadn't worn shoes fit for dancing, and she doubted the men buying them drinks would even notice if the DJ walked away and Waylon Jennings's greatest hits started pouring through the speakers instead.

The space outside the VIP area was getting busier, too, as more and more people approached the bouncer and tried to talk their way behind the velvet rope. She guessed she should've felt special, but mostly she imagined all these would-be VIPs looking her up and down and wondering how she got in when they couldn't.

Sean stood up from the space beside her and Glynn took his place.

"How are you?" he asked, raising his voice above the increasing volume of the music.

They'd seen each other a couple of times since they'd flown back from Boston, but she had an idea he was referring to more than her general wellbeing.

"Good, thanks." It wasn't exactly true. In fact it was a big fat lie. She'd just lost her goddamn job. But there was no point in getting into all of that, no matter how much she liked him.

"You don't look like you're having much fun."

Her face heated. "I am. It's not really my scene, is all."

"Not mine, either, if I'm honest. Jonas is good, though, and you can't argue with free drinks." He raised his in salute.

"True." She tapped her glass against his.

Glynn looked over his shoulder at where Jonas laughed at something Oz said, then back at her. "Can I be really honest?"

After the day she'd had, she'd rather he wasn't. "Of course."

"The fact that you're sitting here in jeans, being uncomfortable and not drinking, is why I like you. And why I'm glad you're with Oz."

She arched a brow. "Thanks?"

"I've been thinking about it since Nedda had her…moment. She would've loved this. She would've known exactly what to wear, what to say, what to drink. Tomorrow she would've taken Ella for lunch and shopping."

"This is supposed to make me feel better?"

"Sorry, I'm circling my point, which is that it's easy to get sucked into the pro-athlete lifestyle. I've known Oz for almost ten years and sometimes I still come close to falling into the trap."

She shook her head. "I don't follow. What trap?"

"The perception of life without consequences. That there will always be more money, more time, another party, someone to pick up the tab. I do think Nedda's feelings for him were real, but there was also a level on which she wanted to be part of the lifestyle. She wanted the clothes, the vacations, the house, the attention."

"She's a doctor," Kate replied incredulously. "That took a lot of hard work. She wouldn't have gone through all that if she just wanted to be someone's arm candy."

Glynn's expression said he wasn't convinced. "If Oz had proposed, she would've quit. At best, she might've continued med school part time for the sake of appearances, but she wouldn't have gone through interning and residency, and definitely never would've worked as a doctor."

She flopped back against the couch as she absorbed Glynn's assertion. Nedda seemed so capable and sophisticated and smart. Maybe Glynn saw her motives even more clearly than Oz had.

"You're saying you don't think I care about that stuff," she supplied.

"Ironically, no."

"Why is that ironic?" she asked, but when she caught Glynn's regretful wince she figured it out.

"Because I need his money a lot more than Nedda did," she answered her own question.

"I'm sorry, Kate, I wasn't trying to imply—"

"It's fine," she dismissed him. "Y'all know what I do for a living. It's no secret that I'm not exactly rolling in cash. I'll take it as a compliment that you don't think I'm a gold digger."

"That's what I meant," he said earnestly. "You're grounded, you're honest, and you're not trying to be anyone you're not. Oz is pretty disciplined but between his intellect and his money, even he gets carried away sometimes. He needs someone to yank him back to earth, and I think you can do that."

She swallowed an unexpected lump in her throat. She'd had a shit day and shittier ones were probably still to come as she looked for a new job, but in that moment she felt lucky. She was lucky to have Oz, lucky he had such great friends, and lucky they accepted her so easily. "Thanks, Glynn. I appreciate that."

He put his arm around her shoulders and gave her a quick hug. "Now, try to do something about his stupid white décor. I'm afraid to touch anything in that damn house."

"Is this man bothering you, Kate?" Oz arrived, gestured for the two of them to slide down, then took a seat on her other side. He slid his arm around her waist and pulled her against him, pressing a kiss to her temple. She relaxed into his firm, lean body, so grateful for his presence, for his very existence, that she had to breathe through another hot swell of emotion.

"I've heard at least seven women claim to be your girlfriend." She nodded to the press of people unsubtly peering into the VIP area. The bouncer had moved the velvet rope to push them farther back but that hadn't stopped them craning their necks.

"Yeah, they look like committed soccer fans. I bet they've all got season tickets and watch every away fixture on TV."

"I'm sure. Anyway, Jonas and Ella seem nice."

"They are. I met Jonas in Stockholm a few years ago at a charity event. He's a big star in Sweden but he's only recently broken through in the US. I'm happy for him. He deserves it."

"When does he go on?"

"Midnight."

She quickly checked the time on her phone and suppressed a sigh. Still two hours to go.

Oz squeezed closer and asked in a low voice, "You're not having fun, are you?"

"I'm just tired. I had a shit day at work."

"What happened?"

She shook her head. "I don't want to get into it here."

"Do you want me to take you home?"

"I'm fine, I promise. Anyway, I drove."

He gave her a sidelong glance, then reached in his pocket and produced a key on a Swedish-flag keychain.

Glynn whistled, which Oz ignored. "You're not enjoying yourself. Go back, help yourself to whatever's in the fridge. I'll see you in a few hours."

"That's the key to the house," Glynn told her unnecessarily, his brows raised. "No one gets to be in there alone. This is a big moment for us all."

"Shut up, Glynn," Oz said without taking his eyes off her. After a second she accepted the key, slipping it into her own pocket.

"I assume you know how to turn off the alarm," he continued. "The code is—"

"You should never tell anyone your code or—"

"Or announce it in a public place. I was listening that day, believe it or not. I'll text it to you, and I'll give you a hint."

He leaned in, pressing his lips beside her ear. "There's no hint," he murmured, his voice deep and sultry. "I just want you to know I can't wait to find you in my bed when I get home."

His words wrapped around her as if she'd slid into a hot bath on a cold evening. Her muscles relaxed, the tension in her spine eased, and the worries that had been hammering her forehead since she left her office went quiet for the first time in hours.

She'd deal with the future tomorrow. Tonight she cared only about the man at her side.

He kissed her goodbye with a long, lingering press of his lips. Normally she would've been embarrassed by such a public display, but knowing all those wannabe-VIP women in tall heels and short dresses were watching, she returned the kiss full force. Oz hummed his approval and raised his hand to her cheek, moving his tongue against hers. She relaxed her jaw to give him better access, sliding her palm up his thigh.

"Should I go? Because this is getting awkward." Glynn's voice snapped her back to the present.

"No, I'm going." She stood and said her farewells to everyone she'd met, including the Swedish visitors. Then, with a last glance at Oz, she left the VIP area and made her way to the exit, aware that every head turned to gawk at her as she passed.

The line to get into the club was even longer than when she arrived, and she marveled that anyone would spend that much time and expense on a few hours of partying, and on a Tuesday night to boot.

She rolled down her windows to enjoy the cool nighttime air, a welcome relief from the scorching summer day. She turned on the radio, then turned it off, preferring the quiet of the deserted streets and the dark, sleeping neighborhoods.

When she arrived at Oz's house she cut the engine and waited in the driveway. Although Citizens First seemed to be embroiled in an internal leadership crisis that had the group splintering into factions, she wanted to be sure no one was watching the house.

She waited five minutes, long enough for a Peak Tactical patrol car to make a circuit down the street. She wondered if they'd phone into the command center with the gossip that they'd seen her car in Oz's driveway, and then get the news she'd been fired. Maybe they already knew.

Satisfied she was alone, she locked her car and walked up the path to the front door. She checked her phone for the code—his jersey number repeated twice. She'd have to talk to him about picking something more cryptic. She unlocked the door with his key, then quickly tapped in the numbers to disarm the alarm.

She flicked on lights as she moved through the open-plan ground floor. The white walls and furniture made everything look clean and bright and orderly, and she understood why Oz liked this style so much. The house felt calm and organized, a haven in the middle of the bustling city and his hectic life.

She drifted into the kitchen and opened the fridge. She wasn't particularly hungry, but the contents impressed her nonetheless. Big hunks of salmon, two packets of ground turkey, a tub of yogurt, and more varieties of fruits and vegetables than she could name.

She filled a glass from the carton of organic orange juice and slid onto one of the stools at the kitchen island. The juice was tart and delicious, the counter surfaces pristine, the house silent except for the barely perceptible hum of the refrigerator.

Glynn's words resurfaced in her mind—his suggestion that she was grounded. Maybe she was naïve not to have thought about it before. She'd been too preoccupied with the emotional bumps and hurdles of their relationship to consider the material side. Of course she liked Oz's house and his car and all the other stuff his salary permitted, including the hand-squeezed orange juice in her glass.

But she liked those things because they were extensions of him. He could live in a trailer with a hole in the roof and drive a wreck with windows that didn't roll down and she'd probably find it endearing.

"Anyway," she said aloud, draining the glass and stowing it in the dishwasher. She climbed the elegant staircase to his bedroom, shucked off her clothes and folded them on top of the dresser, then pulled one of his T-shirts over her head. It smelled like him. The whole house smelled like him.

Not quite ready to settle down, she drifted around the bedroom. She reached for a bottle of cologne on the dresser, then withdrew her hand. Then rolled her eyes at herself.

He'd given her his key. Sent her into his house on her own. She left the military in search of permanency, and now he offered it to her. She just had to find the courage to accept it.

The cologne probably cost as much as two tanks of gas. She picked it up, opened the top, and inhaled. The scent was woody and masculine and tantalizingly familiar.

She replaced the cap and examined the other objects on the dresser. The remote control for the TV. Two rolls of blue kinesio tape. A little red wooden horse with a white- and blue-painted harness and mane.

She touched them each in turn, savoring these glimpses into his everyday life. His house still didn't feel like home, but he did. He felt like somewhere she belonged.

A yawn took her by surprise and she stretched, suddenly tired. She slipped between the crisp sheets and switched off the lights. She exhaled in pure contentment and fell instantly asleep.

* * * *

It was after two o'clock in the morning when Oz climbed the stairs and crossed the hall to his bedroom, but he was wide awake. The high-energy DJ set left him full of adrenaline, and seeing Kate's car in his driveway and knowing she was in his bed doubled his excitement. He had to take a calming breath before opening the bedroom door, which he wanted to fling wide on its hinges.

Instead he slipped into the room as quietly as he could, unlacing his shoes and lining them up inside the door. Normally they'd go back into their spot in the walk-in closet as soon as he took them off, but he didn't want to wake Kate, whose figure he could just about make out in the darkness.

He snuck into the bathroom to brush his teeth and empty his pockets. He always placed his wallet, watch and keys in a neat pile on his dresser, but tonight he arranged them beside the sink instead. He stripped down to his briefs and draped his clothes over his arm to put in the hamper, then grabbed his phone and moved into the bedroom.

After another couple of minutes fumbling in the dark, trying not to make a sound, he finally made his way to the bed and eased in between the sheets.

Kate rolled over and pressed into him. "Hello."

"I was trying not to wake you," he whispered, wrapping his arms around her.

"I'm a light sleeper. Did you have fun?"

He hummed affirmatively. "Jonas was incredible. The whole club was jumping. Awesome vibe."

"I'm sorry I missed it."

"No, you're not. But I don't care," he assured her, tucking her hair behind her ear. "I want you to be happy, not try to make me happy."

"Sounds good. By the way, I rearranged all your clothes to give myself a drawer and moved in a bunch of my stuff."

Panic shot through his chest and he froze, horrified by the mental image of his carefully ordered drawers in disarray.

"I'm kidding." She laughed, propping up on one elbow. "I would never. Oh my God, you should see your face. You look like I just told you I crashed your car."

"Not funny," he informed her, slipping his hands under her shirt to tickle her sides. She squealed and wriggled in his grip, until his fingers brushed over her nipple. Then she grew serious, placing her palms on his cheeks.

"Hi," she murmured before she kissed him.

He inhaled sharply as she ground her hips against him, stiffening his already aching erection. He slid his hands to her rear, pushing down her panties to grip her firm flesh. She purred encouragement against his lips and he tugged the garment down to her knees, then pressed his fingers between her legs.

He growled a curse at the wet heat he found. He started to move his hand but she grabbed his wrist and held him still, nipping lightly at his lower lip.

"I want it fast and hard tonight, and I want it now. Think you can deliver?"

"Anything," he promised, his heart pounding so wildly he could barely breathe.

She pulled her T-shirt—*his* T-shirt—over her head and tugged impatiently at his briefs. He yanked them off and rolled over to open the top drawer of his bedside table. As he rooted blindly for the box of condoms he felt Kate's body against his back, and then she reached around to bob her fist once, twice, three times along his shaft.

He groaned involuntarily, his hands shaking as he opened the packet and rolled down the latex. He turned around just in time to see Kate spread her knees on the bed and brace her hands on the headboard, inviting him to take her from behind.

His dick throbbed and he offered a brief, grateful prayer in Turkish to a God he was confident wouldn't begrudge this happiness.

He moved into position and gently pushed one, then two fingers inside her, assuring himself she was ready. He replaced his fingers with the head of his erection, sliding it along her folds and over her clit, then easing the tip inside.

She shot him an impatient glance over her shoulder. He buried himself in a single stroke.

Her moan was guttural and she repositioned her knees, moving them wider. He took several long breaths, adjusting to the sensation of her warm, encasing flesh, pulling himself back from the brink of climax. Eventually his breathing calmed and he slowly stroked in and out.

Kate met each thrust of his body with one of her own, urging him faster, harder, rougher. He obeyed gladly, sliding one hand up her stomach to thumb her nipple and cupping her sex with the other, holding her against his hips and teasing her clit.

They went from zero to a hundred in only minutes. After a handful of thrusts Kate arched her back, begging incoherently before her inner muscles tightened around him in a way he knew broadcast her impending climax. Just the anticipation of her pleasure rocketed his own to new heights. He rubbed merciless circles over her clit as he increased the pace. She came within seconds, whimpering as her whole body stiffened, then trembled.

The sight of her shoulders heaving with the force of her orgasm pushed him over the edge into his own. He clenched his jaw as he thrust into her and held himself there, pressure building almost unbearably and then exploding into a dizzying climax. He emptied into her, throbbing inside her hot sex, then gingerly pulled out, feeling like every one of his nerve endings was exposed and raw.

Kate flopped onto her back. He tossed the used condom into the trash and stretched out beside her, trailing his fingers through the sheen of sweat between her breasts.

"Good?" he asked.

"Outstanding."

He smiled into the darkness. "Could've been longer."

"Sometimes I like it quick and intense. Plus it leaves time for a second round."

"You're insatiable."

"I'm in bed with a hot man and I want to take advantage. Can you blame me?"

"Definitely not."

She laced her fingers through his. "I haven't always been like this. If anything, sex tended to be mostly awkward. Couple of drinks, guy I was kind of into, twenty minutes of fumbling and I usually had to finish myself off. It's completely different with you."

He kept his voice even, although her words had warmth spreading through his stomach. "Different how?"

"Better, obviously. Way better. And it's not just sex, what we do. It's intimate."

"Deliberate," he added.

"I feel like I know you better after every time. Like we're getting closer and closer."

He squeezed her hand, barely able to contain his excitement for another second. He grabbed his phone from the bedside table. "I have something to show you."

"Something good?"

"Of course." He unlocked the screen, pulled up his e-mail and scrolled to a message. He opened it and passed her the phone.

She squinted at the glowing screen. "I'm confused."

"Read."

"I did. I don't get it."

He took the phone and replaced it on the bedside table. "It's my itinerary for the international friendly this weekend. I booked a second plane ticket. I want you to come with me."

She said nothing for so long he thought maybe she hadn't heard. He was about to repeat himself when she blurted, "I lost my job today."

The phone went into sleep mode, dropping them back into darkness with the same unexpected suddenness as she'd made her announcement.

"What happened?" he asked, not sure where else to start.

"I didn't hit my target, at least not according to Rich's special math. It's probably for the best. I wasn't good at sales and I didn't like it anyway."

He considered the implications of this development, at least as much as a professional athlete who'd never had a job interview could. "So now you look for something else?"

"Pretty much."

"Roland will dump Peak Tactical as soon as he finds out about this." He covered her hand with his own, driven by an unfamiliar instinct to protect her. The possessive urge was startling and brand new. He'd always found independence and self-sufficiency attractive, yet here he was, ready to do almost anything to make sure Kate was all right.

"Do you want me to make some calls?" he offered. "I don't know much about your industry, but I'm happy to pick up the phone to anyone you think could be useful. And your apartment, will you be able to afford the rent? Because if you need a place to stay—"

"I'll be fine," she interrupted. "I've got some savings to keep me afloat, and hopefully I'll find something new soon. It's just annoying to be back to square one."

He closed the space between them, pulling her against him. "The upside is you won't have to use any vacation days to come to Sweden. You can get out of Atlanta, clear your head, be fresh for the job search when you get back."

"Oz," she said softly, her tone broadcasting that she was about to say something he wouldn't like.

He eased back, giving her space. "What?"

"I can't go to Sweden."

Cool disappointment settled on his shoulders, dousing the hot flare of protectiveness that had overtaken him only moments ago. "Why not?"

"Saturday is my sister's birthday. She's having a party in Jasper."

His jaw tightened. "You didn't mention that before."

"It's Tuesday. I didn't realize you needed to know my plans for Saturday."

He withdrew from her, physically and emotionally. He released his hold on her as shutters slammed down around his heart.

"Is it a big birthday?" he asked carefully. "Like her thirtieth or something?"

"She's my younger sister," she reminded him.

"I'm getting an award from the Swedish government the night before the match at a black-tie dinner." He heard himself sounding more and more aloof. He tried to find an anchor in the conversation, to believe that he might still convince her to come with him. "My parents are flying to Stockholm to see it. Yusuf and his wife are coming from London, too. It's a big deal. It would mean a lot to have you there."

Her sigh sounded exasperated. "I've committed to my sister. I can't back out. Why didn't you tell me earlier that you wanted me to go?"

He didn't answer. They both knew why—because earlier their relationship hadn't gone as far as it had in the last two weeks. Earlier they weren't sleeping together. Earlier he hadn't given her a key to his house.

"Forget it," he said coolly. "If your sister's birthday party is more important, you should go."

"It's not about what's more important, it's about keeping promises."

"Fine. So keep your promise."

Her hesitation tightened the air between them. He hoped she was about to relent. Offer to call her sister and explain the situation, then ask increasingly enthusiastic questions about Sweden. Kiss him and fall asleep in his arms, looking forward to their first international trip together.

"Goodnight," she said instead, then rolled over. He pulled the duvet up to his chest and crossed his arm behind his head, staring unseeingly at the ceiling as he fought to understand what just happened.

Maybe he was being arrogant or self-centered—he'd certainly been accused of both before—but he couldn't believe she turned him down. He hadn't just asked her to join him on a weekend jolly somewhere hot and frivolous. He wanted her by his side in front of his family, in front of all his fans, as he was given a nationally prestigious award before strapping on his boots to play for his country. And her reason for staying behind was a party. *A party.* Not work or a family crisis or any other immoveable, justifiable commitment. Her unreliable, unpredictable sister, whom she didn't even seem to like very much, was throwing a birthday party. She chose a night of cheap booze over five days in Stockholm.

He shook his head, astonished and bewildered. There had to be more to it. Maybe an overseas trip to meet his family was too intense.

He liked any opportunity to travel, but he supposed that wasn't the case for everyone. Maybe the idea of hopping a plane to Sweden and putting thousands of miles between herself and her home at a day's notice was intimidating. In the Army she would've had plenty of notice before deployments, and the logistics would've been handled for her. Maybe she was nervous about traveling abroad, especially without time to plan for it.

Then again, maybe it had nothing to do with the destination or the notice. Maybe she just wasn't as all into this as he was.

He devised The Plan to protect himself from the lonely downfall that claimed his uncle, to be an objective framework to ensure he didn't make rash decisions or emotional mistakes. Yet the deeper he got with Kate, the more he ignored it, bending the relationship criteria and reaching to justify why everything would be fine despite their obviously disparate futures.

The whole point was to find a woman who would commit to him forever. Kate wouldn't even commit to this weekend.

Unease and doubt settled heavily in his chest, a pair of uncomfortable, unshifting weights as he saw his uncle's sallow skin and unfocused eyes, his once powerful, unstoppable body bloated and weak. The capable hands that had applauded his childhood soccer skills grown shaky and uncertain. The sure, capable feet shuffling down the hallway in the house where he grew up. The man who was his idol, his inspiration, his everything, slumped in a corner of the kitchen, pathetic and defeated, droning about his lost love with ever more incoherence.

He eased onto his side, turning his back to Kate. He'd rushed into this thing with her, sprinted in with his heart wide open. He had to tighten his grip on the reins, pull himself back under control, recover his detachment and objectivity. He had to evaluate whether this was a good idea or a catastrophic one.

It would hurt—it already did. But a little pain now was better than a whole lot of agony in weeks to come.

Chapter 20

Kate thumbed the screen of her phone to flick to the next picture on Oz's Instagram feed. He wore a slick black tuxedo perfectly cut to his body, and she recognized his parents on either side of him.

Next photo. Oz stood with a man who looked like a slightly heavier-set version of him and a woman in a hijab. His brother and sister-in-law.

Next photo. Oz holding a gold, disc-shaped statuette, his other arm around the shoulders of a Hollywood-starlet Swedish actress who held a matching one.

Next photo. The Swedish Prime Minister, a famous musician, the actress again, and—

"Katie, your sister is talking to you." Her mom's stern voice cut through her distraction. Sheepishly Kate put the phone facedown on the counter.

"Sorry, what?"

"There's another twelve-pack in the trunk. Can you get it? I forgot to bring it in and my nails are wet." Emily held up her alternating pink-and-purple manicure.

"Sure." Kate grabbed the keys for the Sentra from the bowl on a window ledge and headed out to the car, barely aware of her surroundings as her thoughts churned and spun.

She hadn't heard from Oz since the award ceremony last night. In fact, they hadn't had much to say to each other at all since she left his house on Wednesday morning. The pictures on his social-media accounts told the tale, though.

She opened the trunk of the car and stared unseeingly at the forgotten twelve-pack. Oz was insane to invite her. A wedding reception in a hotel was one thing, but a televised red-carpet event was quite another. He obviously hadn't thought it through. For one, she would've had to find something to wear, and she was pretty sure a clearance item from Wedding Belles wouldn't cut it.

He probably wanted to buy something for her, she acknowledged reluctantly. He probably had a grand notion of sending her shopping with his mother and sister-in-law, swirling around the high-end boutiques of Stockholm and meeting him at a hotel with arms full of bags like in *Pretty Woman*.

But this wasn't *Pretty Woman*, and she wasn't in the market for a makeover. Losing her job clarified one thing she knew she wanted, and it was independence. Time to step out of men's shadows and discover the shape of her own.

It was a nice fantasy, a really nice fantasy, but nothing more, she concluded, hefting the twelve-pack from the trunk and slamming the lid shut with her elbow. She was not red-carpet ready and never would be. She wouldn't know what to say to a gossip columnist, let alone one asking questions in Swedish. And sitting for hours at a fancy dinner, the television cameras rolling the whole time—no way. She'd rather spend a week in Baghdad. Far less stressful.

For better or worse, Emily's birthday party was right at her level. She tore open the twelve-pack and distributed the cans amongst the ice-filled buckets, coolers and other improvised containers on the front porch. Sure, it would've been nice to go on a big trip and get all dressed up. It was nice that Oz thought she could handle it, too.

Flattering.

Crazy.

The beer unloaded, she made her way back into the kitchen. Her mom was emptying a bottle of vodka into a jug of fruit punch, her sister was applying top coat to her nails, and Dallas held up Kate's phone, a photo of Oz filling the screen.

"Is this your boyfriend?" her niece asked.

"What did I tell you about taking things that aren't yours? And how did you unlock the screen?"

"I guessed the code," Dallas said sweetly. She extended the phone to surrender it but Emily intercepted, sweeping it out of Kate's reach.

"Damn, Katie, your man is hot. What's his name again?"

"Oz." Kate snatched the phone out of her sister's hand and shoved it into her jeans pocket.

"Oz," Emily repeated, picking up the nail-polish brush. "Weird."

"It's foreign," their mother insisted. "Probably normal where he's from. Bet it's the same as Wayne or Mike in Switzerland."

"Sweden," Kate interjected.

"Same difference." Her mom rolled her eyes, dragging a wooden spoon through the punch. "Anyway, I'm glad you've stuck it out with him. You could do a lot worse."

"Hell yeah you could. Good job, Katie," Emily encouraged her sincerely.

"How far do you think you can push it?" her mom asked, stowing the spoon and pulling out a cutting board.

Kate dropped into a chair at the kitchen table. "What do you mean, how far?"

"Do you think he'll marry you?" Dallas supplied.

"Don't sign a pre-nup," Emily warned.

She laughed bitterly. His Instagram feed spelled out that impossibility in every photo. "No one's getting married. We're playing things by ear. Figuring out whether we can make this work."

Her mom and her sister exchanged glances over the kitchen counter. Then her mom began mercilessly slicing an orange.

"It never works," her mother decreed. "Enjoy it while you can, and get as much as you can get to tide you over 'til the next one."

Emily reached across the table and grabbed her wrist. "You done good, babe. Caught yourself a big fish. Keep him on the reel as long as possible."

Kate didn't have the heart to protest. For once in all of their lives, her mom and sister were right. She wasn't going to change to suit him, and he sure as hell wasn't going to change to suit her. Might as well enjoy it while it lasted and brace herself for the finish.

She pushed up from the table and poured herself a tall glass of punch, then coughed as the alcohol burned her throat.

Her mom grinned. "Strong enough?"

Kate nodded, topping up her glass. "Perfect."

The party was fun for the first two hours. Kate stowed her phone in the room Dallas and Emily shared so she wouldn't be tempted to continually check the score in Sweden's friendly against Slovenia. Emily's friends, most of whom Kate knew from high school, drifted onto the property in clumps. Soon pickup trucks in various states of disrepair lined the driveway all the way out to the road, lawn chairs littered the yard and a gaggle of kids older and younger than Dallas flitted around the house leaving a trail of toys in their wake.

Kate settled into a camp chair beside Pete, a high-school friend she hadn't seen in years. She spent their junior year hoping he'd ask her to prom in the spring, crushing fiercely but secretly on his shaggy reddish-gold hair, his illicit smoke breaks behind the school, and the man-of-few-words temperament that set him apart from their peers. She'd hoped he'd interpret her shyness as mysterious and find attractive virtue in her studiousness and good grades.

Instead he asked out big-breasted, pouty-lipped Whitney, who went to prom as his date but left with another guy. Two months later she got knocked up by her coworker at Dairy Queen. She'd put on a lot of weight since high school, but she'd also found religion, and now ran a home-baking business out of her basement.

Regardless, Kate concluded, Pete picked the wrong prom date.

He was still good-looking, the red-gold shades in his hair now echoed in a couple days' stubble. The hems of his jeans sat perfectly over steel-toed construction boots, and his faded Braves T-shirt was just tight enough to hint at work-hardened arms and a flat stomach.

Two months ago he would've lit her fire. She would've gulped enough liquid courage to make out with him. He might've invited her back to his place, where she'd numbly tolerate five minutes of his thrusting, then another five minutes of his drunken snoring, and then slip out and drive home, sobered by disappointment and regret.

At the beginning of the summer she would've figured that was the best she could get. Now she knew she could do so much better.

But for how long?

"Your mom says you're working down in Atlanta. Private security." Pete popped the tops on two cans of Bud Light and handed one to her.

"Actually I got fired on Tuesday."

"That sucks," he replied, completely without judgment. "What happened?"

"Didn't meet my sales targets."

"So they figure the best solution for you not bringing them enough money is for you to bring them no money?"

"I guess so."

"If that's the kind of thinking these people get paid the big money for, you and I should be millionaires."

She raised her beer can in agreement. "Are you still installing floors?"

"Yeah, but I'm looking around for something else. The business is hanging on by a thread. Not enough new houses going up around here, and not enough people with money to renovate the ones they've got."

"You could move down to Atlanta, or close enough to drive in," she suggested. "Lots of high-end real estate changing hands all the time."

He wrinkled his nose. "I'm not cut out for the city. I'd rather be poor and happy than rich and stressed."

"I'm still trying for happy *and* rich."

"Good." He grinned, clinking his can against hers. "Don't give up."

Emily joined them, and eventually so did Tyler, Dallas's father. Pete excused himself to get another beer but never reappeared, leaving Kate to referee the antagonistic, sexually charged flirtation between the two. After half an hour she gave up and wandered to the porch for another drink.

She fished a beer out of a bucket of mostly-melted ice water and propped her hip against the railing, surveying the party in full swing.

She thought of the sharp disappointment in Oz's tone when she'd turned down his invitation. He'd been a little high-handed to assume she could leave with him at such short notice, but that was Oz—a man unaccustomed to being told no.

What distressed her more was his struggle to see how she could choose her sister's birthday party over a glamorous trip to Sweden. She understood that one seemed trivial compared to the other, and she probably hadn't articulated herself well at the time. But as she looked at each member of her family in turn—her mother laughing at a joke, her sister tossing her hair, her niece twirling in the fading afternoon light—her reasoning crystallized.

They loved her. Sure, they depended on her for money and emotional support and basic common sense. They relied on her to bring some order and calm to the loud, messy, tilting chaos of their lives. But beneath it all they loved her and always would. She could lose everything, make hideous mistakes or totally self-destruct and they would still love her, flaws and bad choices and all. And she loved them too, no matter how frustrated or angry she got.

For years she'd thought of the Mitchell women of Jasper as a three-piece unit, and herself as an orbiting outlier. As she stood on the porch of that old house in the countryside instead of in a five-star hotel on a faraway continent, she realized they'd always been a foursome. If a year in Iraq hadn't put enough miles between them to sever this tie, what would? Not a job in Atlanta. Not a pro-athlete boyfriend. Not even his globetrotting future.

They didn't need her to stick close by. She'd spent years away with the military and they survived. But she'd come to a point in her life where she wanted to be near them. To see Dallas grow up. To hear Emily's melodramatic tales of romantic mishaps. To ride her mother's unfailing optimism that the next man would be The One, and pull her back to her feet when it turned out he wasn't.

Oz was one of the best things that happened to her, and she was pretty sure she would love him soon—maybe she already did, if she was honest with herself. But her future was here, on this scrubby plot of land in the middle of nowhere, with the unruly, unpredictable, beautiful women who made her who she was. She'd spent nearly ten years away. It was time to come home. "Kate?" Pete touched her elbow. His other arm was locked firmly around a young woman she didn't know. "Someone's phone is ringing off the hook in one of the bedrooms. You might want to check in case it's an emergency."

She cringed slightly at the thought of what they might have been doing in the bedroom, then headed into the house. She shut the bedroom door behind her and picked up her phone, which flashed with missed calls and unread texts.

All from Oz.

Hi gorgeous, did you see the result? 3-0, clean sheet!!

Going on TV in 5 mines, you should be able to watch if you want. Google 'sweden slovenia SVT live stream'

How's the party? All good with the fam? Missing you here.

Hi, are u around? Really missing u, can u talk?

Can u txt me when free & I'll call u? Won't keep u long, just want to hear your voice.

She eased onto the unmade bed and checked the time. It was after 11 PM in Sweden—she may have missed her chance already. She thumbed a reply: *Sorry didn't have my phone. You can call now.*

Her phone rang within seconds. She raised it to her ear and answered breathlessly. "Hello?"

She heard fumbling on the other end. "Kate? Can you hear me?"

She squeezed her eyes shut, savoring the distant rumble of his voice. "I can hear you."

"Hold on, I'm going to switch us to a video call. It'll ask if you want to accept. Say yes."

She lowered the phone and watched the screen, wondering if he had any idea what he'd just told her to do.

Say yes.

She wished she could. To everything. Forever. But it wasn't meant to be.

A message flashed on her phone and she accepted the video call. Oz's smile filled the screen, all white teeth and dark eyes, and a surge of affection clogged her throat. She fought it down with a grin and a wave, holding the phone at arm's length so he could see her.

"Hello," he greeted her warmly.

"Hello to you, too."

He extended his arm to hold the phone farther away, and she got a glimpse of his long, lean torso in a blue polo with the collar buttoned up to the top.

"Where are you?" she asked.

"In the hotel suite. Everyone's here."

The image swung around to show his parents, his brother and his sister-in-law seated on both sides of a small breakfast bar in a kitchenette. Oz instructed, "Say hi to Kate," and the chorus of greetings was so loud the audio crackled.

"Hi, everyone," she replied brightly.

"Okay, now I'm moving into the bedroom so you can tell me what you really think of my brother's choice of shirt." Oz pointed the phone at his brother, who raised his hands to protest the criticism of his pink-patterned button-down.

Oz flashed a grin at the camera before the screen bounced with his steps. She caught a glimpse of what looked like a luxurious hotel suite. A built-in seating area piled with pillows, floor-to-ceiling windows, a TV that looked bigger than her kitchen, and then the background noise faded as Oz shut the door and positioned himself on the bed, his face returning to the center of the screen.

"Can you see me?" She shifted.

"I can, and you look beautiful."

She fought her instinct to shrug off his compliment, smiling instead. "Thank you."

"Is this the part where we have phone sex?"

She laughed at his joking, but not entirely unhopeful, grin. "Definitely not. Your family is right outside that door and I'm surrounded by drunk people."

"Party's going well, then?"

"Everyone seems to be having a good time."

"Are you having a good time?"

She shrugged, suddenly uncomfortably aware that she had chosen to be here by herself and not there with him. "Yeah, I am."

"I'm glad," he said quietly, then glanced down. When he looked up again his smile was back to full force. "Did you see the result?"

"Three-nil. Not bad."

"It was a lot harder than it sounds. Slovenia has this striker who plays in the Spanish league. In moments it looks like he's a pro who's wandered into an amateur match, then all of a sudden he becomes super dangerous, throwing himself down the other end of the pitch and—"

Her sister's shriek cut through the thin wall, and it was evidently loud enough to be heard on the phone because Oz paused.

"What was that?"

"Someone being stupid. What were you saying?"

"So this striker, he takes these crazy runs—"

Emily's voice sliced through the room again, shouting something incoherent but so piercing Oz lost his train of thought. Kate shifted so her back faced the door, hoping that would reduce the noise.

"Keep going," she told him.

Oz hesitated, his expression growing serious. "Unrelated, but I had a meeting on Friday afternoon before the gala. My agent got a call from—"

The door burst open and Emily and Tyler spilled into the room, clutching each other and giggling. Kate shot to her feet and her sister's eyes widened.

"Oops, sorry Katie... Wait, is that your Viking lover boy? The Swedish superstar?"

Emily lunged and snatched the phone out of Kate's hand, then skipped into the hallway. Kate darted after her but Tyler shifted his big frame into the doorway, smiling playfully.

"Move," Kate commanded.

Instead he crossed his arms. "Let her talk to him."

Kate scowled as Emily slurred something at the screen, then announced, "I think we need to discuss a few things in private." She cut the video connection and pressed the phone to her ear, so Kate could hear only her end of the conversation, not Oz's responses.

She started to shove Tyler out of the way, then changed her mind. Why should she protect Oz from the reality of her life? Let him see what she'd chosen—and would continue to choose.

Tyler narrowed his eyes, clearly suspicious at her apparent surrender as she resumed her seat on the bed. He braced his feet against the doorframe, ready to stop her attempts at escape.

She smothered a laugh at how seriously he took this assignment, which was emblematic of his relationship with Emily. No matter how often they fought or for how long they stayed apart, they always drifted back together with odd but enduring loyalty.

Emily wandered down the hall and Kate lost the train of her discussion, though she could hear her sister's voice rising and falling, and then her laugh. Her words became clearer as she walked back, demanding, "And what are your intentions for my older sister, sir?" Each *s* was drawn out and sibilant, and Emily swayed as she arrived beside Tyler.

"Really. I hear you. And you're not married, right? Separated? Divorced? Never? No kids, right? No secret love children with flight attendants scattered all over the world? All right. No, I believe you. You sound like a trustworthy guy. Are you a trustworthy guy? Good."

Emily flashed her an unreadable glance, then half-turned, but Kate could still hear her clearly. "I'll let you go, Oz, because I need another drink. I appreciate you talking to me. You seem nice, and you better stay that way. Because if you hurt my sister, I swear to God, I will find you and I will fuck you up. You will not play soccer again, you may not walk again, and you sure as hell won't ever have any kids. I will *fuck you up*. You got me? But we're not gonna go there, because you're gonna stay a nice guy and we're gonna be friends. Right?" She nodded at his response. "Great. Okay. Y'all have a nice night now."

Kate arched for the phone but Emily cut the call.

Her sister wore a big grin when she turned and handed back the phone. "I think he heard me."

* * * *

Oz stared at the silent phone in his hand, trying to figure out what just happened.

He was halfway through texting Kate to ask if she wanted him to call her back when someone knocked on the bedroom door. He called out an invitation and his brother eased into the room, shutting the door behind him.

"Everything okay?" Yusuf asked in Swedish. Although their parents spoke it fluently, they'd always exchanged brotherly confidences in the language they were born into, not the one they inherited from their parents' homeland.

Oz exhaled, setting his phone aside, the text still unsent, and pulled one leg onto the bed. Yusuf moved a pair of Oz's jeans off the armchair and took a seat.

No matter how successful or famous he got, Oz still idolized his older brother. A competent youth player in his own right, Yusuf's promising career as a full back ended with a serious knee injury. He redirected all his focus onto his studies, moved to the UK for university and probably made more money in banking that he would've as a mid-tier professional footballer. Unflappable, strategic, and brutally honest, Yusuf was Oz's first port of call whenever he wanted advice on a major life decision.

"Did you tell her?"

Oz shook his head. "Her sister took her phone. Told me she'd fuck me up if I ever hurt Kate. She was wasted."

"Classy. But at least her heart's in the right place."

"I guess."

Yusuf stretched his legs in front of him. "What's bothering you?"

"I'm not sure," he admitted. "We were going so well until this week. I know I should've given her more notice for this trip, but I feel like this wasn't really about logistics."

"Did you ask her what it was really about?"

"She told her sister she'd be at her birthday party. So, logistics."

Yusuf shook his head. "Don't oversimplify. Not having a valid passport or enough vacation days is logistics. Not wanting to renege on a promise is something else."

"Semantics." Oz waved a hand.

"No, because one is a choice. She chose not to come with you. She chose her sister instead, and that bothers you. You want to be with someone who'll choose you every time."

Yusuf was exactly right, but Oz glowered at him anyway.

His brother leaned back in his chair. "It's natural to want to be the center of someone's universe. You've never had to deal with not starring in someone else's life, adapting to their plans, adjusting your goals to fit theirs. To be honest, I'm not sure it's a bad thing that she didn't drop everything and follow you to Stockholm. You need someone who can stand up to you."

"It's one of the things that first attracted me to her. She doesn't take any of my diva shit." He smiled at the memory of their early, antagonistic exchanges.

"Good. I liked Nedda, but sometimes she was too deferential. Made me wonder how much of it was about you and how much of it was about your career."

Oz propped his ankle on his knee and studied the seam on his sock, nodding thoughtfully. "I told you they met at Jack and Caitlin's wedding. Nedda certainly had some strong opinions about our compatibility."

"Sounds like she felt threatened. She thought you might…" He shot forward in his seat. "You had sex with Kate, didn't you?"

Oz threw up his hands. "Do I have a sign on my forehead? How is everyone figuring this out without my saying a word?"

Yusuf whistled. "Wow. This is serious."

"That's what I've been trying to tell you." Oz sighed, exasperated. "It's serious, and I don't know if it should be."

"Why not?"

"I'm worried." He scrubbed a hand over his eyes, finally giving voice to the thoughts that had been plaguing him for days. "I think I might be falling in love with someone I don't have a future with. We're so different, and that's good, but maybe it's also insurmountable. Like we're two gears that don't quite fit together, and for a while we can rub along and make a big noise and smooth each other out, but ultimately the whole machine is broken and we'll never click enough to push anything forward."

"You can't know that, not yet anyway. Look at me and Hajra," he said, naming his wife. "You and I grew up with parents who see Islam as a broad set of guiding principles, a framework for making ethical and moral decisions, but not really a code of conduct for everyday life. They drink wine, they don't pray, and the house is full of art that fundamentalists would consider obscene. But Hajra's parents? They still ask her when she's going to quit her job now that she's married."

"You're talking about parents, though. The two of you are aligned even if your families aren't. I'm not sure Kate and I are in sync."

"Not so fast." Yusuf raised a stalling finger. "There's plenty of stuff we disagree on. Big stuff. Critical stuff. Our different levels of devoutness. Whether Islam can be about culture as much as belief. How we'll raise our kids in the Muslim faith. But with compromise, respect, and commitment, we make it work. It's not always easy, but it's worth it. We love each other. And we both want to be together more than we want any of the things that could tear us apart."

Hope and optimism stirred in Oz's chest, but he wasn't ready to surrender to them. "Kate and I aren't as convinced about one another as you two."

His brother lifted a shoulder. "Fine, you're less certain. So what? That's not a reason not to try. If it doesn't work out, you'll know you gave it your best, and you'll come out a different person."

"But wouldn't that be a waste of time?" Oz asked.

Yusuf's expression grew skeptical. "You're twenty-seven. And you're reaching. What are you afraid of, truthfully?"

He linked his fingers together and stared at them, unable to meet his brother's eyes. "I don't want to end up like Erdem."

"Erdem? What does he have to do with any of this?"

"You saw what happened after his wife left." Oz shuddered as his uncle's sallow face loomed in his memory.

Yusuf stared at him for a few seconds, then nodded slowly. "That's why you're so hung up on the future. You think she likes who you are now, but she may not like who you'll be in ten years."

"Exactly."

"Özkan," Yusuf said softly, "What happened to Erdem won't happen to you. He chose a woman who didn't care whether he lived or died as long as she got paid. Plan or no plan, you'll never be with a woman like that."

He shook his head. "I know Kate doesn't care about the money. It's the pain. I'll love her harder and harder and it'll be so painful when life rips us apart."

"What if life doesn't rip you apart?" Yusuf countered.

"And what if it does?"

His brother's silence was thoughtful. When he finally spoke his tone was soft but firm, signaling that this would be his final word on the subject.

"You've never been afraid of pain. You've spent your life flying higher and higher, never looking at the ground, never worrying about how far you might fall. Don't start now."

Oz couldn't speak. He could barely think. He knew his brother was right, but that didn't make the situation any easier. In fact it made it harder.

Now he couldn't say no one told him to fight for her. The responsibility was all on his shoulders. If he gave in to fear, capitulated to uncertainty, ran from the best woman he'd ever met and never found one as perfect for him, it was no one's fault but his own.

He couldn't avoid risk, but he had to decide what he wanted to put on the line—his future or his heart. Did he take a chance on being lonely or having his heart broken?

Yusuf said he'd never been afraid to fly, but that's because he'd always carefully constructed safety nets—his education, his backup plan, his constant awareness that soccer careers don't last forever. There was no soft landing when it came to love, and the sudden drop would come with far less warning than the end of a contract.

As his brother quietly let himself out of the room and he was alone with his thoughts, he changed his mind. Yusuf was wrong. He did keep an eye on the ground, he always had, until he met Kate. For the first time in his life he was running blind, with no sense of how much distance he'd covered or how much farther he could go.

That wasn't him. Not at all. The stakes were higher than ever and he'd gotten so caught up he'd lost track of how deep he'd gone. He had to regain control of his life, of his emotions, of the heart he'd so brazenly laid open.

Then he'd make the hardest decision of his life with the same ruthless precision to which he owed everything.

Chapter 21

Kate pressed the doorbell, then stood back and waited. It was a big house—it could take a while to get to the front door. Anyway, she didn't mind the extra few seconds to compose herself.

They'd exchanged plenty of texts in the couple of days since Saturday, but it was clear something had changed between them. In some ways she felt like they were back to the beginning, dancing around each other, cautiously sidestepping whenever the conversation became too personal.

At first she worried that Oz's detached politeness would open the door for that old, insecure version of herself to creep back into her thoughts. It didn't, though, and no matter what happened tonight, or tomorrow, or five years down the line, she was confident that timid, self-conscious Kate was gone forever. Even if Oz dumped her as soon as she stepped inside, she'd always know that a man like him had almost loved her once, and that she'd deserved every second of his affection.

She heard beeps on the other side of the wall as he disarmed the alarm, then the door opened and he stood framed in the light of the entryway.

He smiled, and it was so exquisite she almost burst into tears.

Wordlessly he wrapped his arms around her and held her firmly. She closed her eyes against his sternum and breathed deeply, losing herself in his scent, his warmth. She linked her hands at the small of his back and clung to his narrow waist.

For several minutes they simply stood in silence, their bodies pressed together. Kate luxuriated in the steady rise and fall of his chest, the softness of his cotton T-shirt stretched across hard muscle and harder bone, the slow thud of his athlete's heart.

If she had to pick a moment to stay in forever, she decided it would be this one. Life couldn't be better.

Until he put his finger under her chin, tipped her face to his and kissed her.

I love him. Awareness washed over her with the unstoppable, breath-stealing force of an ocean wave. Strip away all the external stuff, his career and her past and his money and her future, and the truth was bright and clear. She loved him. Oz the man. Oz the lover. Oz the best friend. She didn't care about any of the rest of it, the fame or the house or the car. She wanted him and him alone, more than she'd ever wanted anything.

But not caring about the material things didn't make them go away. Nor did wanting to be with him mean doing so wouldn't come with a price.

Reality settled heavily in the pit of her stomach as she leaned out of his embrace.

"We should shut the door. We're letting bugs in," she told him, trying to force lightheartedness into her tone.

He closed and locked the door after she preceded him inside. Then he reset the alarm, including the motion-sensing beams that ran across each side of the house.

The heat she'd absorbed from his skin dissipated as she followed him through the ground floor. Their physical separation brought back the emotional distance between them, and grim expectation tightened the space between her eyes. This wasn't going to be a fun, flippant, sexy reunion. Something still undefined was pulling them apart, and they had to talk about it before they lost all sight of each other.

"Are you hungry?" He started opening cabinets in the kitchen. She took a seat on one of the stools at the island.

"Not really. I had a late lunch."

"Same here. My stomach's still on Swedish time." He set a tub of hummus and a box of whole-wheat crackers on the island and took a seat across from hers.

"How's the jetlag?"

"The flight last night was delayed, which didn't help, but I'll be fine by tomorrow morning. How was the interview?" he asked, referring to the early-morning meeting she used to justify not seeing him when he arrived in Atlanta the night before.

"I think they'll make me an offer. The money's nowhere near what I was making at Peak Tactical, but it's a steady paycheck every month. No sales targets."

"Remind me what this one was for?"

"Another private-security company, but in dispatch." She wrinkled her nose. "I'm not sure it really maximizes my skill set, but then I'm not totally clear on what my skill set is."

"What about companies that advise businesses on security for their overseas operations? Like oil companies, mining companies, anyone sending employees somewhere unsafe. You'd be great at that."

"That's not a bad idea," she agreed. "I'll look into it."

He looked down at the island's surface. She braced herself.

"Speaking of career changes." He trailed his index finger along the grain in the granite. "I had a meeting in Stockholm. One of the clubs in Spain put an offer on the table. They want to buy me out of my contract with Atlanta in the winter transfer window. I'd start playing for them in January."

He dragged his eyes up to hers and she simply stared. She wasn't sure what she expected, but it wasn't this.

"Wow," she managed finally. "Is it a good offer?"

"Yes and no. The money is better, and the club is prestigious."

He paused. She prompted, "But?"

"But I'm pretty sure they want me as a backup, not a starter. They have one of the best left-backs in the world and he's not much older than me. Unless he got a serious injury, I'd probably only play a handful of times each season."

"And if he did get injured?"

"I'd start against some of the best teams in Europe, for one of the game's most legendary managers."

She exhaled. "Big decision."

He nodded.

"What are you going to do?"

"I'm not sure. I have time to think about it." He cleared his throat. "How would you feel about going with me?"

Shock swelled into disbelief, blacking out her thoughts like drawing a curtain over a window. "What?"

"I'm not asking for a decision tonight, obviously, but I thought I'd put it on the table."

"That's a big step, Oz."

"More like a leap between two buildings. I know." He shot her a feeble smile. "I've given this a lot of thought—it was a long flight. It would be easy to say let's just wait and see, that I wouldn't leave before Christmas anyway so we might as well give it until then to decide. And if you need that much time, fine. But I don't like ambiguity, so I'm putting this out there. If I go, I want you to come with me."

She wasn't sure how long she'd been shaking her head when she finally realized she was doing it. "This is insane. I came here thinking you were about to break up with me."

He frowned. "Why?"

"Because I didn't go to Stockholm. And then Emily—"

He reached across the table and put his hand over hers, warm and reassuring. "That's exactly why I'm saying this to you now. This probably sounds strange, but when you chose your family over me, and once I got over myself about it, I respected you more. Speaking to Emily confirmed what I already knew, that you're loyal and know the importance of family."

"That's also why it would be hard for me to move thousands of miles away from them. I've been so far away for so many years, and I'm only just getting settled back into their lives." She took a steeling breath. "This is what I wanted to tell you on Saturday night and didn't get the chance. I'm at a point in my life where I need to make my own decisions. Be independent. Do what I want, not what I'm told."

His expression faltered slightly, and she could sense him fighting not to shut down. "I'm not telling. I'm asking."

She balked, unsure how to answer, and then the piercing shriek of the alarm cut through the quiet house, sending her heart into her throat and her pulse into overdrive. Oz stared at her, wide-eyed, and she snapped into business mode.

"Your phone," she commanded. She jumped from the stool and armed herself with a knife from the block on the counter as he pulled his phone from his pocket to check the system-monitoring app she told him to install.

"Front beam," he called over the clanging alarm.

"Stay here," she instructed, but inevitably he followed her across the house to the front door. She peered out the windows on either side of the frame but couldn't see much.

"Maybe it's just a—"

The alarm automatically shut off at the end of its sixty-second cycle, plunging the house into sudden silence.

"Cat," Oz offered.

"Where's the patrol car? They should be here by now. And dispatch hasn't called you?"

His expression turned sheepish. "I may have had some strong words for Roland about Peak Tactical after they fired you. They lost the Skyline contract the same day. He's still going through the bids from new providers."

"So no one's coming."

He shook his head.

She swore under her breath and reached around him to disable the alarm so it wouldn't go off again when she opened the front door. Then she eased the door open and stepped outside, every one of her senses on high alert.

She'd barely made it to the edge of the front porch when she saw a shadow disappear around the side of the house.

"Call 9-1-1," she told Oz, adjusting her grip on the knife. Oz's face broadcast his oncoming protest and she shook her head firmly, hissing, "Just do it."

She heard him murmur into his phone as she slunk along the wall of the house, summoning years of military training. She breathed slowly, stilling the frantic beating of her heart, and focused her awareness on what seemed out of the ordinary.

The beams were set high enough not to be triggered by animals, and the shadow she saw was distinctly human. Someone was on the property who shouldn't be, and so help her, she was going to stop them from getting any closer.

She slipped around the corner of the house, freezing as she caught sight of a man hunched over and rummaging in a sports bag near the back door.

She flexed her fingers on the knife handle, shoved aside her fear and shouted, "Hands out of the bag and up where I can see them."

The man looked up in surprise, and although the hood of his sweatshirt was tightened around his face she recognized Wayne Seibert, the Citizens First leader who'd thrown road flares on the pitch.

"You son of a bitch," she seethed, self-control buckling under the weight of white-hot fury.

She lunged for him. He dropped the bag and jerked out of her reach. In the second it took her to regain her balance he sprinted past her. She pivoted, the knife slipping from her hand as she chased him around the corner of the house, sprinting as fast as she could.

She rounded the edge of the garage just in time to see Oz step out from the wall and into Wayne's path. They collided hard, chest to chest, then in a single motion Oz used his foot to destabilize the bigger man's ankles and pushed him over. Wayne landed on his back, the sound of the air leaving his lungs testament to the power of Oz's shove.

Kate leapt on the downed man, pinning his arms with her knees. He stared at her defiantly and she realized he was younger than she thought— young enough not to be the product of a hateful time, to have been raised in an America where diversity was embraced, celebrated, taught in school.

Young enough to know better.

His hood had slipped off, revealing reddish-brown hair that didn't yet have any of the gray in his beard. He wasn't bad-looking. Certainly wasn't a guy you'd glance at twice if you saw him loitering on the sidewalk. The hate hadn't marred his face, not yet anyway, and for an instant she almost felt sorry for him. Maybe something terrible happened to make him like this. Maybe he still had time to change.

Then his mouth twisted. "You're a disgrace to your country, sleeping with this sand-rat terrorist."

"I served my country for eight years. You're the disgrace." She kept her voice level, but her body started to tremble.

"And now you're fucking the same *hajis* you were sent out there to kill? You're right, you're not a disgrace, you're a traitor."

She hit him. Then she hit him again, and again, and again, and when her right hand stung she switched to her left, and then back to her right, bone meeting bone as she barely made out his grunts of pain over the roaring in her ears.

She wasn't hitting only Wayne. She brought her fist down into the faces of every one of those men in Saudi Arabia, every man she regretted sleeping with, every commanding officer who hadn't taken her seriously, finally silencing their jeers and lowering their pointed fingers. He was her disappointment. Her dishonor. Her mistakes, her misdirection. Her catastrophic attempt to build her life after the army.

He was her failure, and she hit him as hard as she could.

A firm grip stopped her wrist mid-swing. Oz wrapped his arm around her chest and pulled her to her feet. She dived toward Wayne but Oz held her tightly, both hands locked on her waist.

"He'll get away," she protested.

"The police are coming."

At his words she registered the sound of sirens. Wayne rolled over to his stomach so she couldn't see the damage she'd done, but if the pain in her hands was any indication, it was bad, and she wasn't sorry. She'd do it again to protect Oz. She'd do it to anyone, any time, to keep him safe.

After a few seconds Wayne got to his feet and staggered toward the edge of the lawn, where he was met by three patrol cars screeching to a halt. She sagged against Oz as uniformed cops took him into custody. Two others swept the property, and she recovered enough coherence to tell them about the sports bag and the kitchen knife behind the house. The commotion prompted neighbors in several houses to emerge onto their front steps or lean out open windows. It would be only a matter of time before the press showed up, too.

An unmarked car joined the others at the curb and Detective Hegarty stepped out, his expression businesslike. He peered at Wayne, now seated in the back of one of the police cars, and then crossed the lawn to where they stood.

"What happened to Seibert's face?" he asked by way of greeting.

"I hit him," Oz said quickly. "I lost my temper, and I hit him."

Kate rolled her eyes. "For God's sake, Oz, you're a Muslim on a green card. Don't be an idiot." She turned to the detective. "*I* hit him, and if he wants to press charges, we'll see if he can find a jury in the state of Georgia willing to convict a female combat veteran. Here, take a picture of my knuckles."

She held out her hands, but before the detective could reply two officers appeared from behind the house. One of them angled the sports bag so they could see its contents.

"Another pig head," he explained.

"Good. Hopefully there's something on the bag that can tie it to the previous one, then we can get him on breaking and entering." He thanked the two officers, then looked between her and Oz.

"I'm sorry to hear Seibert attacked you, Kate," he said carefully. "But of course I'm glad your military training meant you could adequately act in self-defense."

She nodded. "Me, too."

"We'll take your statements, but from appearances this looks clear-cut. And tossing in the bail violation means Seibert will be behind bars until his trial. Citizens First is in total disarray, so with any luck this should be the end of your troubles, Mr. Terim."

"I hope so," he said quietly, looking at her with a significance she didn't understand. She raised her brows in question but Detective Hegarty's partner arrived. As they split up to give their statements she cast a glance at Oz over her shoulder, but his back was turned, his posture unreadable.

She thought of his assertion the first time they met. *I'm a pacifist.* She wondered whether this pacifist still wanted to traipse around Europe with a woman who'd just beaten a man's face to a bloody mess.

This was the end, she concluded sadly as she followed Detective Hegarty around the corner to make her statement. She still had too much baggage from the army, from Saudi Arabia, from everything she'd said and done since the day she left Jasper almost ten years earlier. She couldn't ask him to help her carry it, and she couldn't fall into another situation where all the major decisions were made for her.

It was time to stand tall and sort out her life.

It was time to let Oz go.

* * * *

"And the knife?"

"She picked it up in the kitchen as soon as the beams went off. She must've dropped it when she caught Seibert behind the house, because I didn't see it again. She definitely didn't use it on him, if that's what you're asking."

"Just making sure the details line up." The detective scanned the page in his notebook from top to bottom, then flipped it shut. "That's all I need. Call me if you remember anything else."

"Will do." Oz put the detective's card in his back pocket and showed him out the front door, careful to stay out of sight of the photographers huddled at the curb. Kate was still with Detective Hegarty in the backyard so he moved into the kitchen, put the untouched hummus and crackers away, and took a seat at the island.

It had been only half an hour since the beams went off but it felt like half a day. He'd left his phone on the counter and it blinked frantically with missed calls and unread messages. He scrolled through, discovering that the incident at his house was blowing up the neighborhood block-watch group. More problematically, it seemed one of the members had leaked content to the press. Social media was full of speculation that he'd been targeted by everything from a suicide bomber to the Ku Klux Klan.

He got halfway through a panicked voicemail from Roland before deleting it and calling him. Roland answered on the first ring. Oz quickly talked him down and explained the situation. They hung up so Roland could brief the press team and start to mitigate the damage of the leaked messages.

He fired off reassuring messages to his family, all asleep given the time difference, then turned his phone facedown and gazed at the door to the backyard, wondering how much longer Detective Hegarty would keep Kate.

He couldn't wait to see her. In principle he abhorred violence but seeing her pummel that guy sent a thrill shuddering through him. His uncle's wife hadn't even called when Erdem died. Kate was prepared to take a criminal assault charge to protect him.

He loved her. Improbable, impractical, but the clearest truth he'd ever known. He had to tell her. He would tell her, although the idea scared him to death. You couldn't un-speak something like this, couldn't take it back, but he couldn't let that stop him. He needed her to know. What she chose to do afterward, well, that was up to her.

Car doors slammed outside, followed by the sounds of engines starting up and receding. He heard the front door open and close, and the beep of the alarm being set. Then Kate walked into the kitchen, her face drawn with stress and exhaustion.

"The police are gone. There are still a few photographers outside but they seem to be drifting off, too."

He stood, motioning her into his arms. "Come here."

She obeyed, her slim form fitting into his embrace like their bodies had been designed to slot together. He closed his eyes as he pressed his cheek against the top of her head. The woman he held was so brave, so tough, and then by turns so soft and vulnerable. He wanted to be the man she always leaned on. The one she let in. The one she kept close.

Her breathing hitched. He looked down and realized she was crying. Silent, forcefully stifled sobs.

"It's okay," he soothed, sweeping his thumbs over her cheeks to wipe away her tears. "You heard the detective. It's all over now."

She stepped away from him, wrapping her arms around herself as she nodded to the island. "Let's sit."

He resumed his seat, and when he met Kate's gaze again her eyes were dry and shuttered, her face set in a determined expression.

He arched a brow. "What?"

"I can't move to Spain," she said flatly.

He raised his palm to stop her. "First, we're not making any decisions tonight. Not that we were in a position to do so anyway, but especially not now. Second—and we can go into all of this later—I've thought a lot about how we could make this work, not just for you, but for your family. You did say you took Spanish in school, and if we had enough notice we could get you into a language class before we go. There are quite a few British players at the club, too, so you wouldn't be totally isolated among the plus-ones. We'd make a schedule to fly your family out and for you to fly home to see them, so there's never any uncertainty. Maybe Dallas could even spend—"

"Oz." She silenced him with a firm voice. "I'm not moving to Spain. I'm moving home to Jasper."

He blinked, not sure he'd understood. "Why? Since when?"

"It's something I have to do," she replied testily, then briefly closed her eyes. When she spoke again her tone had softened. "I was so ready to leave the military. I was tired of being told where to live, where to go and how to get there. I was excited to take control of my life, but when I got to Saudi I realized I was still taking orders. I was told how to dress, where to be at what time—the only things that changed were who did the telling and the numbers in my bank account."

"I would never tell you what to do. All I meant was—"

She shook her head. "I can't go from one uniform to another, from

Sergeant Mitchell to a pro athlete's girlfriend. I have to stand on my own two feet. Figure out who I am and what I really want."

Uneasy comprehension cooled his blood. "What are you saying?"

"I want you to know this has nothing to do with you. This is all my problem, my issue. I have to work it out before I can be a good partner to anyone."

His chest tightened. He'd used versions of the same break-up line so many times, and now it came back to rip out his heart when it was at its most vulnerable.

He flattened his palm on the granite, fighting to keep his composure. "Is there anything I can do to change your mind?"

"No," she said, her expression hard and unmovable. He swallowed hard, absorbing the blow like any good defender would. His job on the pitch was to take the hits and stay on his feet. He focused on doing the same now, righting his tilting thoughts, rooting himself in the moment no matter how much it hurt.

"I'm sorry about...what we did," she continued, a betraying waver in the words. "I know you waited a long time. I didn't know I would feel this way or I never would have—"

"Made love to me?" he demanded, anger readily pouring in to replace sorrow. "Let me make that commitment to you knowing full well you couldn't promise to return it? You should be sorry. That's a hell of a cynical way to treat someone who cares about you."

"I know," she agreed, and too late he understood that she wanted him to hate her. She wanted him to kick her out, his fury letting her off the hook.

"You can't stand to be loved, can you?" he realized aloud.

Her attention sharpened but she said nothing.

"This finding-yourself line is bullshit and you know it," he spat, growing more agitated by the second. "I know exactly who you are. You're a coward. You're terrified that I chose you because you're smart and strong and sexy, which means there's no other you to discover. She's been here all the time. And if I love you, it makes it awfully hard for you not to love yourself. You'd have to let go of all your failures and look forward, and that's unfamiliar territory. Am I right?"

Her silent, unwavering glare told him he was, as clearly as if she'd said the words out loud.

"I'm leaving," she said tightly, slinging her bag over her shoulder.

"Of course you are." He pushed off the stool so hard it rocked on its legs, then he followed her to the front door. "Keep running, Kate. You ran to the military, then you ran away from it, and now you're running from me. Maybe you're the exception—maybe you can run forever. But if you ask me, you're going to catch up with yourself eventually, and then you'll have to face who you are—who you've always been. I could've been at your side, but if you'd rather go it alone, I won't stop you."

She punched the code into the alarm panel, her finger shaking but her shoulders stiff.

"Goodbye, Oz." Her voice was icy and unyielding. He set his jaw, waiting for her to see sense, waiting for the moment when she realized she was making the mistake of her life.

Instead she slammed the door behind her. After a few seconds he heard her car start, then the brakes squealing as she spun backward out of the driveway.

She was gone.

He pressed his back against the door, rage and regret and stomach-twisting despair warring within him.

He shouted the filthiest word he knew from his three languages. It rang back at him, echoing around his impeccable, empty house.

Chapter 22

Oz stuck out his hand. "Ready?"

Dallas beamed up at him, a cherubic version of her mother. "Ready."

She held his hand and together they filed out of the tunnel with the rest of the Skyline lineup. Most of the players were escorted by their own children, or nieces or nephews or cousins.

Oz was pretty sure he was the only one who'd brought his ex-girlfriend's niece to the Family Day match against San Diego FC at King Stadium.

But he'd suggested it on the trip back from Boston and he wasn't in the business of breaking a six-year-old's heart, no matter how thoroughly her aunt had crushed his.

He hadn't spoken to Kate in the weeks since she'd shut the door on his fantasies of their future together. He'd bounced between disbelief, despair, and bizarre optimism on a daily, sometimes even hourly, basis. She'll come back, he'd insisted to himself in the pitch-black hours when his heartbeat was the only sound in the four walls of his house. She'll realize she's made a mistake—not about whether or not to move to Spain, but whether or not to be with him. After all, he was the one who loved the very person she claimed she was looking for. She just needed this, er, *trial separation* to understand that she was who she was, that she was worthy of respect and affection, and that he was exactly the right man to give her the stability and support she craved.

Hours became days, became weeks. He'd pushed himself harder and harder in training, enduring physical knocks to numb the emotional ones, excelling on the pitch to counteract the disappointments off it. Yet Kate's absence loomed ever larger, growing more painful as it seemed more and more permanent.

The morning of the Family Day match had dawned bright and clear.

Atlanta was in the throes of an unusual cool front, and the early-September afternoon suggested autumn was well and truly on its way. A refreshing breeze whispered down the tunnel as the players lined up beside their escorts and Dallas clung trustingly to his hand. The audience warmly applauded the appearance of the children and the players.

He swept his gaze across the home fans in the low-row seats, then his vision snagged.

Kate sat in the third row, her smile subdued, eyes concealed by dark sunglasses.

He registered her presence with all the force of a slap across the face. To some extent he figured she'd be here, came close to expecting it, but equally wouldn't have been surprised if she sent her mother and Emily and left her ticket unused.

He wrenched his gaze away and stared straight ahead, trying to keep his expression impassive. Did this mean something? Probably not. Definitely not. If she had something to say she would've called him.

He slipped into his professional focus like putting on a pair of noise-cancelling headphones. For the next two hours he would think only about the match. Mentally he closed a steel door in front of his swirling emotions, pushing them into a remote corner of his brain until the clanging cacophony barely registered as a distant echo.

When Dallas dropped his hand and skipped off the pitch with the rest of the children, she was just another kid. When he scanned the crowd again it was just an anonymous blur of faces.

He took his position on the left side as the announcer on the Jumbotron boomed through the two teams' rosters. Blocking out everything—the noise, the movement, the sun warming the back of his neck—he cupped his hands in front of him, closed his eyes, lowered his face and recited from the Qur'an.

When he finished he pressed his palms over his face, then dropped them and opened his eyes.

Game time.

Over the next hour and a half Oz played some of the best soccer of his life. His speed was unmatched, he saw angles and opportunities with mathematical precision, and San Diego's tricky, clever wingers couldn't get around him. At halftime Atlanta was one-nil up and Roland mentioned his performance in his dressing-room speech, encouraging Skyline's forwards to take advantage of their excellent coverage at the back.

Oz clung to his mental focus as they began the second half, knowing full well who was in the stands and not daring to let his thoughts drift anywhere near her. The whistle blew and he shot into motion again, following the midfield's more aggressive push into San Diego's half, then accelerating at intervals to track back as San Diego counterattacked.

San Diego had a series of near misses as twenty-one men clustered around Skyline's goal. Paulo blocked a dangerous chance and San Diego's right-back caught it on the rebound, toeing a quick, sharp shot at the keeper. Oz read its trajectory before he could even register the ball was in the air. He leapt into its path and headed it out of the way, noticing Rio just in time to spin it in his teammate's direction.

The Chilean winger controlled the ball out of the air with characteristic artistry, slowing it from his chest to his knees to his toes. Then he was off, dribbling past two San Diego players with barely a glance at either one of them.

Oz tore after him, fully aware that the two of them vied for fastest on the team—and that Deon's size and power made him slow, so he was unlikely to reach their opponent's goal in time to create anything from Rio's run.

Rio charged down the left-hand channel in an attempt to evade the San Diego defenders hot on his heels. Oz stayed straight, his gaze clicking between his teammate and the opposing goalkeeper, who already slapped his gloves together in anticipation.

With San Diego's defenders closing in and his angle on goal becoming increasingly unusable, Rio looked up. Oz met his gaze and Rio passed, the ball floating in a perfect, bending arc.

Oz took one last look at the keeper while the ball was airborne. The man was shouting something, full of adrenaline and expectation, but Oz couldn't hear him—he couldn't hear anything except the slight whistle of the ball slicing through the clear afternoon.

He linked his fingers behind his back as his feet left the ground. The top of his head connected with the ball. It flew over the keeper's shoulder and slapped into the back of the net.

Oz's clinical focus dissolved as he shouted his delight. He grabbed the little Chilean tightly as they jumped up and down together, his chest full to bursting with pride. The fans' cheers were deafening as the rest of their teammates caught up to them and joined in the celebration, high-fiving and slapping backs and punching the air in excitement.

Play resumed and they broke up, jogging back toward the center line as the Skyline fans sang "We're Off to See the Wizard." Still grinning, Oz veered toward the manager's box as Roland gestured him over.

"You're so far out of position it's unbelievable. You're a defender, remember?" his manager shouted through cupped hands, but his smile betrayed him.

Oz gave Roland a thumbs-up, then did what he'd resisted since the first whistle blew. He let his gaze drift to Kate's seat.

He didn't expect much. A smile would've been enough. Maybe even a glimpse of her applauding, or nodding encouragement. He'd never needed anyone's approval, but suddenly he wanted hers, and he wanted it desperately.

Her seat was empty.

The sight of the brick-red seatback where she should've been hurt more than a hard ball to the chest. He didn't pause to see whether Emily was there, or Dallas, or Kate's mom—he looked away so quickly it made him dizzy. His legs felt heavy as he ran into Skyline's half, his lungs short on oxygen.

Maybe he would go to Spain after all, he considered, trying to tug up the emotional shields that had served him so well until seconds earlier. Maybe he would get as far away from here—from *her*—as he could.

* * * *

"Dallas, honey, the cutlery needs to stay here, okay? These don't belong to us, they belong to the soccer team." Kate's face burned as she extracted a handful of forks, spoons and knives from Dallas's pink backpack and subtly tried to shove them back into place on the buffet table.

"But Grandma takes knives from the hot wings place," her niece protested. Kate shot her mother a sharp glance.

"I like their steak knives," her mom replied mildly, passing her wine glass to the bartender for a refill.

The match had ended almost an hour ago but the players were still drifting into the Family Day party. Three of the stadium's corporate hospitality suites had been combined to form a space with enough room for a bar and a buffet, with plenty of seating to watch the match at one end and kids' activities at the other. Bored by halftime, Emily insisted they move from their amazing pitch-side seats to the suite during the break. Kate had good intentions of heading back down but they never came to fruition. As a result she'd missed Oz's goal, and as time wore on and he remained absent, she wondered whether she'd missed her last opportunity to speak to him, too.

Not that she had anything in particular to say. She had plenty she wanted to say—how much she'd missed him these last few weeks, how uncertain she was about what she'd said the last time they were together, and that maybe he was right and the only version of herself she needed to find was the one in his arms—but nothing she *would* say.

Because he was right. She was a coward, to the extent that she was afraid he'd already moved on and any capitulation on her part would only open her up to bigger heartbreak.

This Family Day escapade would certainly be simpler if he didn't show up. Maybe it was for the best, she concluded, distractedly removing one of the flower arrangements from Dallas's hands.

Then a hush swept over the room, followed by a short burst of applause. She didn't need to look up to know who'd arrived. It could only be Atlanta Skyline's man of the match, Oz Terim.

"Katie. That's him. He's here, Katie." Her mother repeated her name in a raspy stage whisper.

"Don't make a scene," she muttered between clenched teeth. "He'll come over when he's ready."

"He's much better looking in person, I can tell you that much. Needs a haircut, though. Oh, crap, Katie, he's coming." Her mom dug around in her enormous purse and produced a bottle of perfume, which she spritzed at Kate before she could get out of range.

She wrinkled her nose and batted at the air around her. "Mom, gross, now I smell like old lady."

"Hi."

Kate spun at the sound of his voice, her heart rate already tripling in awareness of his presence. Oz stood before her, long and lean, hands in his pockets. He was so freshly showered she could smell his shampoo and it took everything she had not to fall against his hard body and let him catch her.

She replied, "Hi."

"How are you?"

"Fine. How are you?"

"Good."

She couldn't read his expression fully, but she detected a hint of ice, a touch of detachment. With their Oscar-worthy dialogue running dry, Kate glanced around for inspiration. Instead she found her mother, grinning like a fool behind her newly emptied wine glass.

"Oh, this is my mom. Joanne. Mom, this is Oz."

"Pleasure." Oz extended his hand to her mom, who responded by leaning up and kissing him on both cheeks.

"*Guten Tag*," she drawled, her added wink only intensifying the bewilderment in Oz's expression.

"Great, thanks Mom." Kate inserted herself between the two of them and guided him toward an empty spot by the window. "And you met Dallas earlier. She's running around somewhere with the other kids. Probably convincing them to give her all their goodie bags."

"And your sister? Did she make it?"

"She sure did." Kate nodded to one of the sofas, where her sister was half in Glynn's lap, one leg draped over his as she smiled at him adoringly. "That's Emily. She pounced on him like a tiger as soon as we walked into the room. Didn't even know he knew you. I tried to rescue him but he seemed pretty content."

"Wow. I didn't see that coming." Oz stared at his friend, who trailed a finger down Emily's bare arm.

"I'm sure he didn't, either. Anyway." She shrugged. "Leave it to the Mitchells to put the NC-17 in a G-rated event."

Oz took in the scene around him, then turned back to her with a hint of a smile. When he spoke again his voice was for her ears only. "How've you been?"

"Okay, I guess. Thanks for inviting us today. And for still speaking to me."

"Why wouldn't I speak to you?" he asked softly.

"You know why."

"Tell me."

She inhaled slowly. "Because I hurt you. And I took something you can't ever get back."

"You didn't take anything I didn't give you," he muttered, his bitterness palpable. He straightened. "How's the job hunt?"

"Slow. I'll be out of my apartment in two weeks, so I'm slowly moving stuff to Jasper. Had a couple of interviews. Nothing I'm too excited about. Actually, I've been thinking about going for a commercial truck-driving license. Doing that for a year or two."

He didn't even try to hide that he thought that was a terrible idea. "Why?"

"I like driving." *And it'll keep me away from everyone, give me time to sort through whatever the hell's going on inside of me. Especially that ache in my stomach every time I think of you.*

"You're still set on moving out of Atlanta, then."

She moved on. "Any more trouble from Citizens First?"

He shook his head. "Apparently they've splintered into nothing, at least on the East Coast. Wayne Seibert is in jail, awaiting trial."

"Did Roland find someone to replace Peak Tactical?"

"Yeah, some guys who drive around in Jeeps wearing combat boots. The neighborhood association was so impressed, now most of the houses on the street have men in camouflage pants racing to their front door every time a cat sets off the beams."

She smiled. "I think I know which company you're talking about.

They're good. Make Peak Tactical look like a bunch of suits."

"I think those were the exact words that sold Roland." His expression grew serious as he gestured her away from the buffet table. "I'm still getting those Ausonius comments," he confided in a low voice.

She knew. She scrolled through the comments on his social-media posts almost hourly, quietly monitoring the content for anything alarming—and maybe checking to see whether he responded to any of the more flirtatious messages. Of course he didn't, and although in general the level of ire had dropped far below what it was when they met, each Ausonius comment registered grimly in her mind.

"I've seen them," she admitted. "Does the new security company know?"

"They do, but there doesn't seem to be anything anyone can do."

She nodded. "Peak Tactical's cyber-security guy said as much. I thought maybe a better resourced company would have a solution."

"Evidently not."

They lapsed into thoughtful silence, and after a couple of seconds Kate realized she should wrap up their discussion, drag her mom and niece away from whatever trouble they'd managed to cause in the last five minutes and let Oz move on to speak to other people. To let him move on altogether.

But she didn't want to.

She had more time-wasting small talk on the tip of her tongue when he asked her bluntly, "Do you want to see the boot room?"

"The what?"

"Where all the players' boots are stored. We have a real one downstairs near the locker room, but there's a mini one down the hall."

"Why? So the VIPs can get the real behind-the-scenes stadium experience?"

"And buy wildly overpriced replica pairs, mostly."

"Got it."

"Follow me." He led her through the suite to the door, moving quickly so no one could catch them in conversation. She had to hasten her steps to keep up on the route down the hallway, trailing behind him into a deep alcove. Boot Room announced itself in big red letters, below which a series of hooks, labeled with players' numbers, displayed soccer cleats hung at artful angles.

She drifted toward the pair under number eighteen. "So these are yours."

She glanced at Oz over her shoulder. His expression showed intent so hot, so unyielding that she couldn't stop herself. She reached for his hand and held it tightly.

He pushed her against the wall, sending boots tumbling to the floor as he pinned her body in place with his own. His arousal dug into her abdomen as he raised his palms to her cheeks and kissed her, hard and demanding—everything she'd been missing for these long weeks.

She knew she shouldn't but she kissed him back, tried to tell him with her mouth, her tongue, what she couldn't put into words. That she wanted to be with him, but she was scared, because what she felt for him was too strong, too unshakeable.

That she loved him.

Footsteps echoed down the hall and he pulled away with such force she stumbled and knocked another two pairs of shoes to the floor.

"I'm sorry," he whispered, scooping up boots and slinging them onto hooks.

"It's fine. You're fine." She stood for a second, dazed, then recovered enough to help him replace the boots as the footsteps grew louder.

"Post-match adrenaline. My fault."

She forced a dismissive smile, getting the last shoe into place as a dad with two daughters in tow arrived. The girls squealed in excitement when they recognized Oz, immediately producing match programs for him to sign.

Kate stepped aside while Oz took photos with his young fans, then decided this was her opportunity. She would slip out of the moment—out of his life—with no more unrestrainable lust, no awkward goodbye.

She'd already taken three steps backward when she said, "Oz, I'm going, but great match today and thanks for inviting us."

She managed only half a turn before he called her back.

"Wait—there's something I want to ask you."

She chewed her lower lip as she waited for him to finish with the kids. Was he going to ask her if they could give it another shot? What was her answer?

Nothing had changed since she'd left his house a few weeks earlier. She hadn't miraculously discovered her self-reliance or had an existential awakening. She missed him, but she was still confused and uncertain and isolated, unable to see how anyone else could understand her when she had so little understanding of herself.

Could she offer him what he wanted? Trust. Partnership. Uncompromising honesty.

Maybe.

But maybe not.

Oz left his fans to study the boots and moved beside her, leading them back to the suite.

"When are you out of your apartment?" he asked.

"Next Sunday."

"On Saturday I'm speaking at this interfaith event at the Peace Institute, if you're not busy."

"You want me to come?"

"Only if you want to." His keen expression belied his casual tone. "I thought you might find it interesting, given what we went through with Citizens First."

"I don't know. Is it really a good idea for us to—"

"Please."

She sighed. "Send me the details."

"I will," he promised, already being flagged down by other fans as they reentered the Family Day party. "It was good to see you."

"You too," she replied faintly, watching him move away into the crowd. She raised her fingers to her lips, remembering the pressure of his mouth, the suddenness of his grasp.

She shook her head and set her shoulders, bee-lining for her mother, who still hovered beside the bar.

"Pack it up, we're out of here," Kate announced.

Her mother smirked and accepted a refilled glass of wine from the bartender. "Good luck. Dallas is pinning the tail on the soccer player and Emily's practically marching down the aisle with that guy. Have a beer and relax. These are your people."

"They're really not," she disagreed, but accepted a beer and found a seat on a couch beside her mother.

"They are," her mother insisted. "Look around you. This is where you belong—in this fancy stadium, with these fancy people, on the arm of that sexy guy."

Kate rolled her eyes to look at her mother, but found the older woman's expression uncharacteristically serious.

"I don't know why you want to come back to Jasper, Katie," she said softly. "We're all so proud of you for leaving in the first place. We miss you, sure, but more than anything we want you to be happy. And being with Oz was the happiest I'd ever seen you."

Kate lifted a shoulder. "Yeah, well, sometimes things don't work out."

"Sometimes they don't," her mom agreed. "But that doesn't mean you should quit trying to fix them."

"Nobody's quitting, Mama. Our lives are headed in completely opposite directions. No point in getting stretched tighter and tighter between the two until they get so far apart we can't see each other."

"Excuse me, I didn't realize you had the whole rest of your life mapped out already. Where exactly do you plan to end up?"

"I don't know, but it doesn't matter. It'll be far away from wherever he is."

Her mom narrowed her eyes. "Be specific."

Kate lowered her voice to a whisper. "Like he might be moving to a club in Spain. Is that far enough for you?"

"Hell no," her mom exclaimed. "You been to two different warzones and you're going to split up with him over Spain? Katie, listen to me. Don't lose this man. You trust him, he makes you happy, and he looks at you like you're the only woman on the planet. Your path isn't pointed anywhere it can't meet up with his."

"Now we really are leaving," Kate shot back, bolting to her feet and gathering up their possessions.

"Whatever," her mom slurred, disregarding her as usual.

"Get Emily and Dallas. I'll meet you in the car."

Kate jerked her purse onto her shoulder and stomped out of the room, not daring to look back for a last glimpse of Oz. She wouldn't have seen him anyway—her mother's words had raised hot, blinding tears in her eyes.

She was right. Oz was such a good man—too good. How would she ever live up to him?

She shoved on her sunglasses despite the indoor lighting and mercilessly punched the elevator button to descend to the parking lot.

She needed space to breathe. Time to think. Some sense of purpose around which to align her whole goddamn life.

More than anything, she needed him.

Chapter 23

Kate accepted a program from a smiling woman in a *hijab* and proceeded into the Peace Institute's auditorium. Rows of seats faced a stage set with a podium, behind which a series of flags hung on poles. The room had a dry, stained-wood scent that reminded her of a museum.

With ten minutes before the start of the event the room was already half full, and she'd passed through a large crowd lingering in the lobby. She suspected every seat would be taken soon and selected one quickly, on the center aisle a few rows back from the stage.

She surveyed the people around her with the same intense but largely unconscious instinct that had her locating exits every time she entered a room, a byproduct of years of combat-honed vigilance. Those nearest her reflected the audience more generally, which was one of the most diverse she could remember being part of. A couple of Orthodox Jews, several women wearing *hijabs*, a black woman wearing a West African-style dress, and a handful of white people ranging from a woman with long, beaded dreadlocks to the man directly in front of her who sported a crew cut and a hunting-camouflage jacket.

Her attention snagged on him for a second, but not for any reason she could articulate. She took in his broad shoulders, his face tilted down, his thumbs tapping at his phone.

She filed her reaction to his presence in the back of her mind and opened the program. In recognition of the Eid al-Adha holiday, the event focused on opening up dialogues about Islam in all its forms. The institute's director would give the opening address, followed by a keynote speaker she hadn't heard of—an Emory professor originally from Pakistan. In fact she hadn't heard of any of the names on the list, except the third one—Özkan Terim, presenting a speech entitled "Muslims in the Media: When Private Faith

Becomes Public Discourse."

She closed the program and pulled out her phone, distractedly scrolling through Facebook as she rehearsed, for the millionth time, the speech she'd prepared for this afternoon. It wouldn't be as insightful or academic as any of those delivered on the stage, but as far as she was concerned it was by far the most important.

She'd brushed off her mother's words at Family Day that afternoon, but in the week since they'd echoed louder and louder in her thoughts. For the first time in, well, maybe her entire life, she had to admit her mom was right. She couldn't see the future any more than Oz could, yet he'd been willing to gamble on their potential to meet it together.

Then, on Thursday night, she was sorting through her closet trying to figure out what she could donate so her clothes would fit into the tiny dresser earmarked for her in Jasper. She dug out the plain, black clutch she'd bought for her senior prom and used for every formal event she'd attended since. She'd put it in the donation pile—she wasn't likely to attend a black-tie event anytime soon—then picked it up again and opened the clasp to check she hadn't left anything inside.

A photograph was tucked in the lining. She unfolded it, then sat back to study the image.

It was the formal photo of her prom group, taken when they arrived at the event, then printed and handed back as they left. She'd gone with three other couples, and the eight of them stood in an alternating boy-girl line, uncomfortably pressed together to fit into the frame.

Something struck her as she looked at the photo. Not the fates of the other people with her, or the ill-advised early-millennium fashion, or even a pang of regret that she'd lost her virginity to the spiky-haired boy with his arm around her shoulder despite his refusal to commit to being her boyfriend.

Instead she focused on herself, the faraway look in teenage Kate's eyes. On that warm spring evening she had one foot out the door. She'd met with the Army recruiter, turned in most of her final high-school assignments, and part of her was already driving past the city limits without a glance over her shoulder. Senior prom was a formality, a box to tick, a line to draw across the page to end this chapter and open the next one.

As Kate sat on the floor of her apartment she imagined telling that eighteen-year-old that one day she'd have the chance to travel to Spain with a smart, sexy pro athlete who thought she was smart and sexy, too.

Her teenage self wouldn't have been surprised, she realized with a jolt. She was confident, determined, certain her life held untold adventures waiting just around the next corner.

Over the next couple of days Kate mused over where she'd lost that irrepressible, optimistic eighteen-year-old girl. Maybe it was during her first deployment—it took all of Kate's energy to keep looking forward, to stay alive from one minute to the next. Maybe that girl had slipped off to the side.

Maybe they'd lost track of each other in one of the bedrooms where she'd spent an unsatisfying, purposeless night with a man who didn't want her enough for it to matter. Maybe that girl eased out of the room while Kate stared at the ceiling, wondering why she'd done this again.

Or maybe they still held hands when Kate went to Saudi Arabia. Maybe their grip had loosened but not disconnected. Maybe that girl was yanked away once and for all by the angry mob, her flame doused by their anger, her voice lost amid their shouts.

Kate barely slept the night before the Peace Institute event. She lay in bed and dug deep into her memories, trying to remember how it felt to be eighteen years old and full of hope. To be open and willing and wide-eyed. To be ready to catch whatever life threw at her. Firm on her own two feet.

She wasn't quite there yet, but as she tapped the screen to pull up Oz's picture in the contacts on her phone, she knew how to get back.

Of course she might be too late, but she had to try. She had to tell him how she felt. She would tell him she loved him, and pray that was enough—not only to get him back, but to reopen the heart she'd closed so long ago.

The auditorium was so full people stood at the back, and there was a flurry of activity as the staff members carried in chairs and lined them against the wall. Grateful she'd gotten her seat when she had, Kate flicked through Oz's various social-media accounts, automatically scrolling through the comments.

As she watched, the feed updated with a new comment. *Ausonius 70.*

Her jaw tightened as she tapped to another account. She refreshed the comments. There, at the top: *Ausonius 70.*

She wasn't sure whether it was intuition or sheer luck, but something prompted her to look at the man seated in front of her. His head was bent over his phone, his thumb busy.

She opened another account, scrolled to the comments. The man in front of her stopped typing, put his phone away. She refreshed the page.

New comment. *Ausonius 70.* Time-stamped one second earlier.

It could be coincidence, but her instincts screamed otherwise. Every atom went on high alert and she perched on the edge of her seat, eyes wide, unwilling to blink in case she missed something.

Did she have enough reason to act? She imagined the 911 dispatcher laughing her off the phone as she explained the emergency. *Well, I saw this guy typing on his phone and...*

Doubt fought her hunch as she looked more closely at the man. She put him in his mid-forties, his brutally shaven blond hair showing wide patches of gray at the temples. He wore jeans and unremarkable sneakers, and hadn't brought a bag or satchel as far as she could see. The hunting jacket seemed unnecessary given the hot weather, but then it wasn't unusual for people to bring layers to air-conditioned venues like this one.

The audience applauded to welcome the speakers as they filed onstage and took seats along the back, but she was so buried in her thoughts she barely noticed. She would be no better than Citizens First if she falsely accused this man. Who said white guys in their mid-forties who wore hunting camo couldn't be interested in a scholarly event about Islam? Probably the same people who insisted all Muslims were hateful fundamentalists.

But she couldn't shake the nagging sense that she was dead right. That the man seated in front of her was the one they'd been looking for all along, and he was here to cause serious trouble.

She watched Oz ease into the chair on the stage. In black trousers, a snug blue button-down and a gray blazer, he looked every inch the young academic he could've been—although the loafers-without-socks look gave away his celebrity, as few normal men would dare it. He hadn't seen her, she didn't think, his arms crossed patiently across his chest. As always he looked calm, cool and slightly aloof, and a rush of anger heated her nerve endings as she thought of anyone trying to hurt him.

Her gut had gotten her out of plenty of scrapes during deployments. She couldn't mistrust it now, with the stakes higher than ever.

As the director of the institute took his place at the podium and began his address, she scrolled through her contacts to Detective Hegarty's number. Deciding a call would be too urgent a reaction given the lack of evidence, she began tapping out a lengthy text message explaining the situation, admitting it might all be paranoia but wanted him to be aware regardless.

She wasn't listening to a word the director said in his pleasant, resonant voice, but a rustle in the seat in front of her snapped her attention up from her phone. The man slipped out of his jacket, revealing a white button-down shirt underneath. She could see the outline of the short-sleeve T-shirt he wore underneath and the faint suggestion of writing on the back, but when he leaned backward the chair obscured whatever was printed on the T-shirt.

She returned her gaze to her phone, quickly reviewing the message before hitting send. Then she tried to listen to the director's speech, glancing between the podium and the man in front of her. After a few minutes her phone buzzed in her hand. She opened the message from Detective Hegarty.

I trust your instinct. Keep your eyes on him. I'm on my way.

For a moment she sagged in her chair, drained with relief that she wasn't losing her mind. Then she snapped to attention and did as she was told. She watched the man like everything depended on it—hell, maybe it did. And although the man did nothing more sinister than scratch his nose during the director's speech, her inner alarm bells clanged louder and louder.

He appeared to listen attentively, but he showed no reactions. He didn't smile at the director's jokes or nod along with everyone else when the speech became solemn. Though fairly confident he wasn't a suicide bomber—she'd met a few in her time and he didn't have that air, plus there was no way he could sneak anything under such a thin shirt—she didn't like the way his jacket sat bunched around him instead of pooling on the seat, as if something stiff inside one of the inner pockets kept it propped up. Quickly she checked her phone—no more Ausonius comments since he'd put his away. So while the timing might have been a coincidence, nothing proved he *hadn't* been posting them, either.

Suddenly the man's posture stiffened. Kate bolted to alertness, watching him keenly.

Distantly she heard the director introducing Oz. "And for those of you who aren't soccer fans, you may have seen his occasional contributions to our quarterly journal, most recently an editorial on progressive Islam in our winter edition. Without further ado, let me welcome a pillar of our interfaith community, Özkan Terim."

Applause warmed the room as Oz stood, shook the director's hand, and took his place at the podium. Every one of Kate's senses focused so intently on the man in front of her that she didn't hear a word Oz said. The man had visibly tensed, and began unbuttoning the white shirt he wore over his T-shirt.

Her heart pounding, she inched to the edge of her seat, craning her neck to look over his shoulder. He finished with the buttons and shucked the shirt off his shoulders, but sat back too quickly for her to see the writing on the back of his T-shirt.

He remained still for a minute, his hands folded in his lap. Adrenaline surged through Kate's veins, tightening her jaw and roaring in her ears. She didn't dare look behind her to see whether Detective Hegarty had arrived. She wouldn't spare a glance for anything or anyone until she was sure this man posed no threat to the love of her life.

She choked back the sob that erupted unbidden in her throat. Goddammit, she loved Oz more than she ever thought possible. She couldn't imagine living without him—the very thought had tears stinging the corners of her eyes. She would do whatever—*whatever*—it took to keep him safe.

The man moved again, sliding forward on his chair. He was careful, quiet, as if deliberately trying not to draw attention to himself. Any normal person would simply shove off their extra layers or fidget at will, but his incremental movements filled her with suspicion.

She narrowed her eyes. Every motion he made seemed slower than the one before. He leaned forward almost imperceptibly. Snaked his right hand across his lap to reach into the inner pocket on the left side of his jacket. Made a fist around what was inside and began to withdraw it. Leaned forward a tiny bit more...

She saw it, and time lurched from agonizing slowness to stomach-dropping light speed. The writing on his T-shirt wasn't writing at all. It was a symbol, and as he arched forward she made out every one of its thick black lines.

A swastika.

Her emotions shut down as her training took over. She flung her phone into the lap of the person next to her with the command, "Call the police." Then she scrambled over the back of the chair and wrapped both hands around his right wrist. She caught his arm just in time to see the Desert Eagle semiautomatic handgun he was pulling from the pocket.

"He's got a gun," she shouted, vaguely registering the thunderous sound of people leaping from their seats as she threw all of her weight in the opposite direction of his grip, trying to dislodge the weapon.

The man heaved to his feet and she tightened her fists, twisting his hand so the weapon pointed toward the ceiling. He used his free hand to yank on her hair, grunting with the effort, but her focus was so singular she barely felt the pain.

She would protect Oz, whatever it took.

She took advantage of his proximity and jammed her elbow into his throat. He released her hair to cover his neck and she risked taking one hand off his wrist to use it to shove him off-balance and drag him to the ground. It didn't work. He caught her palm on its way to his chest and twisted it mercilessly, forcing her to turn her body so he didn't break her wrist, weakening her grip on the hand holding the gun.

Fear weaved through her chest in icy ribbons. For the first time she considered that she might not be able to overpower this man. She might not be able to save the man she loved. She might be about to die.

The chaotic sounds of the auditorium suddenly seemed louder, the noises of stampeding feet and voices raised in fear, and chairs tipping over. She kept the man's arm pointing the gun skyward but she couldn't for much longer. She hoped the police were on their way. At least she'd bought time for Oz to get out, even if she couldn't—

A strong arm wrapped around her waist and shoved her to one side, her fingertips brushing the butt of the gun as they slid off. She whirled in time to see Oz tackle the man to the ground and plant his knee on his chest, fighting to tug the gun out of his fingers. Panic stole her breath when she saw the man's gleeful expression and realized what Oz couldn't.

He didn't have to make his shot from a distance, now. His target was in point-blank range, and that realization fueled her back to her feet.

She brought her sneakered foot down on the man's forearm with as much force as she could muster, channeling every scrap of rage and fear and desperation into the strike. It worked—for a second. He released the gun, then threw himself after it. Oz clambered on top of him, trying to hold him back while going for the weapon at the same time.

She started after him when someone grabbed her arm. She turned—a woman in a *hijab* was trying to pull her to safety.

"I can't leave him," she managed, breathless and desperate, but the woman tugged harder on her arm and Kate realized she probably couldn't hear her over the noise in the room.

"Hurry," the woman mouthed. Kate shook her head and tears welled in the woman's eyes, clearly distraught at the possibility of leaving her behind. Panic, urgency and empathy warred for dominance in Kate's heart, but she had no choice but to wrench free from the woman's grip and shove her toward the door. The woman looked over her shoulder one last time before joining the running crowd, and Kate knew that if she died in the next few minutes her would-be savior would never forgive herself.

That was incentive enough to—

The gun went off, the *crack* of the shot echoing around the room momentarily silencing the shouts of the crowd, then amplifying them. Kate screamed as she spun around, her heart freezing in terror. Plaster rained from the bullet hole in the ceiling, cloaking everything in white fog. She made out two figures, one prone and motionless on the floor, the other raising the gun in triumph.

She hurled herself forward, ready to kill the man with her bare hands if it was his body on top.

Instead she collided with pure muscle, a chest she knew better than any other, a face she wanted to wake up to every morning.

She breathed his name as his arms came around her shoulders. It was the only word she knew—the only one left in her vocabulary as sheer joy and relief loosened her muscles and clouded her brain in a fog of incoherence.

"I don't know how you spotted that guy, Kate, but if you hadn't—"

She shushed him, collecting her senses, dimly aware of sirens squealing outside and the bang of the auditorium doors slamming open to admit a stream of uniformed officers. Within seconds one of them had taken the gun from Oz's hand and ushered them both out of the room. Kate looked back in time to see three other officers crouched over the man's body, one of them declaring he was out cold but otherwise unhurt.

They moved through the exterior doors and Kate began to drift in the direction of the police van where most of the audience seemed to congregate but Oz stopped her, pulling her in tightly, the two of them a rock in the sea of motion on the sidewalk.

"They're going to separate us to take our statements, and I need to tell you this now," he told her urgently.

She shook her head. "I have something I want to tell you first."

His eyes were wide with impatience. She thought of her carefully prepared speech, her meticulously organized thoughts, the rarity of the fact she'd actually planned this statement instead of winging it as usual— and the irony that not one second of her planned moment would make it into the real one.

"I love you, Oz. I don't need to figure out who I am, because I know, and I've always known. What I didn't know, and what scared me, was how much better I was with you than without you. I'll move to Spain. I'll move to Sweden. I'll move to Antarctica if that's what it takes to be with you."

He tightened his hands around her upper arms. "I'm not moving to Spain. I turned them down."

Surprise lifted her brows. "Why? What about your plan?"

"Fuck my plan," he insisted harshly. "You're my plan now. Sure, I would've earned a bit more in Spain, maybe gotten to play a couple of big teams. But I'm happy here. I'm happy at Skyline, and I'm never happier than when I'm with you. I love you, Kate, and I want you to be happy, too. I'll do whatever you need to get you there."

"You already did. Those three words. That's all I want."

He grinned. "Then I'll say them again. I love you."

"And I love you."

Her voice broke on the last syllable but she didn't care. She didn't care about anything—not the police streaming through the building, the stretcher carrying the assailant to an ambulance, the wildly flashing press cameras already bunching up along the police tape—except the man in her arms.

And when he kissed her, and she closed her eyes, she saw the future. Two paths winding together until they merged, inseparable and inextricable, stretching all the way to the horizon.

Epilogue

"Wait, don't put that there. You can put it—Actually, could it go in a drawer or something?"

Kate shot Oz a sharp glance, holding the bottle of hand lotion an inch off the surface of the dresser.

He exhaled, unclenching his hands. He forced a smile. "Put it anywhere you want. I don't mind."

She placed it squarely on the dresser and pushed aside the empty cardboard box, then reached for a pair of scissors to open the one beneath it.

"I'm pretty sure this box is all clothes." She glanced up. "Did you clear out a drawer for me? And some closet space?"

His anxiety thrummed again. "Do you need a whole drawer?"

"More like two."

"Are you sure?"

She sighed. "We've been through this a hundred times since you asked me to move in. This is going to require compromise. We can't all live in Swedish minimalist wonderland. Some of us need daily access to, you know, *objects*."

"I know." He yanked open the drawer he'd half-emptied for her and studied its contents. He'd earmarked this for screen-printed T-shirts, ordered by color, but he supposed he could integrate them with plain T-shirts. Although…

"Hey." Kate moved beside him, slipping her arm around his waist. "It's okay."

"I'm trying," he told her, turning to pull her against his chest. She was warm and soft, the perfect fit he never expected.

"And you're doing great. But maybe we could get through this box a little more quickly than the last one. Say, less than two hours?"

"Don't push it." He tilted his head to kiss her. In the month since the incident at the Peace Institute he'd gotten used to having her in his house. The gunman turned out to be a man who'd legally changed his name to John Ausonius and was already on an FBI watch list due to his online participation in a number of racist and xenophobic forums. Oz slept better than ever now his stalker was in prison—and because he no longer slept alone.

They'd spent the day before driving her stuff back to Atlanta from Jasper and this whole Sunday morning and early afternoon unpacking her things in his house. At first it was difficult, but as the day wore on he grew to like seeing her possessions mixed in with his. Her feminine-labeled cosmetics between his masculine ones. Her shoes alongside his own. Her surprisingly racy lingerie collection jumbled amidst his austerely folded briefs.

Remembering the sight of her bright red, sheer bra tossed into the drawer gave him an incentive to get through this box faster after all. Releasing her he dropped to his haunches, pulling open the folds and assessing the contents.

"You have that second interview tomorrow, right? For the corporate security advisory company?"

She nodded, sitting on the floor and taking out a couple of pairs of folded jeans. "But it's mostly a formality. I think the managing director would've hired me on the spot if he didn't need to get signoff from HR. He said he has a great track record hiring veterans, and he's been dying to get a woman on staff. So many of their executives are women, and they face completely different challenges trying to do business in the Middle East."

"You're going to be so good at this, Kate, it's almost scary." He grinned. "What time is the meeting?"

"Eight-thirty, why?"

"You probably need to get to bed early, then. So you're rested and ready to go."

She narrowed her eyes. "Your point being?"

"You know me, always planning." He shrugged. "And my plan was to make you come at least twice before we went to sleep, so if we work backwards from, say, eleven o'clock…"

"I'm sure this can wait." She shoved the box aside and scrambled into his lap, straddling him, her mouth finding his with heat and hunger.

He smiled into the kiss, threading his fingers through her hair. Kate certainly wasn't the woman he could've ever imagined he'd end up with, but that didn't matter. She was here, she was his, and he couldn't have planned it better.

Don't miss book one in Rebecca Crowley's Atlanta Skyline series!

Crossing Hearts

FEVERED FATES

New to the U.S. soccer scene, not to mention the English language, compact yet explosive Chilean soccer legend Rio Vidal is driven to define a role on his new team, Atlanta Skyline. But he must also adapt to a new culture—and accept that he can't do it alone. His beautiful interpreter, Eva, has been his voice, his refuge. But she is becoming so much more. If only he could convince her he isn't like the other men she's worked with, players on—and off—the field.

As a translator for pro athletes, Eva Torres is used to dealing with self-interested super stars. But Rio seems different, and she's blindsided when he locks eyes with her across a church pew. By now, after weeks of close contact with the endearing athlete with whom she shares a language, her thoughts are far from holy. She must remind herself flirtation is probably just his default style. Plus, she's the only one he can really talk to. But when his ambition threatens to derail his career—and their deepening connection—they'll both have to lay their hearts on the center line . . .

Chapter 1

"Rio! Rio! Rio!"

His name was the only word he could decipher as he entered the arrivals area of Hartsfield-Jackson Airport. He was hungry and tired after the overnight trip from Antofagasta and five minutes earlier he'd almost asked a security guard to sneak him out a back door so he could spend the first several hours of his new life in America soundly asleep.

Now, as flashbulbs lit up the already bright airport and a group of reporters thrust a bouquet of microphones toward his face, he thought this might be one of the best moments of his life.

His grin came easily as he surveyed the crowd. Members of the press vied for proximity, a group of fans waved Chilean flags, and a welcoming committee wearing brick-red Skyline jerseys turned in unison to show his name and number printed on their backs: Vidal, 17.

He focused on each photographer in turn, flashing the practiced smile that showcased his expensively straightened teeth. The fans' cheering grew louder, the reporters shouted over them, and by the time Skyline's manager, Roland Carlsson, waded over to him, Rio couldn't make out what the stylish Swede said as he clapped him on the back.

Not that he would've understood the words if he'd heard them.

He blinked up at his new boss, who returned his stare expectantly. He took in Roland's perfect haircut, the touch of grey at his temples, his tailored clothing—he couldn't be more different from the pudgy, tracksuit-wearing manager he'd played for in Chile. After several uncomfortable seconds Roland raised his eyebrows behind his hipster glasses and repeated himself loudly enough for Rio to hear.

"Bzzz Atlanta, Rio. Bzzzbzzzbzzz."

Rio widened his smile, hoping it was an appropriate response as anxiety quickened his breathing. It would be so embarrassing if he turned out to be grinning like an idiot at the man who'd just asked him a question—or fired him.

Roland's friendly expression faltered. Rio's mouth went dry. He quickly inventoried the few English words he could deploy.

Soccer. Bon Jovi. One, two, three…

"Señor Vidal, buenos dias." A woman appeared at his elbow, her Skyline jersey so oversized it nearly met her knees. *"Soy Eva Torres. Su traductor."*

"Eva the translator, just in time to save my career," he gushed, grateful to be back in the safe waters of his native Spanish. "Please don't say Roland just told me to get on the next plane home to Chile."

Her smile was more magnificent than the flashbulbs sparkling around the room. He took in her small stature, olive complexion, dark hair falling thickly over her shoulders. Her eyes were wide-set, the exact shape of almonds and slightly hooded, as though their black-coffee depths were so accustomed to keeping secrets it had ceased to be a challenge.

From nowhere he thought of his grandmother's obsession with the Virgin of Guadalupe, the paintings and candles and statues that cluttered her curtained-off corner of the tin-roofed shack where he'd grown up. She used to insist the eyes of the Virgin changed, that it was possible to read warnings and reassurances and answered prayers in those heavy-lidded orbs. As a child he'd spent hours nose-to-nose with one of her figurines. Watching. Waiting.

He always blinked first.

But this Eva… He bet the cool eyes she tilted up to him could give that ceramic Virgin a run for her money.

"He welcomed you to Georgia, as does everyone here." She swept an arm to indicate the increasingly frantic crowd. "The plan is for us to make our way to the auditorium for a brief press conference, then you'll be taken home to rest for the evening. I'm sure you're exhausted after your journey."

So polite, so professional. He stole a glance at her ring finger.

Bare.

Encouraging.

"Who could be tired with all this excitement? Lead the way, I'm all yours." He gave her his trademark cheeky grin, which she returned with a slight dip of her chin before ushering him toward a corridor.

He resigned himself to her indifference as she turned her back and walked so briskly he had to quicken his pace to keep up. Evidently his hopelessly romantic side had made it through all those long flights. His celebrity status in Chile certainly hadn't aided his love life, so he was silly to think that would change in the United States. As if the woman of his dreams was going to be the first one he spoke to off the plane—ridiculous.

Signing to one of the best Championship Soccer League teams in America was the biggest leap of his career. He couldn't mess it up, couldn't let it pass him by. Definitely couldn't get distracted by a beautiful woman with secretive eyes.

At that moment Eva glanced over her shoulder, probably checking to make sure he was keeping up. Their gazes locked and in the split second before her expression resettled into cool disinterest, he saw it. Barely a flicker, almost imperceptible, but bright enough to sear onto his memory: the same shimmering, teasing flame of bald lust that began roaring in his gut the instant he'd laid eyes on her.

"This way." She snapped her attention back to the front, walking even more quickly as a door labeled *Auditorium* loomed ahead. The corridor echoed with the shuffling din of onlookers finally being allowed to follow them, and before he could process the sequence of events the heavy door swung open. He was shown to a seat at a table dressed with the Skyline banner on the stage, and the horde that had greeted him just minutes earlier was filing into the room.

Roland dropped into the seat beside him and leaned in, winking conspiratorially. "Bzzzbzzzbzzzbzzz."

Rio glanced around for Eva, who was standing behind the seat on his other side, speaking to a man holding a microphone. Roland seemed to be waiting for a reply, so Rio nodded and smiled. Roland winked again and Rio released an anxious breath, knowing full well that these head-bobbing responses would only suffice for so long.

Eva took her place beside him and he smiled at her for longer than he probably should have, unable to shake the memory of what he'd seen in her face. She gave him a muted nod before turning her attention to the audience, where hands were already raised to ask questions.

Roland spoke first, hushing the onlookers as tiny tape recorders clicked on and pens scratched across notepads. Rio kept his camera-friendly grin fixed firmly in place as Roland buzzed on and on. He caught a few of the manager's words—his own name, the team's name, the name of his fellow midfielder, Nico Silva—but for all he knew Roland could be singing his praises or apologizing to the fans for signing a total unknown from an obscure team in Chile.

When Roland finished Rio glanced at Eva for some clue as to what his boss had said, but there was no time for her to translate as members of the press began firing questions.

"Bzzbzzbzzbzzbzzzzzz?" The reporter barely looked up from his notepad as he spoke in rapid, urgent tones.

"He'd like to know how it feels to join a Championship Soccer League team," Eva murmured.

Rio blinked at the journalist, then at his translator. "Are you serious? That's his question? He sounded so angry, I thought he was accusing me of cheating on my wife."

"But you're not married."

"Exactly."

A suggestion of a smile flickered across Eva's mouth. "That's his question."

"Tell him I'm delighted to be joining Atlanta Skyline. It's the highlight of my career so far. I just hope I can live up to the fans' expectations."

Eva nodded, leaned into the microphone, and buzzed a response to the audience. Approving smiles spread across the room and he sighed with relief. He'd gotten the first answer right, at least.

Another reporter barked a question, extending his tape recorder above the head of the person seated in front of him. Rio looked expectantly at Eva.

"He wants to know whether you've had adequate time to rest after the South American Cup tournament, and if you'll be appearing for Skyline right away."

Roland spoke before Rio could, hunching his big frame over the microphone.

"He's telling them you're fully fit and will start playing immediately," Eva whispered. Rio nodded gratefully, his head beginning to spin with the back-and-forth of translations.

The next question was from a woman who introduced herself in Spanish, explaining she worked for a Spanish-language newspaper. He grinned at her, relieved to be back in control, even if only for a minute.

"I think most of us learned your name for the first time during the South American Cup, from those assists in the early rounds to the goal in the final. You've been playing soccer for twelve years, since you were scouted at the age of fourteen. Why has it taken so long for the world to discover Rio Vidal?"

He exhaled heavily, buying time as he considered his answer. What to tell them? As he looked out over the rows of seats in the dim auditorium he saw his childhood home slouching amidst hundreds of identical shacks on the edge of the desert, the packed dirt in the empty lot where he and his friends played five-a-side, the trail of exhaust from the car his mother borrowed to drive him to youth-league training in Calama, the stomach-dropping lift of the airplane as he took his first-ever flight to Santiago to make his professional debut.

Should he tell them how hard he'd worked to overcome his height, his size, to channel his frenzied energy on the pitch?

Maybe he should tell them it was all thanks to the mining accident that killed his father, the life insurance payout that arrived in the mail, the move to the apartment in the school district where an involved coach made a phone call that changed his life.

Or should he admit that he'd been conflicted about leaving Santiago to join an American team, and that it felt a lot like selling out? Should he remind them of the footage from the Cup final, the famous shot of his eyes welling as he hefted the trophy? Should he explain that nothing he could win at Skyline would compare with the pride and privilege of playing for his country?

He cleared his throat, shifted in his seat. Cameras rolled, pens hovered, and the Spanish-speaking journalist smiled patiently. These would be some of his first words on American soil, his introduction to the fans he was asking to trust him, believe in him, and support him through the season ahead. He wanted to show them his heart. Tell them his story. Share the joy and tumult of his journey to this career-defining moment.

He leaned toward the microphone, summoning every last shred of recollection from the hour he spent half-watching YouTube language lessons.

"I...excite...to play...Skyline."

Laughter and applause warmed the auditorium. The inquiring reporter inclined her head in thanks, blatantly charmed by his broken English. It wasn't his most eloquent statement to the press, but it seemed to have done the job.

Roland interjected in his characteristically thoughtful tone, and Rio sat back in his chair. To think he'd thought the long-haul travel from Chile had been exhausting. Now he knew he was in for the ride of his life.

Chapter 2

Eva led Rio down the carpeted steps to the cinema room, where oversized posters of classic Mafia movies loomed over plush theatre seating. "I don't know if it's exactly to your taste, but hopefully you can deal with it until you find a place of your own."

"Are you kidding?" Rio's jaw slackened as he took it in. "I love it."

Eva bit her lip for the millionth time that day, trying to hide her endeared smile at Rio's enthusiasm. From the middling turnout at the press conference, to her two-door hatchback instead of the limo that had broken down on the highway, and now this ostentatious house, Rio's excitement hadn't waned.

The mansion had been built by former Skyline player Hector González, who'd sold it to the club for a bargain-basement price when he signed a bountiful new contract with a club in his native Spain. He'd been so delighted to get away from Atlanta—and her, by extension—that he probably would've given it away for free if Roland had been more patient.

She hated the seven-bedroom monstrosity in the exclusive Buckhead neighborhood. Every ornate cornice and embellished light fixture reminded her of the two years she'd spent as Hector's interpreter. Two years traipsing behind the most self-centered man on earth, being treated like the semi-human equivalent of a can opener: absolutely essential when you needed it, utterly forgettable when you didn't.

Hector's English was better than Rio's—which wasn't saying much, from the look of things.

Rio would undoubtedly require much more from her, and her contract didn't include overtime, but she didn't mind. Two years with Hector made her hate the job she'd worked so hard to get in a sport she'd loved since childhood. Two hours with Rio had already turned that around.

It didn't hurt that he was easily ten times more attractive than Hector—

to her at least.

Hector was classically handsome, and probably spent more time in magazine photo shoots than he did on the pitch. Whenever people found out she was his translator, the first question was always whether she had the inside scoop on his love life. Although she always said no, the answer was yes.

She knew full well how many young, inebriated, dubiously consenting women came and went from his bed. She'd even raised it with Roland, who'd been visibly concerned but said his hands were tied until someone made a complaint. No one ever did, but she still lost sleep over that parade of women and whether she should've—or could've—done more for them.

Every instinct she possessed told her Rio was completely different. For one thing, he was unlikely to grace the cover of a glamorous men's magazine unless it was a special South American issue. At barely five-foot-seven he was short and compact, nowhere near the statuesque, six-foot-two Hector.

And as much as she chastised herself for indulging the stereotype, she liked how Rio looked, well, Latino. She liked his dark-olive skin, his nut-brown eyes, the thick, black hair shaved closely on the sides and coiffed on top. She liked the way he spoke Spanish with a working-class Chilean accent, full of dropped consonants and distinctive vocabulary. She especially liked his smile, its lopsidedness, the way it showed his back teeth, and the frequency with which it appeared. Hell, she even liked his horribly pronounced attempts at English.

Whereas Hector had artificially tanned skin, light eyes, and all the airs and graces of a royal-blooded European, Rio looked and acted authentically, never contradicting exactly who he was: the son of an industrial port city caught between the desert and the sea, where copper mines made people unbelievably wealthy and crushingly poor by turns. The local soccer star who'd caught the world's attention—and hers—with his boundless energy and creativity on the pitch. The new signing trying to make his way in a foreign city, in a foreign language.

Me gustas, Rio. I think we're going to get along just fine.

"Oh my God." Rio pulled open the drawers built into the wall beneath the screen to reveal row after row of DVDs. "I thought I had a big collection but it's nothing compared to this. Why didn't he want to take any of these with him?"

"I don't think American DVDs work in European DVD players." She perched on the edge of one of the leather-upholstered theatre seats, trying and failing to settle her internal debate. She should get going, give Rio space to check out his new house, take a nap, have a shower—she slammed on the mental brakes at that last thought, fighting back an image of the chiseled torso he'd shown millions of viewers when he ripped off his shirt after scoring a goal in the South American Cup final.

She should definitely leave. She'd see him bright and early on Monday morning, and he needed time to decompress after everything that happened today. He was probably jet-lagged, desperate to unpack his essentials, decide which of the seven bedrooms he wanted to sleep in…

He glanced at her over his shoulder. "Are you hungry? Should we order dinner?"

"What? Why? Aren't you tired?"

"Not really, but I am starving. Do you have to be somewhere?"

Say yes.

"No."

Dammit.

One corner of his mouth lifted. "Are you sure? It's Saturday night. I wouldn't ask you to cancel your plans."

He wouldn't? Really? Apparently Rio wasn't just different to Hector, they were total opposites. She doubted it ever occurred to Hector that she had a life outside her employment as his interpreter. If it had, he certainly hadn't let it bother him.

Anyway, why shouldn't she stay for dinner? It would be good for them to get to know each other before he started training with the team on Monday. He'd invited her—why should she feel uncomfortable? Just because he was the hottest man she'd ever been this close to, and she was having intrusive thoughts about touching the bicep tightening the sleeve of his sweater, and she hadn't gotten any action in over a year, well, unless you counted that guy on Halloween, and she totally didn't count him, and—

"So?" Rio's expression suggested she'd overrun the normal-people time limit on accepting or declining in-person dinner invitations. "Do you have plans?"

"I do now," she replied way too perkily, regretting her high-pitched tone as soon as it hit her ears.

Get a grip, Torres. It was going to be a long season if she couldn't pull herself together. Where was the immutable professionalism her professors had raved about during her MA in Translation Studies? Where were the discretion and levelheadedness that had launched her career in sports interpreting? Where was the unflappable ice queen who had sat across the desk from Roland, unshaken by his unyielding, pointed interviewing until he leaned back in his chair and announced, "You're hired"?

Oh right, she was back at the airport, her knees knocking and her heart racing as weeks of Internet image searches in the name of "research" appeared live, three-dimensional, and even sexier than she imagined.

"Eva?" Rio waved a palm to get her attention. "You okay?"

"Yes, sorry, just thinking about dinner." *And your legs. And your chest. And wondering if I should quit now or wait to be fired for sexual harassment.*

"What would you like?"

She shook her head. "It's your first night in Atlanta, so you pick. You can get almost any kind of food here. Chinese, pizza, barbecue—Mexican?"

He rose from his seat on the floor, stretching his arms over his head. Eva tried very, very hard not to notice the way his thin sweater pulled taut against his chest.

"Are you from Mexico?" He shoved his hands in the pockets of his jeans.

"I'm from Texas," she replied stiffly, automatically bristling at the question before considering its context. More gently she added, "My parents are Mexican."

He nodded. "I can tell from your accent."

"I'm not doing a good job, then." She smirked. "I spent a lot of years learning to speak with as little accent as possible."

"I didn't mean it like that. It's nice, the way you talk. Fancy. Not like me."

His playful grin was back. She swallowed hard.

"You speak just fine."

"Not English, though." He began a slow wander around the room, pausing in front of each of the expensively framed posters Hector had left behind. "I tried to learn a bit before I arrived, but I hate studying. I was terrible at school. I skipped class as often as I could. I don't know what I would've done if I wasn't good at soccer." He traced the letters at the bottom of one of the posters. "Been a miner, I guess."

"We'll work on your English at a pace that suits you," she assured him. "I'll teach you differently than you would learn in a class. For a start, we'll focus on the vocabulary you need on the pitch. Then we'll look at conversation as it's relevant to your career, like answering post-match questions from the press. Nothing too technical, at least not until you get the hang of the basics."

He turned back to her with a smile. "That's great. Much better than the ten minutes I spent learning to ask where to board the train."

"Yeah, that's not going to get you too far in Atlanta."

"So, your parents." He was on the move again, continuing his tour of the room's circumference. "Where in Mexico are they from?"

"North," she replied with forced casualness. This was not a topic she liked discussing with anyone, let alone her brand-new client. "In fact, there's a restaurant in town owned by a family from Monterrey. I don't know if they deliver, but—"

"Is that where your parents are from? Monterrey?"

"Juarez," she told him quickly. "I've got the number on my phone, I'll give them a quick call to see if they'll deliver out here. Their beef *empanadas* are absurdly good."

She had scrolled halfway through her contacts when she realized Rio hadn't responded. She looked up to find him studying her from across the room, his high forehead creased in thought.

"What?" The single word carried more annoyance than she'd intended, and she pushed her lips into a smile to soften it.

"I'm just surprised." He propped one shoulder against the wall. "I didn't think I'd ever meet a woman more beautiful than the ones in Chile, yet here you are."

"Rio," she chided, praying the heat climbing her neck wasn't showing on her skin. "Save your smooth lines for the women in the nightclub. They're wasted on me."

"Why?"

"Because I'm your interpreter, and they don't pay me enough to be anything else."

She hoped her joking tone defused the situation without offending him. It worked—he moved back to the front of the room and flopped down on the floor with an exaggerated sigh.

"You break my heart, Eva."

"You'll live." She held up her phone. "Do you want to see the menu?"

He gestured for her to toss him the phone, but she lowered it instead.

"Are you kidding? You play soccer, not baseball. I don't trust those hands."

He hauled himself to his feet with a comical groan and crossed the short space between them. He dropped into the chair beside her and reached across the armrest, but instead of taking the phone, he wrapped his hand around hers where she held it.

"These are the safest hands you'll find," he murmured. He was right beside her now, his face so near she could see the amber flecks in his brown eyes, his body so close she could feel his heat, catch his scent.

Tea tree oil. Saltwater. Asphalt in the sun. She let her lids fall closed as she inhaled, and when she opened them again he was watching her.

He slid his thumb over hers. His skin was warm, dry, slightly rough.

They spent a full minute frozen in this tableau. Her heart raced yet her thoughts had ground to a halt. If Rio had asked her name she probably couldn't have told him. The only word her multilingual mind seemed to retain was yes.

Yes.

He snatched the phone from her hand, shattering the stillness. She dragged air into her lungs as he threw her phone high above their heads and caught it one-handed behind his back.

"See?" He held it up with a wink. "Hands you can trust."

She cleared her throat, tugged at the cuff of her long-sleeve shirt. Hector must have the heating programed on a timer. No way was it this hot when she'd first walked in.

"Beef *empanadas*," she repeated firmly, "With *frijoles negros* for me. Best in town." She grabbed her phone from his hand and started dialing, ignoring the way her fingers trembled.

She raised the phone to her ear. "It's ringing. Last chance to tell me what you want."

He arched a brow.

She ordered without waiting for his answer.

Meet the Author

Rebecca Crowley inherited her love of romance from her mom, who taught her to at least partially judge a book by the steaminess of its cover. She writes contemporary romance and romantic suspense with smart heroines and swoon-worthy heroes, and never tires of the happily-ever-after. Having pulled up her Kansas roots to live in New York City and London, Rebecca currently resides in Johannesburg, South Africa. You can find her on the web at rebeccacrowley.net or on Twitter at @rachelmaybe.